Everything You Need
To Know

Emily Brott

Published by Emily Rose Brott, 2023.

Contact www.emilybrott.com

Cover design © Christa Moffitt

ISBN: 978-0-6457496-2-5

For my family and friends,
I'm so grateful for your support and encouragement
on my writing journey

Chapter 1

Nora

I t feels like I'm trespassing as my fingers run along the oak veneer entertainment unit. Open for inspections really are quite the invasion of privacy. Strangers touching and looking at every crevice of another person's home. A potential buyer opening a wardrobe to check the inside fittings and space for their clothing and being confronted with someone else's shirts, dresses, shoes. Other people's toiletries on full display. Even the innocent act of opening a pantry door is like snooping on another person's life. But I guess I shouldn't feel that way considering I lived in this house, once upon a time.

The current owner has clearly gone to a lot of trouble getting the house ready. It looks immaculate. There's a neat pile of magazines styled on the coffee table in the living room and the cushions on the couch are fluffed. A vase sits on the dining table filled with yellow tulips. The fruit bowl on the quartz kitchen benchtop is layered with an assortment of colourful fruit and a few cookbooks are stacked next to the stove. There's even a faint smell of cinnamon and vanilla, like biscuits have been baking.

A couple move past me and walk through the open glass doors that lead to the garden, the real estate agent hot on their tails. The lawn is freshly mowed and looking lush. The deciduous tree in the back corner is shedding its leaves. In full bloom it's filled with gorgeous plum-coloured leaves.

I glance over the flyer, as though I don't already know every inch of this house, self-conscious and feeling out of place compared to the agent dressed in a grey suit, his dark hair styled, the potential buyers in their nice clothing. Most likely I'm wearing clothes from someone who is deceased. No matter how many times I wash this plaid jacket, I can't seem to get rid of the smell of mothballs. Absently I brush a hand through my hair, continuing to run through it, even after I've reached the ends, still expecting more hair to be there. I'm not sure I'll ever get used to it being so short, but it's easier to manage this way.

Normally I wouldn't be inspecting houses. Why would I bother? Buying a home is completely out of my reach. But when I saw the photograph of this house for sale in the weekend magazine, I had to come. Knowing someone else lives here now, it felt safe to see it one last time.

I briefly glimpse into the backyard and am relieved to see the cubbyhouse is still there. I check my watch. There's only twenty minutes left for the inspection and I can't just stand here in the living room. I don't exactly look like I fit in this world.

Buying time, I make my way up the staircase, on the side of the living room, my hand trembling as it brushes the timber banister. My stomach clenches. It's all too familiar. One step at a time, I tell myself.

I walk to the bedroom on the left of the landing, my shoulders slumping in relief that it looks completely different to how I last saw it. The room clearly belongs to a teenager. There are posters on the wall, one of Justin Bieber, the others I don't recognise. A wooden desk sits in front of the window, and when I move closer I see a maths textbook. There's a pink lip gloss and a teen magazine. The bedspread is mauve and a cream throw sits over the bottom corner like it's effortlessly fallen there, but I imagine it took the owner several attempts to get it looking so natural.

Crossing the landing to the room opposite, my heart thumps in my chest even before reaching the doorway. An ache engulfs me as I stand at the entrance. This room looks more familiar. Instinct takes over and my eyes close as I inhale deeply, hoping for a familiar scent. There's nothing.

Lego buildings and children's books are displayed on the shelf. A blue teddy lies against the pillow on the single bed. Forcing down the lump in my throat, I leave the room, continuing past the bathroom until I'm standing in front of the master bedroom. It's been ten years since I've set foot in this room. If I'd come when the house had been sold back then, there's no doubt I wouldn't have even attempted to enter. But I'm a different woman now, so I do. There's no love left inside me, but when I step through the doorway the burst of anger is too overwhelming. Swiftly I turn around and leave, heading back downstairs.

The voice of the real estate agent, making one last attempt to draw in potential buyers before they leave, reverberates down the hallway from the front door. The living room is empty as I make my way out the back door to the cubbyhouse. There's a small patch of grass on the other side of it and I'm completely out of view, hidden.

Falling to my knees, I remove a dessertspoon from the worn red tote bag my friend Heather gave me.

Then I dig.

With my heart pounding, I dig beneath the grass, deep into the layers of the earth, searching for the only tangible item left from my past. But there's nothing there. My hands fill the hole back up with dirt then gather the grass, patting it on top in a fruitless attempt to leave it neat. The back door closes with the click of a lock. I take a breath. 'Come on, Nora, you're not leaving here without it.' My fingers trail along the grass. It could be anywhere. I stop and close my eyes, remembering the day my children and I buried our secret treasure.

It was summer, the last week of the school holidays. The weather had been scorching and I'd spent the morning spraying the boys with a hose as they ran in their bathers along the inflatable slip and slide I'd set up for them in the backyard. The afternoon had reached forty degrees so we moved indoors, the air conditioning running at full capacity. We made mint ice-cream from scratch, letting it churn in the ice-cream maker before adding the chocolate chips, and when it was setting in the freezer, I was running out of ideas to occupy them. Two young boys without entertainment can become terrors. So I suggested we make a time capsule.

We had emptied a wooden domino box of its pieces and the boys drew spaceships and rockets on both of the long rectangular sides. I wrote the date on the sliding top in black marker. We each wrote a letter to our future selves, folded them up and put them in the box, and then each of us had chosen a special keepsake that could fit inside: a matchbox car, a Bob the Builder figurine and the beaded bracelet the boys had made me for Mother's Day the year before.

When the sun began its descent, taking with it the blazing heat, we came outside with the time capsule. We had used the boys' plastic spades, still covered in remnants of sand from our holiday at Torquay, to dig the hole. I decided we should bury it on the far side of the cubbyhouse so that if we made a mess ploughing through the grass, it would be out of sight. The boys had wanted to put it right below the window so when they played in the cubbyhouse, they could keep watch and make sure the capsule was safe.

The window.

I look up at the window on the brown weathered cubbyhouse, kissed by daylight rays, and I know exactly where it will be. I dig with the spoon until there's a knock of metal hitting wood. My hands take over, like a dog searching for a buried bone. Pulling out the box, I brush away the dirt as best as I can, letting go of the breath I didn't realise I'd been holding on to. The date on top reads 23 January 2012. I slip the box into the tote bag. As desperate as I am to look inside, I can't yet, not here at the place where I lived. It would be too much. I also don't want to rush the moment but savour it.

So I fill the hole back up with dirt and grab tussocks of grass, piling them on top in another futile attempt to tidy it. I brush my hands together to remove the dirt, but it remains underneath the tips of my nails and in the corners of my nailbeds. I check my watch: the inspection finished twenty minutes ago at two o'clock, so I'm sure the real estate agent will have left by now. Just in case, I peek around the side of the cubbyhouse. The coast seems clear. I run down the side of the house and unlatch the gate that leads to the driveway. Once again I check there's no one there, then, as casually as possible, like I actually belong here, I stride through the front gate onto the footpath and keep walking.

It's only when I've walked past a few houses that it registers that the 'For Sale' sign that was on the fence when I arrived has been removed.

Chapter 2

Elle

I notice the woman watching me straight away. Ever since I was robbed at an automatic teller machine five years ago, I always check my surroundings before I withdraw money. My son Olly was only a few months old at the time and I'd been up all night with him. I'd taken him for a walk so he'd fall asleep and decided to get my shopping while we were out. As I waited for the money to dispense, out of nowhere a huge hand attached to a man who seemed twice my size grabbed the notes as they came out then sprinted. I hadn't expected that my body would freeze when faced with that situation, but by the time I thawed, the guy was already a block away.

So naturally I'm aware of the woman standing a few metres from me, near the pedestrian crossing. At first glance I assume she's homeless. But then, when I surreptitiously glimpse in her direction again, I'm not so sure. There's some effort in the way she's dressed: the red tote bag held in place over her shoulder, her hair neat, clothing clean and tidy. But it's odd the way she's just standing there, staring at me so intensely. I look back at the ATM. My card comes out of the slot and I place it in my purse, waiting for the cash. Ever so slightly I turn my head, and in my peripheral vision I can see she's coming towards me. I'm momentarily alarmed, but I don't think she's going to take my money. For starters, she looks like she's in her late fifties. But it's not just that, it's the way she's looking at me, like she's known another life. I retrieve the cash, place it in the side of my purse and turn around. I haven't had a chance to zip it up before she's standing right next to me.

She seems hesitant, but then she asks, 'Do you have any money?'

'Um,' I say, zipping up my purse and slipping it inside my cross-body handbag. 'I don't have any change.' My withdrawal came out in fifty-dollar notes. I feel awful; her skin is so pale, almost tinged with green. Maybe she's not well. I glance across the street at the bakery. 'But I can buy you some food.'

'Thank you,' she says.

'I'll be back in a minute.' I cross the road at the pedestrian crossing and she follows me. I had expected her to wait there, outside the bank, but maybe she thinks I won't come back. Stepping inside the bakery, we stand together in front of the counter, an array of cooked food in the display section, fresh loaves in the racks behind. The bakery is warm from the ovens out the back and filled with the sweet smell of yeast. The couple being served stare at us.

'Would you like a pastie?' I ask her. I want to buy her something of substance.

'Um, something with tuna, please.'

The couple leave with their coffees and Danish pastries.

I check the display, looking for something with tuna. 'Could I please have two tuna patties for the lady?' I ask the young man behind the counter.

I feel like I should say something to her while we wait, but what would be the appropriate thing to talk about? The weather? Or if she has somewhere to sleep tonight or needs essentials like sanitary items? So I say nothing and we stand in silence.

The guy serving hands me a brown paper bag and I pass it to the woman. When she takes it, my heart sinks as I notice the dirt under her nails and that her hands are shaking. There are often homeless people living on this shopping strip, every possession they own within their small space of footpath. Their whole existence relying on the kindness of others to toss them a few coins or buy them some food. I often wonder what led them here, to sleeping outside in the cold, completely vulnerable. Especially the women. It tugs at my heartstrings.

'Thank you,' she says, looking straight into my eyes.

I shift on the spot, feeling slightly uncomfortable. 'My pleasure,' I say. I turn my attention to the young man behind the counter. 'Can I please have four wholemeal rolls?'

'With sesame seeds or without?'

'With, please.'

The woman stares at me a second or two longer and then walks out the open door of the bakery.

After I've paid, I wait inside the bakery for a moment. I feel silly standing here, but there was something about the way she looked at me that was unsettling. And her eyes. Even behind the glasses, too big for her petite face, there was a familiarity to them. I step outside and look in both directions, relieved she's nowhere to be seen.

. . .

When I arrive home, I drop my handbag and grocery bags on the bench and go back to the car to retrieve the rest of the shopping. My phone is ringing on the bench as I come back in, my business partner's name flashing on the screen.

'Hey, Georgie. I'm just unpacking the shopping for tomorrow,' I say, cradling the phone between my ear and the top of my shoulder. I shop for any ingredients we need for our small corporate catering business after the lunch order goes out, so that the mornings are free to cook.

'We didn't get time to chat about it this morning, but I wanted to see if you'd given some thought to the idea,' says Georgie.

I sigh. 'I don't know, George.' She wants us to expand the business into larger events, conferences and work cocktail parties, especially for Christmas time when we miss out on the big corporate functions. But expanding means renting a commercial kitchen, hiring and managing more staff and working after hours. And it will require a financial investment in the business. 'Right now, with two young kids, it's not a great time to take on more.'

'Have you spoken to Richard about it? Maybe you can hire a nanny to help out?'

Argh. 'I haven't brought it up with him yet.' As it is, my husband would prefer I didn't work at all. And he doesn't believe in nannies or me working in the evenings when he gets home from work. I also run the business side of things, managing the administration and client accounts. Georgie is responsible for the marketing and social media. It's difficult enough finding time in the day to catch up on admin. Fortunately, Richard goes to the gym most mornings, so if I get up early I can sneak in an hour before the boys wake. And it's a godsend when he has work dinners or has to stay at the office late. 'He's been so busy at work, I've hardly seen him this week.'

'Okay, but I'd really like to get moving on this so I can have the marketing organised for Christmas.'

'I'll run it past him on the weekend but I don't know if it's going to work for me. Maybe in a few years' time when the kids are a bit older.'

'Look, I'd be happy to take on the extra load,' says Georgie.

'I don't feel comfortable letting you do more. As it is you fill the breakfast orders.'

'I have Sarah helping me, and we can hire more staff.'

Sarah is our only employee. She delivers and sets up the food for us at our clients' offices and assists Georgie with the morning orders. The lunch orders we do here. 'I don't know, George.' I sigh again. It's always been my long-term goal to have our own commercial kitchen and be able to cater for larger events, but the timeline in my head was for when Olly and Charlie were in high school, which is years from now. I'd hoped by then the boys would be more independent and Richard wouldn't mind. The thought of even discussing it with him now when Olly has only just started prep and Charlie year three causes heart palpitations.

'Just speak to Richard, see what he says.'

'Okay. I better go – I want to marinate the duck before I pick up the kids.'

'See you tomorrow,' says Georgie.

I carry the shopping bags to the laundry behind the kitchen, where there's an extra fridge and cupboard that's purely for work, and stack everything away except the duck. I grab the five-spice powder, soy sauce and rice wine and then head back to the kitchen. For a client lunch tomorrow we're making duck pancakes with hoisin sauce, bao buns with chicken and Asian salad, artisan rolls filled with roast vegetable and pecorino, and mini roast tomato, kale and feta frittatas. For dessert, fruit platters and raspberry muffins dusted with icing sugar.

I prepare the marinade and rub it over the duck, massaging firmly into the skin. Probably too firmly – my fingers digging and palms kneading isn't really necessary to enhance the duck's flavour, but I have to let my tension out on something and this poor duck seems to be the recipient. The thing is, I know there's no point in even bringing up the expansion with Richard. He won't go for it, and I can't invest more money without him as all the money I earn from the business goes into our joint account. Not that I can't withdraw from it, but if I do, Richard will see it. He sees everything.

Chapter 3

Nora

My hands are trembling. I clasp them together on my lap, but they're still vibrating. In fact, every inch of me is vibrating, as if I've been hit with an electric charge. The nausea that washed over me in an instant, the moment I stood face to face with Elle, lingers.

I'm not sure what's happening, how I could possibly be seeing her. And Elle didn't even flinch. There was absolutely no sign of recognition. How could she not have known who I was? Of course, I look different now, my hair short, fringed and bottle copper. My skin is heavily wrinkled; having your life turned upside down will do that to you. I don't wear make-up and obviously I dress differently – my clothes now cheap and worn. But still, I find it hard to believe that she didn't stand there staring at me in shock and confusion the way I had stared at her. Maybe it was the unfashionable red-framed glasses obscuring my face.

When I saw her on Glenferrie Road it was like time suspended, my limbs stopped working. I'm mortified that I asked her for money, but I had to speak to her, my stomach literally tugging, imploring me to do something, and it was all I could think of to say. The pitying way she looked at me, like I was homeless, was a punch to the gut. Although it is true, I don't have a home.

After she bought me the patties I wanted to explain, but anything I uttered would have sounded completely ludicrous. I thought about following her, to make sure it really was Elle and I wasn't dreaming, but she'd likely call the police. The police getting involved will cause a whole host of problems for me to my husband's advantage.

I lean back into the tram seat, taking several long inhales and exhales to calm my ragged breathing and stop my hands from shaking like a leaf in a gale. Maybe it wasn't Elle that I saw. Maybe it was a hallucination because I've spent the afternoon revisiting my old life, which she was a part of. Being in my old neighbourhood has triggered something in my brain to create an illusion of Elle. That must be it.

The brown paper bag rests on top of my tote. I open it, inhaling the smell of dill and tuna. Perhaps that's what I need, some food in my stomach. I haven't eaten since breakfast. The first mouthful, the burst of lemon, the denseness of the potato, is like a hit of home.

Staring out of the tram window as I eat, watching the cars driving by, people walking the streets, going about their day, I'm trying to make sense of what happened. I used to believe I had a purpose in life, that there was a reason for my existence on this beautiful planet. But that all changed in a day. Maybe it wasn't exactly a day, but at the time it felt like I lost my whole life in the sweep of a moment. It wasn't just my home that I lost but my children and the people closest to me, not to mention my livelihood. Everything that gave me meaning and direction.

It's been ten years since that day, but I'm still not used to it. I can't imagine that I ever will be. My mind is my worst enemy. It's on constant repeat, having conversations with itself, not letting me accept the now, as if by going over the details of then will somehow change the present. But no matter how many times I go over it, the ending is the same. I live in a shelter for women.

The tram pulls up at my stop and I walk the quiet side streets to the shelter. From the outside it looks like all the other buildings that line the street, plain and unassuming, to ensure the safety of the residents escaping domestic violence and other dangerous situations. A security camera is tucked in the corner above the doorway. I put my code into the keypad and the door clicks open. Inside, the entrance to the refuge looks like a small foyer, but beyond those walls there's a homely, welcoming feel.

'Hi,' I say to Sheena, who is sitting behind the reception desk, as I make my way to my room.

'Hi,' she says, not looking up from her computer.

I don't stop to chat. Emotion is brewing inside me. I know as soon as I slide off the lid of the domino box, memories will flood like a dam gate lifting. I barely remember what I wrote in the letter to myself and I didn't read the letters my kids wrote. I don't know how I'll react when I see their raw handwriting, straight and circular lines forming to make letters and words. They were so young, innocent and untouched by real life. It tortures me every day thinking of what they've gone through without me, like a repeated stabbing in my chest that never stops. It's been agonising knowing I can never hold them again, not while they're under their father's care. I'm holding out for the day when they turn eighteen and become adults. It's the one thing that's kept me going, the knowledge that one day I can try to reconnect with them.

I put my key in the lock to my bedroom door, but it won't turn. I take it out and try again and when it still won't budge, turn the handle several times, but it's locked. I walk back down the hall to the reception.

'Sheena, my key's not working for some reason.'

She looks up at me with a strangely blank expression. 'Can I help you?'

'Yes, my key won't open my room. Do you have a spare?'

'Are you staying here?' she asks.

'Of course I am.'

'What's your name?'

'My name? Sheena, it's Nora. I work here.'

'Surname?'

'Plankett. Sheena, what's going on?' This is ridiculous – why is she acting like she doesn't know who I am? 'Look, I just want to go to my room. It's been a long day and I have to get to the kitchen soon to start prepping for dinner.'

Sheena's busy typing on the computer, presumably searching the register for my name. I notice now that she's dyed her hair red. It's usually light brown and this colour doesn't really suit her.

'If you can take a seat, someone will be with you in a moment.' She hands me a clipboard and a pen. 'Please fill out this form while you wait. Do you have a referral?'

'A referral?' I ask, confused. She already has all my information, but I take the clipboard.

'From the crisis centre? You need a referral from your case-worker at the crisis centre to stay here.'

'No,' I say, perplexed.

'Won't be long,' she says, returning to her computer and picking up the phone.

This is infuriating. Why's she acting like she doesn't know me? Straight away I think my husband is involved somehow. What if he saw me at the inspection earlier today and he's messing with me, sending me some kind of warning? I sit down on a chair in the waiting room, placing the clipboard on the small coffee table, and pick up a magazine. While I'm flicking through the pages I hear Sheena on the phone to Mary, the in-house counsellor.

'There's a woman who says she lives here but I don't have her information on file ... Yes, only a few minutes, she just came in.' Sheena glances my way and lowers her voice, but I can still make out her next words. 'Ah, she looks okay, but I think she could be on drugs.'

Chapter 4

Nora

A hand with red-painted fingernails extends in front of me. 'Hello, Nora, I'm Mary.'

'Mary! Thank goodness,' I say, grabbing her hand. 'I'm not sure what's going on but my key wouldn't open my room and, for some reason, Sheena didn't recognise me.'

Mary sits down in the chair next to mine, crosses her legs and threads her black shoulder-length hair behind an ear. She reaches for the clipboard, which I haven't bothered to fill out, then looks down at the form. 'Is it just you or do you have children with you?'

I let out a sigh. Something doesn't feel right. I pull my tote bag across my body and the corner of the domino box digs into my ribcage. 'Mary, why are you talking to me like we've never met? You know I have children and they're with their father.' There's no way Mary would let my husband get to her too, but maybe this is some sick plot of his to make me think I'm going mad. What if the staff here have been in contact with him all along? He did manage to find me, after all. I wouldn't put it past him – he'd go to any lengths to keep me from my kids, and now that my eldest is in his final year at school, he must know it's only a matter of time before I try to reach out. If my children find out that he's been lying to them this whole time, and I'm not tucked away in a mental institution, there's sure to be consequences for him.

'Nora, are your children safe with your husband?'

'My husband wouldn't hurt them, if that's what you mean.' He wouldn't physically harm them, just mentally scar them for life by taking them from their mother.

'Good,' she says. 'That's good. How long have you been out of home?'

'Mary, I've been living here for ten years! I work in the kitchen, remember?'

'Do you know the name of your caseworker? Which crisis centre have you been staying at?'

'I don't have a caseworker! I'm not staying at a crisis centre.' This is exasperating. I vaguely recall her asking me similar questions the day I arrived here. Most of my memories from those first few weeks at the shelter are a blur. But I do remember it was a problem that I'd walked in straight off the street and not been referred by one of the state crisis centres.

'We have a waitlist for accommodation here,' she continues.

There's a tsunami in my stomach, rolling waves being displaced from my core and radiating in all directions. My home is here at the shelter. I have nowhere else to go.

Mary must sense my distress because, light as a feather, she places her hand on my arm. 'I think we can arrange a spare bed for the interim. Why don't we get you settled and just leave it to me to organise a referral for you? Perhaps after a rest and a cup of tea, things will be clearer.'

'Okay,' I say, completely shaken. I've known Mary for years and she's also behaving like we've never met. But I'm wary of whatever is happening and know that I have to remain on guard. If I don't play along, they might call the police. 'That would be great,' I say, the quake in my voice evident. 'I am feeling a little light-headed.' I need time to work out what's happening and what I need to do to keep safe, assuming my husband is involved in this.

Mary stays close to me, in a motherly way, as we walk down the hall and up the stairs to where there are more bedrooms. My private room is on the ground floor. We stop outside the door to a room with four beds. The bed closest to the doorway is neatly made with a fresh towel, a folded pair of flannel pyjamas and a pack of toiletries.

'I hope you find everything you need. There's a bathroom down the hall and a communal lounge and dining room downstairs. I'll organise a cup of tea and some biscuits to be brought to you, so you can settle in.' Mary looks me directly in the eyes. 'You're going to be okay, Nora. We're here for you.'

She seems so genuine – maybe I'm wrong about this being some far-fetched plot that my husband has schemed. When she leaves the room, I let go of my breath and sit on the bed, tote bag clutched to my chest. I feel like I'm back at the beginning and don't know what I'm supposed to do with myself. This process was daunting enough the first time.

I open my bag to retrieve a stick of chewing gum and see the time capsule, still lightly dusted with dirt. An image of Elle flashes in my mind, her honey-gold hair, long and wavy, her flawless make-up, dressed in denim jeans and a dusty pink shirt. Maybe there is something wrong in my brain. I conjured Elle up earlier today. What if

Sheena and Mary not recognising me has something to do with me? Maybe this is some kind of delusion and going back to the place I once lived has triggered a weird reaction, causing the wiring in my brain to go haywire. I think Mary's right – a rest and a cup of tea will calm my nerves and hopefully reset whatever's happening in my head.

There's a knock on the open door and Heather is standing there with a mug and a plate of biscuits, a magazine under her arm. I fill with relief.

Heather has worked at the shelter for as long as I've been here. Her role is somewhere between supervisor and housekeeper, keeping an eye out that everything's running smoothly. She's also the night manager and sleeps here. She has this amazing ability to make people feel comfortable in her presence and you just know that you can tell her anything and she won't judge. She's my closest friend here.

'Hello, Nora,' she says.

Finally, someone who knows me. She comes into the room and places the tea and biscuits on the bedside table.

I reach for her hand. 'Heather, I don't know what's going on but Sheena and Mary are acting like they don't know me. I'm so relieved to see you.'

Heather reaches into her pocket and retrieves a foil packet, pushing two tablets into her palm. 'Take this, you'll feel better.'

'Panadol?' I look up at her, confused.

'You'd be surprised how well it works to relax your muscles. We prefer not to give you anything stronger until you've had an assessment.'

'I don't need to see a doctor,' I say.

She places the tablets next to the biscuits on the plate.

'Mary will decide that with you after your initial assessment with her.'

My shoulders slump. 'You don't know who I am,' I mumble under my breath.

'It takes time to settle in,' she says. 'But I promise you, in a few days you'll start feeling better. I thought you might like this.' She hands me a magazine. If she doesn't know me, how does she know that almost every day for the last ten years I've flicked through these women's magazines in the communal lounge?

'Thanks,' I say, taking the magazine from her, a picture of Angelina Jolie and Brad Pitt on the cover.

'I'll come check on you later,' says Heather before leaving.

I lie back on the pillow and close my eyes. One second later they're wide open. I sit up and stare at the magazine cover. Angelina and Brad are back together? How did I not know this? I flick through the magazine until I reach the double-page spread with images of the happy couple and their brood of children. But then it registers that their children are young, and Brad Pitt's grey goatee isn't so grey. I close it and check the date on the cover: 10 April 2012. Sometimes the magazines they keep in the lounge area might go back six to twelve months, but they shouldn't be this outdated unless one got lost amongst the pile. But even as I tell myself this, my hands are trembling. My gut is again telling me something is off. We're very in tune with each other now, my gut and me. For so many years I didn't listen to it, even when it was practically shouting at me, warning me. My heart and even my overthinking brain would tell me to do something else. Unfortunately, it took me becoming homeless to connect with the intuition that sits right in my centre, that knows my very being and what's right for me.

I walk out of the bedroom, down the staircase and head straight to the communal lounge. It's always busy at this time of the day. There's a woman sitting on the carpet playing a board game with two young children. A table holds a group of women, knitting and chatting. A young mother sits on the couch reading to her daughter. There's a small kitchenette in the corner near the windows and a pile of newspapers are on the bench. I pick up a *Herald Sun* from the top and, as I read the date, my lungs feel like they're closing up and my heart races so fast I think it's going to explode through my chest. I pick up the newspaper underneath and check that too: 11 April 2012. There's a photo of Julia Gillard on the front page, referring to her as the prime minister. I pick up the newspaper underneath that one, 10 April 2012, and again and again until it's 7 April 2012 and there are no more newspapers left.

This can't be right.

My breathing is heavy. My legs feel like jelly, but I manage to walk to the couch. 'Excuse me,' I say to the woman reading to her child, 'I'm sorry to interrupt, but can you tell me today's date please?'

She looks up from the picture book she's reading. 'I think it's the twelfth.'

'Of April? What year?'

She looks at me oddly and I see her surreptitiously tighten an arm around her daughter. 'It's 2012.'

My hand grips the back of the couch to steady myself. If my legs felt like jelly before, now they're completely numb. I drop my head and take a few quick breaths in and out. Keep it together, Nora, I tell myself. If I become hysterical I really might end up in a loony bin this time.

In a daze, I turn around and make my way down the corridor to my bedroom. I turn the handle and it's locked. 'Shit,' I mutter under my breath and climb the stairs to the new bedroom Sheena allocated to me. I sit on the edge of the bed and drink the lukewarm tea in one go then stuff a biscuit in my mouth, chewing furiously until it's digested. The sugar works instantly and blood pumps once again to my brain, restoring warmth to my cheeks along the way. I must be caught up in a dream that feels completely real. One of those dreams where you're trying to pull yourself out of it, but no matter how many doors you open, you just can't wake up.

My tote bag lies on the bed. I rummage through it and pull out the domino box, my heart thundering against my ribcage as my hands clutch the only tangible object connecting me to my old life and my children. Surely *this* is real – I can feel it in my hands, the roughness of the wood, the graininess of the dirt. Like a child tearing through a birthday present, I pull it open and empty the contents on the bed, picking up the car, then the figurine and finally the bracelet, an assortment of yellow, purple, green and blue beads. My hands run over the beads, before slipping the bracelet onto my wrist. Then I pick up one of the letters, the paper not yellowed at all. In fact, it looks exactly as it did the day we wrote them. I unfold the small square and my heart cracks into a hundred tiny pieces that I don't think I'm ever going to be able to put back together. I read both my boys' letters before scanning the one I wrote to myself then scrunching it into a ball and throwing it on the ground, the tears that were absently cascading down my cheeks now flooding as I sob.

This must be a freakin' nightmare. That's the only explanation. I just have to go to sleep and then I'll wake up tomorrow and none of this will have ever happened. Seeing Elle was just a dream, the staff here not knowing me all a dream, the date on the newspapers just part of this nightmare I'm having.

Fully dressed, I climb under the covers, curling my knees into my chest as my hand cradles my aching head. I close my eyes and when the sobbing eventually calms, I drift off to sleep.

Chapter 5

Elle

I'm woken at dawn by a flock of chirping birds. Maybe not exactly a flock, but it sounds like it. I think there's a nest in the tree outside our bedroom window, and it's the third day in a row that they've woken me. When I complained to Richard on the first day he told me to ask the gardener to get rid of the nest, but I can't do that. What if there are eggs waiting to hatch? They'll be motherless. And even if there are no eggs and the gardener relocates the nest, a family of birds would come back and find they had no home. They may not even be able to find each other.

I roll onto my back to meditate, hoping I'll nod off.

Next thing I know my husband is half-lying on top of me, nibbling at my ear, his hands roaming.

'Good morning,' he says.

'What time is it?' I lift my head to check the clock next to the bed. It's five-fifty. Richard sets his alarm at the same time every morning to go to gym. Sometimes I'm already up, getting a head start on work, other times I'm in bed asleep, which is why Richard allows himself an extra ten minutes.

'Maybe not this morning,' I say, rubbing my eye. 'I'm so tired, the birds woke me again.'

'I told you to get rid of the birds,' he says, his head hovering over me, dark eyes staring down.

'I haven't yet.'

'Call the gardener today.'

'I will.' I look up at his face, knowing he's going to get his way, but I give myself one more shot. 'But really, I'm too tired and I've got a lot on today.'

'You know what they say, a good roll in the hay is a great start to the day.'

I give in and reach to kiss him.

'Morning breath.' He turns his face away and kisses my neck.

Five minutes later, we're done. Well, he is.

After I've showered and dressed, I go downstairs and take the marinated duck out of the fridge to bring to room temperature and start on the boys' lunches.

At six-thirty, Olly runs into the kitchen in his pyjamas, rubbing sleep from his eyes.

'Is it school today?' he asks.

'It is,' I smile. He's still getting used to the routine of going to school every day. Last year he went to kindergarten three times a week, and on the other two days he'd mostly spend the morning with Nick Jr. or the Disney Channel. Bad parenting, I know, but there wasn't much alternative.

I run my hands through Olly's dishevelled hair. One cheek is still rosy from where he lay on it, and when I bend to kiss the smooth skin, it's deliciously warm. 'Coco Pops or toast with peanut butter?' I ask him.

'Coco Pops!'

'Okay.'

He runs to the couch and turns on the television and the *Peppa Pig* tune replaces the morning quiet. 'Come on, buddy,' I say, placing the bowl on the kitchen table. 'You can watch from here.'

Covering the duck with foil, I slide it into the oven on a low heat. At seven I run upstairs to wake Charlie.

'What time is it?' he asks, stretching his arms out to the side.

'The same time that I wake you every school morning. Get dressed and come have brekky. Do you want eggs?'

'Yuck.'

'Toast?'

'Ugh.'

'Weet-Bix?'

'Weet-Bix!' he grizzles. 'I know Olly gets Coco Pops every morning. I see the chocolate milk in the sink.'

'I only let him have it to keep him quiet so he doesn't wake you. Coco Pops isn't a nutritious breakfast. Weet-Bix will give you energy.'

'It's so unfair,' whines Charlie.

'You know the rules, you can have it on the weekend. Take your pick, eggs, toast or Weet-Bix.'

'Fine,' he says, sitting up and throwing off the covers. 'I'll have Weet-Bix.'

We're in the car by eight. Somewhere in between Richard has come home, made his morning smoothie, chatted with the kids for a few minutes and taken himself off to shower and get ready for work. By the time I come home he's already left. Every other day he leaves a list on the kitchen bench, of things he'd like me to do: errands to run, organising someone to fix something around the house. Then there's the pile of bills that I not only have to pay but enter into a spreadsheet so he can cross-reference them with the bank statement. Fortunately, the only item on his list today is to organise the gardener to remove the nest. I scrunch up the note and toss it in the rubbish bin. The birds waking me won't be mentioned again.

I have half an hour to clean my kitchen to commercial standards before Georgie arrives at nine. She lets herself in as I'm loading the kitchen bench with ingredients. Georgie has her own key, although Richard doesn't know about this. It was just easier that way. If my hands are covered in mincemeat, I don't waste time stopping to wash them to answer the door.

'Morning,' I call, rinsing the zucchinis and eggplants. The capsicums are already in the oven roasting.

'Good morning.' Georgie drops a bag of artisan rolls on the bench. Gathering her long brown hair into a ponytail, she pulls on an apron embroidered with our logo, Notch Catering. The name was Georgie's idea, because our aim is to be a notch above the rest when it comes to our food quality and work ethos. I shift an eggplant away from the running water and she washes her hands before grabbing chopping boards, mixing bowls and knives from the cupboards and drawers. She knows my kitchen like her own and this is how we work, in symmetry, everything just flowing.

I slice the zucchinis into long slivers as we talk. Fortunately, I've bought myself some time with the whole business expansion topic – I have until Monday to get back to her after supposedly discussing it with Richard. There has been something else on my mind though. The homeless woman I met yesterday keeps invading my thoughts. If I told Richard about this need I've been feeling since I met her, to give back in some way, he'd put a stop to it before my ideas became a plan. But Georgie I can brainstorm with. I tell her about the woman I met yesterday. 'I don't know,' I say, 'I just feel like I have to do something to help. Maybe we could make food to drop off to a shelter?'

Georgie scans the bench full of produce as she trims the snow-pea sprouts before adding them to the shredded Chinese cabbage. 'Food costs money. We'd need funding.'

She's right. 'What if we supply them with leftovers from our catering?' I turn on the gas, drizzle olive oil into a pan and spread the zucchini strips over its base.

'We make maybe two extra portions of each dish as a backup. Everything gets used.' She glides her knife through the carrot and then the capsicum as though the vegetables are as soft as butter. 'The only thing you can really do that doesn't require funding is give your time.'

My time I can give, although I am strapped for it as it is. 'What are you thinking?' I turn over the zucchini slices with the tongs, rubbing them in the oil and juices in the pan as I do.

'Do what you do best – cook.' Her fingers effortlessly tear the coriander and mint leaves before lifting the chopping board and using the knife to slide the ingredients into the salad.

'Cook?'

'Yes. Do a cooking class at a shelter. I'm sure they'd love it. It'd be great for morale.'

'You really think they'd like it?'

'Sure. Try it once, and if you enjoy it and feel that it's helping, do it again.'

It does make sense and would only require a few hours of my

time. Even if once a week was too much, I could run the workshop every fortnight or even once a month. And if I wait until everything is running smoothly before I tell Richard then he'll have nothing to protest about. 'Will you do it with me?' I give her my best puppy-dog eyes.

'How about you do the groundwork and I'll come to the first few workshops and get you started.'

'I'd love that. See, you're brilliant, George. I knew you'd think of something.'

'That's me, full of ideas. Speaking of which, I've put all my plans to paper for the next stage of the business, so if you want models and projections for when you speak to Richard, they're good to go.'

'Thanks,' I say. I feel awful knowing Georgie has put so much time into this already. But I know Richard, and he won't want me investing any more time into the business than I already do. It's not like I haven't brought up my dreams for the business over the years with him. And whenever I have, he brushed them off, like that's all they'll ever be – unfulfilled dreams.

'I'll bring them with me tomorrow,' says Georgie.

'Okay,' I say. As much as I'd love to see her plans, I have no intention of showing them to Richard.

Chapter 6

Nora

I open my eyes, my head feeling heavy. The room is dark other than the light seeping under the door from the hallway. I press a palm to my forehead as the nightmare I had last night plays through my mind.

A high-pitched snore suddenly fills the quiet. I jolt, turning my head sideways to take in the shapes of three other single beds in the bedroom, two of them occupied. 'What the ...' I mumble under my breath. I'm not in my room. This is not happening. This is *not* happening! I pull back the covers and I'm wearing the same denim jeans and long-sleeved top I went to sleep in. It can't possibly be the day after yesterday, the day after 12 April 2012. Am I stuck in some kind of time loop or am I still dreaming? I pinch the skin on my forearm. Definitely awake. Climbing out of bed, I shuffle in my socks to the door, quietly closing it behind me before dashing down the stairs to the communal lounge.

The urn is switching on and off as it heats and I open the jar of instant coffee, placing a heaped spoonful of granules into a mug.

My hands are shaking as I push down the lever on the urn, and when the boiling water hits the granules, I deeply breathe in the familiar smell in a misguided attempt to calm myself. Not bothering to add milk, the coffee scalds my tongue as I take a sip.

I eye the newspapers on the bench, petrified to even look. The coffee mug begins to quake in my hand so I place it on the bench before daring to glance over the paper. My breath escapes me: the year is the same as it was yesterday. I close my eyes, questions flooding my mind. What's happening to me? How can I be in 2012? Am I going crazy? And if I'm not going insane then why am I here, back in the past? Living that year was hell enough the first time around.

My eyes flick open and I take in my surroundings: the kitchenette, the clean dishes drying in the rack, the board game on the coffee table, the shelves in the corner stacked with books and more games. My fingers brush back my fringe and I glance down at my body, taking in every inch. That hasn't changed; I'm definitely not the size six I was in 2012. Everything about me looks the same as it did when my day began yesterday and I visited my old house. And if I'm still here at the shelter, I guess that means I'm not back in my old life as it was in April 2012. I'm the same person I am in 2022.

I pick up the mug and take it to sit on the couch by the window. Dawn is breaking around the edges of the surrounding buildings, bringing with it a new day. I'm just not sure I'm ready to handle what my day brings.

I sigh and take a sip of my coffee, trying to process what's happening to me, but I'm not sure it's explainable. I need answers, but who would believe me if I told them I've gone back to the past? I'm struggling to get my head around it myself.

I can only think of one way to get some answers.

Standing, I walk over to the shared computer at the desk in the far corner of the room. I've barely touched it in the last ten years. I had no reason to. I click on the mouse and the screen comes to life. I think for a moment and then type 'time travel is it possible' into the search field, and the screen fills. I scroll down the list, clicking on random links, scanning the abundance of information that is mostly like reading another language.

There's a pen and notepad on the desk. I rip off a sheet of paper and jot down notes. I write down Einstein's theory of special relativity, that time and space are linked together, and the faster you travel, the slower you experience time. I read other theoretical scientists' views that time travel is possible but it's a one-way ticket, you can only go to the future. They talk about intense gravitational acceleration of black holes and travellers rocketing into space at the speed of light. None of it makes sense to me, but I keep writing. I don't know what else to do. When I read about wormholes to the past, I throw down the pen and run my hands through my hair. This isn't helping.

When I look up, I notice that other residents have filtered in, some sitting at tables eating their breakfast. A mother is buttering a slice of toast for her child. There's a sense of calm, the exact opposite of what I'm feeling inside me right now. Inside I'm in complete disarray. I look back at the screen and check the time, it's already after nine, then stare at it like it's going to magically give me the answers I need. Having nowhere to be and still not knowing what I'm meant to do, I type in another search. One search leads to another and I end up reading about parallel universes and the multiverse. Maybe this reality is a variant of my own? But if that's the case, I'm still not in 2022 – I'm back in 2012.

'Nora, there you are.'

I startle and abruptly turn to find Heather behind me.

'Heather ...' I grab the mouse, dragging the arrow over the red dot to close the page on my search.

'Mary is waiting for you.'

'Mary?'

'Yes, you met her yesterday. She's the counsellor here at the shelter. You have an appointment with her.'

'Why do I need an appointment?'

'All the women have an initial session with Mary when they arrive. Counselling sessions are very beneficial to your stay here. We also have group sessions. They're a great way for residents to connect with each other and share their stories – sometimes the women have experienced similar challenges, and it helps to know you're not alone.'

I breathe out in frustration. I've already been through all of this. I couldn't share my story with others the last time so, it's unlikely I'm going to share it now with a whole new set of strangers. Heather was the only person who knew my history, although even that was only snippets of what I allowed myself to share. I couldn't trust anyone with the whole truth. There was too much at risk for me.

Heather smiles at me and I stand up to go with her. She takes in my socks and rumpled clothing from yesterday. If it wasn't Heather, I'd be embarrassed.

'We have a clothing cupboard in the hallway that you can help yourself to later. There's every size in there.' As she talks, she turns to walk to Mary's office. I'm sure it's a tactic to avoid eye contact and make me feel comfortable. 'All that we ask is that items are washed and folded after they're worn and returned to the correct shelf.' I'm about to follow her when I remember I haven't turned off the computer. I click the mouse pad to put it to sleep and notice the pages of notes on the desk. I pick them up and shove them in my back pocket.

Heather knocks on the open door of Mary's office. 'I have Nora for you.'

'Great,' says Mary, getting up from her desk. 'Please, come in.' She gestures to the couch underneath the window on the far side of the room. Heather leaves, closing the door behind her. There's a round table that seats four opposite Mary's desk, but other than a print on the wall next to the table it's pretty sparse. The clutter of plants that liven the room in my time haven't made an appearance yet.

I sit down on one side of the couch and Mary takes the other, a pad resting on her knee and pen in hand. She asks the basics – name, date of birth – before heading into old territory. As familiar as it is, this time its feels completely different too.

The first time I sat here on this very couch, ten years ago, I was in a completely different state. I'd come from spending almost two weeks sleeping on the streets and hadn't been well. In fact, there had been moments when I thought I was literally going to die because my body was shaking so violently. One moment I'd be pouring with sweat, the next, every inch of me frozen and shivering. The staff had checked on me throughout each day after I arrived, but my body was so heavy, I was so physically and mentally shattered, that I couldn't get up. It was several days before I was even able to have a consultation with Mary.

'How are you feeling today, Nora?' Mary had asked back then.

'A little better.' I had wrapped the woollen cardigan Heather had given me from the shared cupboard tighter around my frail, shivering body, breathing in the scent of laundry powder. I'd left home with a backpack, two spare t-shirts, a few changes of under-wear, and a toothbrush and toothpaste. There was no time to prepare. I'd slept on the steps of shop doorways, shielding myself from people of the night. It was only when I arrived at the shelter that it felt safe to breathe again. All those small things, being able to shower, wear fresh clothing, to sleep in a bed and have a warm meal, were a gift.

My finger had jerked upwards of its own accord and Mary's eyes had darted to my hand. It had been doing that sporadically, since I left home, and I had no idea why and couldn't control it. Self-conscious, I had placed both hands between my thighs.

'Do you feel comfortable talking about why you left home?' she had asked.

My eyes filled. My body ached everywhere, but the stabbing pain in my heart was unbearable. 'I had no choice. I had to leave.'

'Are your children safe at home with your husband?'

I nodded. Tears flowed down my cheeks. I had no strength left in me to even attempt to hold on to them. Mary passed me a tissue box. 'Thank you,' my voice was shaky, almost broken. I pulled out a tissue, blew my nose, then scrunched it into my hand. I needed something to hold on to.

'Nora ... are you safe with your husband?' she had asked gently.

I shook my head, looking at my lap, every nerve ending in my body going at a million miles an hour.

'Nora,' she had continued, leaning over to place her hand on my shoulder. 'You're safe here. Within the walls of the shelter, you're safe. We have security cameras and no one will find you here. You're safe,' she reiterated, as though repeating the words would make it true. 'Do you understand?'

I'd sniffed and nodded, but still I couldn't stop crying. I'd never felt so weak in my life. This was not me, this was not who I was.

'Can you tell me the names of the medications that you're taking?'

'I'm not on any medication.'

Mary's eyebrows had raised. 'Any herbal medication?'

I shook my head.

She had carefully placed her notepad and pen down on the couch next to her. 'Are you sure? Maybe your doctor prescribed something for you?'

'No, nothing.'

She had seemed hesitant, watching me kindly but intensely before she said, 'These last few days, when we've been caring for you, you have displayed all the symptoms of someone withdrawing from drugs – the violent shaking, changes in body temperature, paranoia.'

'Drugs? I've never taken drugs in my life. And if I'm paranoid it's because I'm afraid my husband will find me.' The man was planning to incarcerate me in a mental institution, but I had held that information back. I thought I knew how these places worked: if Mary suspected abuse, she'd contact the police or legal aid, and that would only cause more problems for me. My life was in the hands of my husband. He was pulling all the strings. All that mattered in that moment was that I was safe and had a place where I could recover.

Mary's lips had pursed, clearly unconvinced.

'I had some health issues for a while before I left home. I saw several doctors but they couldn't work out what was wrong with me. I think it just intensified over the last couple of weeks, that's all. I'm already starting to feel better,' I had lied.

'Okay,' said Mary. 'Let's put in another session for later in the week, and when you feel up to joining the group sessions, the times are listed on the noticeboard in the communal lounge. She went to her desk and wrote a time and date on a small card and handed it to me.

'Thank you,' I had said, then walked out to the lounge area and found a place to sit where the sunlight seeped through the window. I closed my eyes, absorbing the warmth. Mary was right, since I left home I'd been experiencing all the symptoms you hear about drug addicts experiencing when they abruptly stop taking recreational drugs. My nervous system was a mess. The only problem was, I'd told Mary the truth, I'd never taken drugs in my life.

'Nora?' Mary interrupts my thoughts as I sit on her couch, having an initial assessment, for the second time now.

'Sorry, what did you ask?'

'Do you have anyone in your life who it would be safe to stay with? Any other family?'

'No,' I say. My parents are both dead. But then it hits me: in 2012 my father had passed the year before, but my mother ... my mother is alive. If I am really back in 2012, as insane as that sounds, my mother will be living in a residential care home in Balwyn. I swallow. 'My mother lives in a home. She has Alzheimer's.'

'Perhaps we can organise for you to visit her, once you've settled in.'

'Yes – yes, that would be good.'

'The most important thing for now is keeping you safe. We don't want you to go anywhere your husband might find you until you're back up on your feet, so to speak.'

'Yes, right,' I say, completely distracted. All I can think about is that my mum is alive.

Chapter 7

Nora

It takes me an hour, two bus rides and a few short walks to get to the residential care home in Balwyn. Even though it's been years since I've been here, as soon as I walk through the doors to reception, the musty smell that greets me is familiar. Checking in at the front desk, I'm relieved that I don't know the nurse.

'Hi,' I say. 'I'm here to see Rosalind Plankett. I'm her ...' I hesitate. It may be confusing if I tell the staff here I'm her daughter, they won't recognise me. 'I'm a relative,' I say. My heart palpitates as I wait for her response. If the receptionist tells me to go in, it will confirm that I really am in 2012 and my mum is actually alive. Years of not just grieving for my mother, but aching for her presence in my life once I found myself all alone will obliterate in an instant.

'Sure, love, go right in,' she says.

'Thank you.' I practically choke on the words. My palms are sweaty. In a moment I'll be face to face with my mother. I can see her and hold her again. I pass the dining hall, filled with dozens of small round tables that seat four to six residents. Staff are setting the tables with cutlery for lunch. I thought I'd be sprinting to her room, but I seem to be crawling, conscious of moving one foot in front of the other. My mother died in 2017. She was eighty-five years old. She had me late in life at thirty-nine and called me her miracle baby. Mum developed Alzheimer's in her early seventies, but my dad insisted on looking after her at home until he became sick. They moved to the residential care home together a year before he died.

It's crazy that I'm so nervous to see my own mother, but in my world, she's been dead for five years. I pass the communal lounge room, armchairs occupied by residents watching the news on a large television screen. Several are sitting on sofas in front of the floor-to-ceiling windows that overlook a leafy green courtyard, playing a game of Rummikub.

As I near Mum's room on the ground floor, my fingernails dig into my palms. Her room overlooks another courtyard, which was nice because she used to love to garden. On good days she'd be out of bed, sitting at the small table that faced the courtyard and working on a needlepoint, usually a canvas that came with a ready-made design. On those days she'd remember me. Even if she kept repeating herself and asking me the same question over and over, she knew who I was. She'd recall stories from her childhood in such detail that it left me amazed that this disease could also cause her to not know her own child, more often than not.

The door to her room is open. I brace myself against the doorframe, taking in the basic room, the dresser, the small table with two chairs, the slight figure under the covers of the adjustable bed, staring out the window.

I've forgotten how to breathe.

'Mum,' I whisper.

She doesn't respond. I creep to the edge of her bed, but she doesn't seem to notice me. Picking up one of the chairs, I take it to the far side of the bed and sit down in her field of vision. Sometimes she would do that, just stare into space, and it would take her time to notice that someone was there.

'Mum,' I say again, too afraid to touch her in case she doesn't know it's me. It's not only because of the Alzheimer's that she may not recognise me – she also never got to see me at fifty-one years old. Everything about me is so different now.

Her eyes move and focus on me. They look almost grey, vacant. Her face is wrinkled and sunken. She looks empty, like her body is here but her soul has moved on.

'She's not having a great day,' says a nurse standing at the door.

I don't recognise the nurse, but it was such a long time ago. For a moment I wonder if she remembers me but she doesn't show any signs of recognition.

'Oh.' I'm desperate to reach over and wrap myself around my mother. I want to climb on the bed, curl into her and release the sobs I'm holding on to. But I know if I do, I'll only frighten her.

'I'm Ronny,' says the nurse, coming into the room.

'Nora,' I say. 'How has she been?'

Ronny takes one of Mum's hands and begins massaging it. 'She's doing great, aren't you, Rosalind?' She moves her hands up Mum's arm, gently kneading.

Mum turns to face the nurse. 'Who are you?' she asks.

'I'm Ronny, your nurse. How are you today, lovely?'

'Tired,' says Mum.

Ronny moves over to the side of the bed I'm sitting on and picks up Mum's other arm to massage.

Mum's eyes follow her and then they land on me. 'Are you a nurse too?'

My chest constricts. I'd forgotten how hard it was when she didn't recognise me. I can't even remember what I used to say to her when she was like this, whether telling her who I was made her more agitated, calmed her, or if she absorbed the information at all. 'It's me, Nora.'

'Do I know you?' she asks.

I look up at Ronny for guidance.

'Nora's come for a visit,' she says. 'Would you like her to read to you?' Ronny picks up a book from the bedside table and hands it to me, a weathered copy of *Pride and Prejudice*. 'This is her favourite,' she says.

I know it is. I open it to a random page.

'I'll come back later to check on her,' says Ronny.

'Thank you.' I start to read and Mum stares at me as she listens.

'He's so handsome, Mr Darcy.'

'He is,' I say. I can imagine him too.

She's peaceful while I read, and after fifteen minutes or so, her eyes begin to flutter and eventually close. I place the book on the bedside table, leaving it splayed open on the page we were at.

'Mum,' I say, gently touching her frail hand, skin so thin it's translucent. My fingers trace her polished nails, which the staff redo weekly for her. There are a few chips but they're beautiful. I move my chair closer and bend my head so that my cheek rests on her arm. The scent of her skin is my undoing, the familiar orange blossom of her soap, that I would replenish for her. I quietly let the tears flow, listening to the sound of her gentle breathing.

'You're still here.'

My head jerks up at the sound of Ronny's voice. I must have dozed off. I sit up and automatically wipe underneath my eyes, but whatever tears were there have dried. I check my watch; it's already eleven o'clock. There's a tray with morning tea on the dresser but I didn't hear anyone come in.

Ronny places her hand on my shoulder and squeezes it. 'I know it's hard, lovely, but you're doing great. Why don't you take a break and grab a coffee? There's a fresh cake in the lounge.'

'Thank you. I think I will go get a drink.' It's not like I have anywhere else to be right now. My friends and my job at the shelter don't exist. I can't even reach out to my children because I'd only frighten them if they saw me. To them I'd be a stranger, not their mother. The only person in my life right now is Mum.

In the lounge I make a coffee and cut a slice of the cake. It smells like banana and cinnamon. I take the plate and coffee to the couch, giving myself a moment to digest what's happening, that I'm here with Mum again. I'm still comprehending that it's April 2012. Even though I'm not homeless yet, I can't go home. That doesn't seem to be how whatever this is works.

I finish the cake and make my way back to Mum's room. She's sitting at the table looking outside, the teapot and plate of biscuits set up on the table for her. Ronny must have woken her so she could have morning tea. I remember now that they like to keep the residents in a routine during the day so they feel safe and secure. The teacup shakes slightly in her hand as she moves it towards her lips.

The chair I'd moved to the side of her bed is back at the table. I hesitate for a moment before I enter and stand with one hand on the back of the chair. I'm about to sit down, when Mum looks up at me. There's a glow in her eyes; they're sparkling blue again. Her mouth forms into a smile and that's when I realise she recognises me.

'Eleanor,' she says, reaching her free hand out towards me. 'My darling Elle.'

My knees buckle to the carpet and I crumble before her, resting my head on her lap. Her hand brushes over my hair.

'Darling, what have you done to your hair?'

I can't help but let out a laugh amongst the tears. The comment is so like Mum, it's absolutely perfect. I'm exactly where I need to be right now.

Chapter 8

Elle

I dab a smudge of concealer on my chin then brush over it with some bronzer.

'The babysitter's here,' Richard calls out from the bedroom. 'Are you ready?'

'Coming.' I close the mirrored cabinet door before swiping on some lip gloss. 'Ready,' I say as I come out of the bathroom and pick up my clutch from the bed.

Richard's eyes draw down over my cream silk blouse tucked into black pants and strappy heels. He walks to the closet and opens the door, rummaging through my clothes, then pulls out a short black dress, long-sleeved and with ruching at the neckline, revealing plenty of chest. 'Why don't you put this on? It looks great on you.'

'I feel like wearing pants,' I say, taking the hanger from him and placing the dress back in the cupboard. 'And it's too dressy for a dinner party.'

'You look like a prude in that, all covered up.'

My mouth gapes.

He moves closer, his eyes never leaving my face, and places his hand on my waist. 'You know what I mean. You've got great legs, you should show them off. Can't let all that gym time go to waste.'

Richard has me working out with a personal trainer twice a week. He even makes me his protein smoothie every morning, which is about the only time he uses the kitchen. He doesn't eat a proper meal until lunchtime and thinks I should do the same to keep my figure. Fortunately, coffees before twelve are admissible.

'Let's just go, I don't want to be late.'

'There's plenty of time. I'll meet you in the car,' he says, then walks out of the bedroom.

I look down at my outfit, then to the closet, and shake my head.

Georgie's husband, Tye, greets us at the front door, giving me a hug and shaking Richard's hand. I hand him the bottle of red wine and carry the scented candle I bought for Georgie to the kitchen.

'Hi,' says Georgie. 'Look at you! That dress is stunning.'

'Thanks,' I say, handing her the gift, feeling uncomfortable being so dressed up. Georgie's wearing black pants and a blouse.

'Thank you. You didn't have to get me anything,' she says, placing it on the bench.

'It smells delicious in here.'

'Tye,' she calls out, 'get Elle and Richard a drink. He's made martinis. I'm on my second.' Her cheeks are flushed and she's grinning like a Cheshire cat.

We go into the living room where two other couples – Brooke and Jeremy, and Courtney and Dion – are sitting on the sofa, nursing drinks and picking from the platter of hors d'oeuvres on the coffee table. They're not close friends, and Richard and I only socialise with them when we're with Georgie and Tye.

After exchanging hellos, I join them on the sofa and pick up a crostini topped with a kingfish tartare. It smells of ginger, lime and soy. I grab a serviette and bite into it. 'George, this is delicious.'

'You like? I concocted it today.' She comes to sit on the sofa next to me, cocktail in hand.

Tye comes over with Richard and hands me a martini. Richard perches himself on the side of the sofa and rests his hand on my shoulder. I take a sip of my drink, the balance of olive brine to gin perfect.

'Cheers,' says Tye, holding up his glass.

A chorus follows.

We make small talk while we drink and nibble, and then Georgie announces that dinner is ready.

The table looks immaculate, set with wineglasses, chopsticks and cloth serviettes. Georgie has made an Asian feast. There's a bamboo basket with steamed prawn dim sum, a platter with vegetarian san choy bow and another with duck spring rolls. Georgie's been talking about her menu with me all week.

'Wow, this looks amazing,' says Courtney. We're standing around the table, all eyes on the display of food.

'Sit, sit,' says Georgie, placing herself at the head of the table. Tye sits opposite her and I take the seat next to him. Richard sits down next to me. 'Don't be shy. Tuck in.'

I reach for a san choy bow, cupping the lettuce leaf and taking a mouthful. The juices ooze into my hand and I wipe it with the serviette. 'George, you've gone all out.'

'What can I say, I like to cook.'

We all laugh.

The prawn dim sum are perfection. With everyone so busy eating and commenting on the food, the conversation slows. Tye opens a bottle each of red wine and white and walks around the table filling everyone's glasses.

'Georgie, you've outdone yourself,' says Richard, wiping his serviette across the side of his mouth.

'Thank you,' she says.

'She's been slaving away all day,' says Tye. 'She had the kids and I running to the shops and back every time she forgot an ingredient.'

'I didn't forget to buy any ingredients.' Georgie pouts. 'It was only after I taste-tested and realised I could make it even better that I sent you out. I wanted everything to be perfect.'

'It is, babe,' says Tye. He turns to me and winks. 'I'm used to it.'

We do occasionally call Tye to pick up something for us when we've forgotten an ingredient; his office is less than ten minutes from my place and he's his own boss. But we always send him away with some samples, so he's mostly pretty happy with the arrangement.

'You love it,' I say. 'You get lunch.'

'I do,' says Tye.

Richard, listening to our easy banter, places his hand on my thigh.

'Can you please pass me a spring roll?' I ask him. The platter is on the other end of the table.

He squeezes my thigh, ignoring me. 'There's so much food, I'll have no room for the main course,' he says to Georgie.

I assume that comment is a reminder for me not to overeat.

'I'll make sure to pace the dishes,' says Georgie. She gets up from the table and reaches for the spring roll platter. Like a waitress, she offers one to Courtney, sitting on Richard's other side, then Ben sitting opposite and continues on her journey around the table until she gets to me.

'I think I'll save myself for mains,' I say.

'Elle, you have to try one. I was thinking we could add it to our menu.' She places one on my plate.

'Thank you,' I say.

She fills a teaspoon with hoisin sauce and drops a large dollop on my entrée plate.

I dip the spring roll into the sauce and take a mouthful. It's deliciously crunchy and oily on the outside and the duck melts in my mouth. Paired with the hoisin sauce, it's perfect.

Richard removes his hand from my thigh, and when Georgie offers him another spring roll, he declines.

She sits back down at the table. 'So what do you think?' she asks.

'They're unbelievable. Is that a hint of cinnamon I can taste?'

She points at me, clearly thrilled. 'I knew you'd pick that up.'

I smile at her and take a sip of red wine. Richard is quiet beside me.

Georgie gets up to clear and I pick up Richard's plate, Tye's and mine along with the empty bamboo basket from the centre of the table and join her in the kitchen.

'What was that all about?' she asks, rinsing the plates at the sink.

'What?'

'Richard and the spring roll? He clearly didn't want you to have one.'

'I didn't notice,' I lie, taking over stacking the dishwasher so she can assemble the mains that are keeping warm in the oven.

Brooke pushes open the swinging door to the kitchen. 'Do you need any help?' she asks.

'No, all good,' says Georgie. 'Actually, can you take this to the table?' She hands Brooke a steaming bowl of sticky fried rice.

'Sure,' says Brooke, taking the bowl and pushing backwards through the swinging door.

I close the dishwasher and wipe my hands on the tea towel. 'Anything else ready to go?'

Georgie hands me a deep plate filled with beef and black bean sauce on a bed of Asian greens. I can see the concern in her warm brown eyes, but I look away and carry the plate to the table.

Richard is sitting on the sofa with Tye and the other guests. I only catch a few words of their conversation, something about expansion and Christmas parties, but it's enough to guess what they're talking about. My body tenses, and after I place the dish on the table, I veer straight back to the kitchen.

'Are you okay? You look like you've seen a ghost!' says Georgie.

There's a rock lodged deep in my throat. 'I haven't discussed it with him yet.'

'Discussed what with who?' she asks, garnishing the crispy lemon chicken with finely sliced spring onions.

'Expanding the business. With Richard.'

'That's okay, we have time.'

'No, you don't get it.' My heart is racing, my voice becomes agitated. 'He's hearing about it for the first time now, from Tye. They're discussing it in there, with everyone.' My head points towards the swinging door.

Georgie wipes her hands on her apron and comes around to the other side of the bench, placing her hand on my arm. 'Elle, you're trembling.'

Looking down at my hands, they're visibly shaking. I place them on the benchtop, telling myself to snap out of this. I'm probably getting worked up over nothing. 'I'm sure it's fine. I just wanted the chance to talk to him about it before discussing it all together.' Although the truth is that five minutes ago I had no intention of ever bringing it up with Richard. The expansion is a moot point. There's no way he would approve.

'Let's go back in there. I'm sure they're onto another topic by now.' Georgie picks up the platter of chicken and I follow her into the dining room. 'Dinner is served,' she says.

I sit down at the table and the other guests come over from the sofa. When Richard passes my chair I feel a cold gust of wind sweeping by. He's quiet for the rest of the evening, and when I try to engage him in conversation on the car ride home, he turns up the volume on the radio and ignores me.

He pulls up in the driveway, slams the car door and strides into the house. I pay the babysitter and walk her out, and when I come back to the living area, Richard has poured himself a Scotch.

'So this is how it is now? You make decisions without me, behind my back?' He leans against the kitchen bench and turns to look at me, eyes blazing.

'Richard, it's not like that at all.'

'Explain it to me then.'

Consciously keeping the bench between us, I stand opposite him and choose my words carefully. 'I didn't tell you about it because I'm not going ahead with the expansion. The timing isn't right for us. I don't want to work more hours, I want to be here for you and the boys.' Surely that will placate him. There's nothing there to argue with.

'But you didn't tell me you were thinking about it?'

'I wasn't thinking about it. It was Georgie's idea.'

He moves around the bench to stand right next to me. His face is so close to mine, I can smell the Scotch on his breath. 'Do you have any idea how embarrassing it was for me to hear about my wife's business plans from her partner's husband? And in front of other people? Tye seemed to know all about it, and in detail.'

'That's because it was Georgie's idea. She obviously discussed it with him.'

'But you decided not to discuss it with your husband.'

It doesn't matter what I say, every word I utter will be a waste of breath. Richard is clearly not listening to me, and when he gets like this it's better to let him have the last word.

'I'm going to bed.' I move past him but he reaches for my wrist, pulling me back into his body.

'We're not finished here. You embarrassed me tonight.'

My heartbeat gains momentum. 'I'm sorry. I didn't mean to put you in that situation. But you have nothing to worry about, our business model is staying exactly the same.'

He loosens his grip on my wrist and I take the opportunity to retrieve it and go upstairs.

When he comes up to the bedroom, I've already changed into my nightie and I'm in bed, leaning against propped-up pillows, reading my book. The main bedroom light is off, the room lit with the golden glow from the bedside lamps.

I keep my eyes on my book, rereading the same sentence while Richard unbuttons his shirt and throws it in the wash basket in the corner. He sits on the edge of the bed and unties his shoes, then stands, undoes his belt and pulls off his trousers. He moves to his side of the bed and reaches to turn down the covers. I can feel his eyes on me, waiting. I rest my book on the doona cover and look up at him. He motions with his head in the direction of the door.

My shoulders lift with tension. 'Really?'

'Yes. I'm not sleeping in the same bed as a woman who's deceitful.' His voice is icy but at the same time eerily calm. Definitely too calm for Richard. Usually he loses it and gets it all out. But the way he's looking at me chills me to the bone.

He does this when we're not on good terms. They say couples shouldn't go to bed angry, and technically we don't. Richard just makes me sleep in one of the boys' rooms or on the couch downstairs when we've had an argument. Sometimes it can take a few days for him to let it go. The longest he's gone is eight nights when Olly was eighteen months old. Eight nights I had to sleep on a narrow couch after I told Richard I wanted to go back to work and start the catering business with Georgie. The idea wasn't well received, to say the least.

'Richard ...'

'I can't trust you.'

'Of course you can. I already explained. There was nothing to discuss because I wasn't going ahead with Georgie's plans. My family comes first, you know that.' It's exhausting this back and forth, having to constantly explain myself and hope to be forgiven. I'm so used to it, though, that it's become normal behaviour in our household, although I am aware that it's anything but. I grew up in a home with parents who were in love and spoke to each other with kindness and respect. Even on the occasions when they did have an argument, there was no anger in it, no hate. When Richard and I fight, I feel as if he doesn't even like me, that he only tolerates me.

He continues to stare, waiting for me to get out of the bed. 'Come on, Elle, I'm tired. I want to go sleep.'

I climb out of bed and take my pillow with me, turning off the bedside lamp and closing the door on the way out.

Olly is sound asleep as I carefully move him over, placing my pillow next to his and turning onto my side so there's enough room for both of us. I nestle my face close to his so I can breathe him in. The night-light is on in his room and my eyes focus on his beautiful round face, long golden lashes fluttering against his cheeks; his breathing makes a little purring noise. I keep staring at him, hoping to bring back all the good in my life.

Chapter 9

Elle

I wake to a soft, warm hand resting on my cheek. Olly's face is right next to mine, his big blue eyes smiling at me.

'Hi, Mummy.'

'Hi, sweetheart.'

'I like it when you sleep in my bed.'

'I like it too.' I wrap my arm around his little body, drawing it to mine and nuzzling into his neck. 'You smell so good.'

He giggles.

'Shh, we don't want to wake Daddy and Charlie.' It's barely light outside and I'm sure it's not even six-thirty. 'Should we try to fall back asleep?'

He shakes his head. 'I'm hungry.'

'Okay.' I lift the cover to get up.

'Can I have Coco Pops?'

'Sure.' My dressing-gown and slippers are in my bedroom, and even though it's only autumn and the weather has been nice, the living room is cold. I turn on the heating unit and put on the kettle. Olly runs to the couch and clicks the remote for the television.

'Not too loud,' I say, pouring cereal into a bowl. I make myself a peppermint tea and join him on the couch, letting him eat at the coffee table. I curl up and cover myself with a throw blanket.

I must have fallen back asleep because my eyes open to bright light filtering in through the windows. My hand instinctively shields them from the glare. Olly is lying at the other end of the couch, watching television. I sit up and turn my head towards the kitchen.

'Hey, Mum,' says Charlie, sitting at the kitchen table, munching on cereal. He picks up the box of Coco Pops and tops up his bowl, knowing it will annoy me.

'Hi. What time is it?'

He turns to check the clock on the oven. 'Ten past ten.'

'I must have fallen back asleep.'

'Dad said not to wake you.'

'Where is he?' I ask, getting up from the couch and planting a kiss on top of Charlie's head.

'He said to tell you he had to go to work and that he'll be home later.'

Usually Richard lets me know in advance if he has to go in to work on the weekend, but this is the first I've heard about it. I make myself an instant coffee and sit down at the table with Charlie.

'So what do you boys want to do today?'

'Can we go to the playcentre?' calls out Olly.

The last thing I feel like doing is being cooped up inside a play-centre. 'Why don't we go to the park?'

'I'm too old for the park,' says Charlie.

I'm not sure if he's too old or just too cool for the park. 'Okay, what do you want to do?'

'Can we go to the movies? There's a new Spiderman out.'

'Hmm, Olly's a bit young for Spiderman. Why don't we find something we can all see?'

'I'm not watching a baby movie,' says Charlie. He takes his bowl to the sink and joins Olly on the couch.

'Fine, but pick something that's PG. We'll go visit Grandma after the movie.'

'I don't want to go to Grandma's,' says Charlie.

'Me either,' says Olly.

'Why not?' I ask, getting up to go sit with them.

'I don't see why we have to go – she doesn't know who we are anyway,' says Charlie.

'Yeah, she doesn't know who I am,' mimics Olly.

I pull Olly onto my lap and pat the spot next to me for Charlie to move closer, placing my arm around his waist. 'I know it's hard, boys, but sometimes Grandma does remember you when we visit, and when she does, it makes her so happy to see you.' My heart aches. 'And even though she doesn't always recognise us, isn't it worth it for the times that she does, to see how excited she is?'

'I guess,' says Charlie.

'I guess,' says Olly, in the same tone as his brother, which sounds ridiculous coming from a five-year-old.

'And she gives you presents whether she remembers you or not.' I plant gifts for Mum to give them when we visit. Even if she doesn't know who we are, she's always delighted to have children visiting her and to see their faces light up when she gives them their presents. It doesn't really matter that she doesn't realise they're her grandchildren, it still makes her so happy.

'I want to go!' Olly beams up at me.

'Fine, I'll go too,' says Charlie.

'Great.' I kiss the tops of both their heads and ruffle Charlie's hair. 'Thanks, mate. Let's go get dressed.'

It's just after two o'clock when the movie finishes and we head to the coffee shop next door to the cinema.

'Do you want a sandwich for lunch?' I ask the boys.

'No, my tummy hurts,' says Olly, stuffed from a choc-top and popcorn.

'What about you, Charlie?'

'I'm not hungry.'

'Well, I am,' I say, picking up a salad wrap from a counter display and taking it to the cashier. When I place my purse back in my handbag I retrieve my mobile phone, turn it off silent and check my messages. There's nothing from Richard. Not even a text with a time when he'll be home. He was pretty cold with me last night. I'm going to have to broach the subject with him later so we can move past it, though I'm not looking forward to the conversation. But I know if I put it off I'll be sleeping in Olly's bed for a while, and Charlie's now old enough to ask questions.

'Come on, boys, let's go.' I take a mouthful from the salad wrap and finish it on the drive to the residential care home.

When we arrive, I take Olly's hand as we walk through the carpark to reception. Charlie takes my other hand, which he rarely does anymore. I'm sure he thinks he's too old to hold my hand, but I relish the moment and hold it tight. One of the nurses who often takes care of Mum is standing at the desk, next to the seated receptionist. 'Hello there,' she says to the boys and me.

'Hi,' they answer.

She leans over the high desktop. 'Would you like a lollipop?' she asks the boys.

'Yes, please,' says Olly.

'Thanks,' says Charlie, when she hands him one.

'How's Mum doing today?' I ask. It's better if the boys are prepared for what state she'll be in before we visit.

'She's having a good day,' she says. 'Go on in.'

'Thanks,' I say, filled with anticipation. There's every chance she'll recognise us. I usher Olly and Charlie towards the room and am relieved to see Mum sitting at the table with her needlework. The boys are hesitant and stand in the doorway. 'Mum,' I say, testing where we're at, just to make sure.

She turns her head towards us and her face fills with a huge smile. 'My darlings!' Mum's open arms draw the boys in, then with both hands she grabs hold of Charlie's cheeks. 'Look at how big you are.'

Charlie is clearly thrilled. Olly climbs onto her lap and, while they're getting reacquainted, I place two gifts on the dresser near the door.

'What did you get us?' asks Olly.

'You can't ask that,' Charlie scolds him.

Mum looks over at me, unsure what they're talking about.

'He's asking about the presents you bought them, Mum.' I make a show of picking them up from the dresser, giving them a rattle and taking them to Mum so she can give them to the boys.

'This one says Olly on it, so I presume it's for you.' Mum hands it to Olly and he gives her a kiss on the cheek.

'Thanks, Gran,' he says, jumping off her lap.

'This must be for you, young man,' Mum says to Charlie.

'Thanks, Grandma.'

The boys drop to the floor and rip at the wrapping paper while I sit down on the other chair at the table. 'How are you, Mum?'

'Fine, darling. How are you?'

'I'm good.' I'm too stressed to be good, but I don't want to worry her. I do miss our talks, though. We used to talk about anything and everything. It was easier when Dad was alive and I knew that he was with her all the time, taking care of her. It's still difficult to process that he's gone. It's been almost a year, but I think of him every day, and I worry about Mum more, here without him. I hate thinking of her alone at night. I guess that's silly with twenty-four-hour care, but it's not the same as living with someone who loves you. I pick up the needlework that she placed on the table. 'This is looking great.'

'Thanks, darling.'

'Mum, look what Grandma bought me!' Olly holds up the Lego box. 'It's a truck.'

'Aren't you a lucky boy! Charlie, what did you get?'

'A model car.'

Charlie loves to make model cars. It can keep him busy for hours and he displays a collection of them on the shelves in his bedroom. Sometimes Richard helps him work on them, which is partly why I buy them for him, so they can have time together one on one.

'Would you like a biscuit?' Mum asks them.

Olly's eyes light up.

'They've had so many treats already at the movies,' I say to Mum.

'Oh, just one won't hurt them.' She reaches for the plate from her afternoon tea with several biscuits still left on it. Her hand shakes and with it the plate. I have to stop myself from taking it from her. These small independent moments are so important for her wellbeing.

The boys look up at me, waiting. 'Go on,' I say.

Olly stuffs a biscuit in his mouth. 'Thanks, Grandma,' he says while chewing.

Charlie politely thanks Mum before picking up the biscuit and taking a bite.

When Olly reaches for another one, I shake my head at him. 'It's for Grandma.' He hands it to Mum.

'Thank you, young man,' she says.

We don't stay too long; Mum tires quickly. I help her into bed for a rest before we leave.

When we get home, there's still no sign of Richard. The boys spend the afternoon assembling their presents from Mum and I set up my computer on the kitchen table to get a head start on admin for the week.

Later I make us tacos with saucy beef mince and guacamole for dinner. The boys are both fed, showered and in their pyjamas, sitting on the couch watching television, when Richard walks in the front door.

'Hi, I'm home,' he calls out.

I close my laptop, place it in the kitchen drawer and go to sit on the couch that faces the garden.

Richard plonks himself between the boys. He's dressed in denim jeans and a shirt. 'How was everyone's day?'

'We went to the movies and had ice-cream and popcorn!' says Olly.

'Lucky you!' says Richard, pulling Olly onto his lap and tickling him.

Olly giggles, and Richard looks over at me and smiles.

I'm taken aback that he's so cheery – I'd expected cold stares and abruptness when he came home. Often when he's mad with me he takes it out on the kids too and gets snappy with them, but he's behaving like last night's argument never happened.

'Gran bought me a model car,' Charlie tells him. 'I've done most of it, but there are a few pieces I couldn't work out.'

I sense Charlie's hesitancy in asking for help.

'Come on,' says Richard, lifting Olly off his knees and placing him back on the couch. 'I'll help you finish it.'

The model car is set up on the kitchen table over pages of newspaper. I get up and go to the kitchen and open the fridge to take out the leftover taco ingredients. 'We had tacos for dinner. I'll heat it up for you.'

'No need, I've eaten.'

'Oh ... okay.' I put the food back in the fridge and look at my watch. It's only seven. He must have ordered in at the office.

After Richard and Charlie finish making the car, I take the boys up to bed. I tuck Olly in and put on his night-light for him and then go into Charlie's room to give him a kiss goodnight. As old as he thinks he may be, goodnight kisses I will not budge on.

'Mum,' he says, as I'm about to turn off his bedroom light, 'you buy the presents, don't you?'

I place my finger over my lips. 'Shh, don't tell Olly. Love you.'

'Love you too.' He rolls over onto his stomach, pulling the doona up over his ears.

When I go back downstairs, Richard is sitting on the couch watching television.

'They work you too hard,' I say, dropping onto the other end of the couch from him.

'Huh?' He draws his eyes away from the television.

'Work. You've been at the office all day.'

'Yeah, it's been busy lately. You fine to watch this?' He gestures at the episode of *Curb Your Enthusiasm*.

'Sure.' But I don't watch the television screen, I watch Richard from my peripheral vision. He's laughing at the show and seems way too jovial considering what happened last night. His phone beeps and he checks it. He's smiling as he types his reply. When he looks up, he notices me watching him.

'Work,' he says.

When did work become so fun?

'I'm going up to bed,' he says, getting up. 'Are you coming?'

'I'll be up soon.' I assume that means I'm allowed to sleep in our bedroom tonight. In fact, usually when he asks if I'm coming up with him it's because he wants to have sex. This is very unusual and freaking me out a little. But isn't this what I always want to happen after we've had a fight, for everything to resolve quickly and for Richard to get over it, so we can move past it? Clearly Richard has, so I should let it go too.

I turn off all the lights and make my way upstairs. My bedside lamp is switched on, the lamp on Richard's side of the bed is off. He's lying on his side, his back to me, facing the closed curtains.

I change into my nightie and climb into bed. He hasn't moved. I reach over and turn off my bedside lamp and lie on my back, staring at the dark ceiling. Obviously he didn't want sex. I seem to have gotten that wrong too.

Chapter 10

Nora

I've been blessed with the gift of more time with my mum, so I grab hold of this miracle and spend every day by her side. Mum didn't recognise me this morning, but she still enjoyed the company.

'Bye,' I say to Ronny, sitting behind the desk at reception with another staff member.

'Bye, Nora, see you tomorrow.'

When I arrived at the shelter the first time round, I was so scared and confused, not to mention completely paranoid, that I didn't want to give my real name in case Richard found me. So I told them my name was Nora and used my maiden name, Plankett. I was named after my grandmother Eleanor, and everyone called her Nora. Growing up, my parents called me Elle so that it wasn't confusing when we were together. Of course when I was scolded, it was Eleanor.

Walking through the carpark, I freeze at the sight of the oak tree standing on its lonesome on the lawn at the side. I exhale, remembering everything that happened here that day.

Giving a different name to the staff at the shelter turned out to be futile: Richard found me anyway. It was four months after I'd left home. I'd been visiting Mum, the only connection I had left to my old life by then. I thought I was being discreet. I wore a scarf around my head when I walked in, my clothing was unrecognisable and I'd gone there early in the morning as soon as visitors were allowed. Mum wasn't having a good day. She didn't recognise me, and I kept pressing until she became completely agitated, screaming so loud for me to get away that several nurses ran in. I left in tears, which was why I wasn't on my guard and didn't check my surroundings. I practically walked straight into Richard. I actually said, 'excuse me,' my eyes were so focused on the ground. I'm surprised I hadn't smelt the danger in the air.

'Well, look who we have here,' he'd said.

My pulse raced. I'd forgotten how to speak. He grabbed my wrist, pulling it against him so his face was inches from mine. I was so frail, barely eating those first few months, while I was recovering. My weight had plummeted. Bones protruded through my skin and the clothes I wore fell off my body. I was mentally weak too, traumatised by the ordeal I'd gone through that I hadn't really processed yet. I was still asking the why. Why had it happened? Why did he do this? Why wasn't I enough? As much as life at the shelter aimed to help me recover, I fell into a state of depression.

I was sure that Richard was responsible for the sequence of events that led to me ending up living on the street. I was physically off before I left home, my mind would get hazy, my thoughts unclear and I felt unsteady half the time, bumping into things. I could barely function. The doctors didn't know what was wrong with me, each doctor referring me to the next.

'Richard ...' My voice was barely audible. Unlike me, my husband looked exactly the same. His jawline was hard, like a sculpted marble figure, his dark eyes impenetrable, his thin lips pursed. He looked fit and healthy, well groomed in his expensive work suit and black woollen overcoat.

'You think you're so smart,' he said.

My eyes went wide while every other inch of my body constricted. Now that he'd found me, I was sure I was done. He'd finish what he'd planned for me at the outset and deliver me to a mental institution. I tried to wriggle free from his clutch.

'Did you really think I wouldn't find you?'

'Let go of me.'

'That's what I've been trying to do, Elle, but you keep showing up here.'

He'd seen me here before then. What if he'd followed me back to the shelter? The fear in my face must have given me away.

'Yes, Elle, I know where you sleep at night.'

I felt my body cave, and he clearly felt it too because he tightened his grip, holding me up like a rag doll.

'Why did you do this?' I cried weakly. 'You could have just divorced me.'

'Why do you think? I want the boys.'

'We could have shared them. We could have worked it out.'

'Don't you get it, Elle?' He stared coldly into my eyes. 'I don't want to share them with you. I want them full-time. Would you have allowed that?'

I was in shock, but at least I finally had his reason, however unfathomable. Although it was hard to believe that the man I once shared my life with, slept next to every night, would go to such lengths to have me out of his life. It wasn't that long ago he'd done everything he could to have me in it. Of course I wouldn't have handed my children over on a silver platter. I probably wouldn't have let him have them half the time either. He was unfaithful to me. He was the one who left our marriage.

Anger had surged inside me and with it an ounce of strength. I yanked my arm away. 'No, I wouldn't have allowed that. You would have had to kill me to get sole custody of my children.'

He had laughed. 'That can be arranged.'

I swallowed. I didn't doubt him.

'Take this as a warning, Elle. I'm watching you. You go anywhere near the boys and the police will be all over that homeless shelter. And if you move, I will find you.'

'Maybe I should go to the police.' I'd thought about it. But the day I ran, Richard told me that his lawyer was organising a restraining order against me and if I went anywhere near him or the boys he'd contact the police and I'd be arrested.

'I'd have a long, hard think before you make any rash decisions,' he replied.

Rash, was he serious? It was all I thought about, being reunited with my children. But I was still regaining my strength. I needed to get my life in order and be able to provide for my boys before I tried to get them back.

'You think a restraining order means the police won't listen to me?'

'Elle, sweet Elle. You always were so naïve. It's not just a restraining order, the police have a warrant for your arrest.'

'What are you talking about?' I stared at him, completely confused.

'Don't you remember? You sliced me with a knife!'

'What? You're insane!'

Richard had untucked the bottom of his shirt, baring the left side of his torso to reveal a five-centimetre wound, red and raised, as if time hadn't had a chance to heal it. He tucked his shirt back in. 'And then there were the bruises. The police have photos of everything. Doctor Bolton gave them a full report of your condition and every single assault on me. Why do you think he signed off on admitting you to a mental hospital? You were a danger, Elle, to me, to the boys, to yourself.'

Our family doctor had been managing my care when I'd been unwell. He'd referred me to a neurologist and for testing, but I can't believe that he thought I was crazy or that I'd harm anyone.

'The house looked like a crime scene the day you left. You destroyed everything. It really was quite the tantrum.'

'What did you do?' My house was in perfect condition when I left it, my home was destroyed, but they're two different things.

Richard laughed. 'I didn't do anything. You're the one who attacked me and then threw everything you could get your hands on. Don't you remember?'

My lungs constricted, I could barely breathe.

'Probably hard to remember, what with all the drugs you were on.'

And there it was. The drugs.

'You did this, didn't you? You drugged me. You actually drugged me!' In those first couple of weeks when I was living on the street and then at the shelter, I just thought that whatever had been wrong with me was intensifying. But Mary had been right – my body was actually detoxifying from drugs.

A smug look filled his face.

'How could you do that? How could you drug me?'

'I told you, Elle, I wanted our boys.' He moved to go. 'Just remember, I know where you are. I'll always know.'

And then he had walked away, leaving me standing there shaking from head to toe. I had shuffled over to the lawn at the side of the carpark, where I'm standing now, and dropped to the ground, too shocked to even cry. I didn't know how to stop my body from shivering. I wrapped my jacket around myself in an attempt to get warm. My breathing was so shallow, I wasn't sure enough oxygen was making its way to my head. I lay back on the grass, still damp with morning dew, focusing on the leaves of the tree above my head, trying to calm myself. Eventually my body followed suit.

I had managed to make my way back to the shelter and went straight to the communal bathroom. As my hands clutched the bench and my eyes bored into my reflection, I tried to process everything that had just happened. I'd been holding onto a shred of faith that once I got myself together, when I was stronger, I'd be able to get my boys back. But now all that was shattered by Richard's lies and actions. If I sought legal aid, Richard would send the police for me. If they had my medical records, like Richard said they did, implying I was delusional and a danger to myself and others, I could end up in a mental institution or even in jail for assault. What kind of mother would I then be to Charlie and Olly? The only way to keep them from seeing all that was to give in to Richard's threats.

I had already become accustomed to the safe environment the

shelter provided, cocooning me from the world. The only time I stepped out was to visit Mum. Holding onto her was the only thing keeping me from feeling completely rootless and if I let go of Mum too, I was sure I'd wither away.

I pulled at the scarf, which fell around my neck, and looped my hands in it. How stupid I had been to think that wearing this over my head would disguise me? I needed to do something more drastic.

I had pulled open the bathroom door and gone to the communal lounge where an arts and crafts table was set up for the women and children to use. Art therapy, Mary had called it. I had rummaged through a box of materials – coloured paper, beads, glue, rulers – until I found what I was looking for. I grabbed the pair of scissors and headed back to the bathroom.

Standing in front of the mirror, the scissors shaking in my hand, anxiety coursing through me, I grabbed a chunk of my long, wavy golden hair and cut. The hair fell to the floor, but I couldn't bear to look. I hacked into the sides, then pulled at the hair at the back, bringing it forward and snipped.

The bathroom door had swung open, and Heather stopped in her tracks at the sight of me. 'Nora, what are you doing?'

My mouth gaped. 'I ... I needed a change.'

She took the scissors from my hand. 'Here, let me help you.'

In that moment our eyes connected, and it was like she knew everything without me having to utter a word. I nodded.

'I'll be back in a minute.'

She had returned with a chair and a hairbrush. I sat down, closed my eyes and succumbed, allowing myself to trust Heather just for that moment.

'There,' she said when she'd finished. 'That looks better.'

I had opened my eyes and tears had welled. My hair now fell just below my chin. The floor was covered in my beautiful hair.

'Do you know what I think would suit you? A fringe. I used to cut my kids' hair when they were toddlers. I'd pop them in the highchair so they couldn't run away. I wasn't half bad at it.'

I had shrugged. 'Okay.'

Heather stood in front of me, gathering some hair from either side and brushing it before she snipped a few times. She checked it was even then said, 'Perfect.'

The haircut did make me look different, but I didn't think it was enough. I wanted to be unrecognisable. I wanted to fade away, so no one knew who I was.

'Do they keep any hair colours here?'

Heather went and opened a cupboard. 'There are usually some bottles that haven't been finished.' She pulled out several, placing them on the bench. They were mostly shades of red and one black.

I picked up a bottle – copper. 'This one.'

She had grabbed an old towel and a pair of plastic gloves from a box in the cupboard and draped the towel around my shoulders. 'You know, you're not the first woman to stay here who wanted to change her appearance.'

In my reflection I saw my half-hearted smile.

'It's okay, Nora. You're going to be safe here.'

I had nodded. I'd be safe as long as I kept quiet.

A car horn breaks my trance and I realise I'm still standing in the carpark staring at the oak tree. I hold up my hand and mouth 'sorry' before moving out of the way. I instinctively scan the parking lot looking for Richard, thinking he might find me.

But then I realise that to the Richard of 2012, I don't exist, only his version of Elle does. He'd have absolutely no reason to perceive me as a threat. And although the Richard of this time may already know his intentions for Elle, he doesn't know I escaped his plans for me. Right now, I'm completely safe from him.

But Elle isn't.

Chapter 11

Elle

'Can you see a number?' I call out to Georgie from a few metres away.

'No,' she calls back. 'Are you sure it's four ninety-seven?'

I double-check the address I've written on the manila folder holding copies of recipes to hand out. 'Yep.'

Georgie comes over to me. 'I'll check the location on my phone.'

'We should have left earlier,' I say, glancing at the time. I don't want to be late and it's almost one o'clock.

'It should be the next one down.'

'I already looked that way.'

Georgie walks to the next building and I follow her. She looks up at the number and then walks back in the direction we came from. 'Well, it has to be between these two buildings. Wait, there's a door here. I can't see a number though.' I follow her towards the door and see an intercom on the side with the street number above it. 'Tada,' she says, pressing the buzzer.

'Can I help you?' a voice says through the speaker.

'Hi, we're here for the cooking class. Georgie and Elle.'

The door clicks and Georgie pulls it open. 'After you,' she says to me.

We're greeted by a short, stout woman, her hair threaded with grey.

'Hi, I'm Carla – we spoke on the phone,' she says, shaking each of our hands. 'Thanks so much for coming.' She turns and leads us down a hall. 'The women are in the kitchen ready for you.'

I glance at Georgie. I'd hoped we would have some time to set up before we started. Carla has bought the ingredients for the session but I wouldn't have minded a little time to get organised and familiar with the space.

We follow Carla into a small kitchen with at least twenty women cramped together in the centre. A bench with a stove runs along the wall side of the room and a trestle table has been set up in front of it. Some ingredients for the demonstration have been laid out on the table, but there are no utensils or cookware in sight.

I panic, realising we're completely unprepared. From the expression on Georgie's face, she's feeling the same. Both of us function best in order. I feel responsible, like I've let her down. This was my idea and I was the one who was meant to organise everything for today's session.

'Ah ... could you show me where the utensils are?' I ask Carla. 'We'll need a chopping board, some bowls and a saucepan as well.'

Carla opens a cupboard and rummages around while Georgie pulls out drawers to find knives and a few different sized spoons. We'll have to make do.

We put on our Notch aprons, pull up our sleeves and begin. 'Hi, everybody, my name is Elle and this is my business partner,

Georgie. We're both qualified chefs and run a small catering company.' All eyes are glued to me. 'We're very excited to be here today to show you a few easy dishes to make.'

'Right, I'll leave you to it,' says Carla, smiling as she backs out of the kitchen.

Georgie takes over, showing the women how to make the spice mix for the Moroccan vegetable tagine, while I start chopping the carrots, potatoes and onions. The women watch quietly, no one speaking. I feel awful that they're just standing there, watching while we cook, especially when I notice the young woman near the front with a fading bruise around her eye. She looks frail and worn out. Maybe she recently arrived here at the shelter.

While the tagine is cooking on the stove, we prepare the blueberry muffins, both Georgie and I making a batch so there will be enough for each of the women to taste.

An hour passes quickly and the muffins are baking in the oven while the tagine is still cooking. The women have filed out of the kitchen and it's just Georgie and I left, cleaning the dishes and tidying up.

'That didn't go as I'd envisaged,' I say, wiping the bench. 'I thought they'd get more into it. Maybe for next week we should have the women cooking with us.' I've booked a session at another shelter to give us a chance to assess if it's something that would be beneficial to the women and doable for us.

'I agree,' says Georgie.

'We could make it more of a workshop rather than a demonstration. I think if they were involved in the cooking it would be a distraction for them and they'd feel more comfortable with us.'

'It's worth another try,' says Georgie, drying the bowls.

'I'll make a list of the cookware we need as well and then if they don't have something, we can bring it.'

'Great idea. And it would be good if we can make at least one dish that cooks in time for the women to sample while they're in the kitchen. Eating food brings people together,' says Georgie.

'It does.'

'A little bit of tweaking, that's all.'

I hope Georgie's right. I'd love to make this work.

By the time I pick the boys up from aftercare, I'm exhausted. I make them a snack and sit on the couch with them while they watch television.

'Can you turn it down a bit? Mummy's tired,' I say to Charlie, then lean back into the cushions and close my eyes. Just for a minute.

'Mummy, I'm hungry,' says Olly, crawling onto my lap.

I open my eyes to his little face in front of me. I must have fallen asleep. 'What's the time?' I ask him.

'I don't know,' he says. I look out towards the garden, the sky shades of pink and orange.

'Where's Charlie?' I ask.

'Upstairs.'

'Okay, I'll get dinner ready.' In the kitchen I turn on the oven and see it's six o'clock. Adrenaline courses through me. Richard will be home soon and I haven't even started cooking. I grab some potatoes from the pantry, not bothering to use a peeler, I wash them and cut them into fine chips, hoping they'll cook quicker. Tossing them in olive oil and salt, I pop them in the oven, then prepare a plate with flour, a bowl with egg wash and another with breadcrumbs to make the chicken schnitzels. While the schnitzels are frying, I put together a garden salad and a dressing.

Charlie returns downstairs. 'When's dinner?'

'Soon, mate. Sorry, I fell asleep. We can all eat together tonight. Won't that be nice?' Most nights I feed the boys at five-thirty and Richard and I eat after they're in bed.

Charlie doesn't answer and goes to the couch. Both boys are lying there watching television when Richard walks in. He loosens the tie around his neck and takes in the mess in the kitchen.

'Why are the boys still in their uniforms?' he asks.

'It's been a busy afternoon. Can you take them up for showers while I finish here?'

Richard screws up his face at me, like I've suggested something outrageous. 'I just got home from work.'

I turn the schnitzels over with tongs and line a plate with paper towel, avoiding Richard's gaze. I've been working since six-thirty this morning, taking care of our children, then at my job, but of course I don't say any of that.

'Boys, turn off the TV and come set the table,' I call out.

Charlie and Olly saunter to the kitchen and take out the cutlery and plates. When we sit down together, Olly picks up a potato that is barely golden. 'Is it cooked?' he asks.

'Yes, it's cooked,' I say, popping one in my mouth. I reach over to his plate and cut up his schnitzel, leaving a piece on his fork.

Olly eats the mouthful and then pulls up his legs, his feet on the chair.

'Feet on the ground,' says Richard.

'They don't reach,' says Olly, looking up at Richard with his big, sweet eyes.

'Eat your dinner,' he says to Olly.

'I'm not hungry.' Olly pushes away his plate.

'Come on, mate, one more mouthful,' I say, placing another piece of schnitzel on the fork.

He pushes it away.

'If you're not eating your dinner you can go to your room,' says Richard, his voice stern.

Olly makes a face at his dad then runs upstairs.

I let out a sigh. 'He's just tired,' I say to Richard.

'Because he should be in bed by now, but instead he's having dinner and hasn't even had a bath. What were you doing that you didn't have time to get them ready?' he asks.

I look over at Charlie, diligently finishing every mouthful on his plate.

'I had a busy afternoon with work.'

'Were you working after school? Elle, I thought we discussed this already. When the boys are home, you leave the catering behind.'

Charlie's teeth are gnawing at his lower lip.

'Sweetheart, why don't you go upstairs and have a shower,' I say to him.

'Okay,' he says, taking his plate to the kitchen.

'See if Olly will go in with you.'

He nods and makes his way upstairs.

'Richard, I wasn't working. I was tired and must have dropped off when I was sitting with the boys on the couch.'

He leans back in the chair. 'And here you were thinking of expanding the business when you can't even manage what you do already.'

'Richard, that's not fair,' I say, feeling defeated.

'Well, clearly it's true.'

I place Olly's uneaten plate on top of mine and get up to clear the rest of the table, piling everything on the kitchen bench. Then I go to the sink and start cleaning the dishes. I feel pathetic that I have to justify to Richard why I dozed on the couch and why I'm late getting dinner ready. I'm relieved neither of the boys mentioned that they were at aftercare. I don't want to even think about how Richard would react to that.

Chapter 12

Nora

'Thanks so much for helping out today,' says Sheena. 'I know you're still settling in here, but Lloyd said you're a wonder in the kitchen.'

'Thank you,' I say. 'I like feeling useful.' The fact is I've been working with Lloyd, the cook here, preparing dinner for the residents for the last ten years.

This time around, I let the staff here know right away that I'm a chef and spend my afternoons assisting in the kitchen. I have no idea if I've been planted back in the past temporarily or forever. If it's the latter, I'll need somewhere permanent to live. The refuge offers short-term accommodation for women, usually up to six months, so I'm going to need to cement myself in the kitchen so they offer me a job and, with it, board.

When I initially began helping out in the kitchen all those years ago, I hid my skills. My old life was too fresh, and working as a chef would have been a constant reminder of my past. I was also so fragile at the time and I didn't feel confident enough taking on any responsibilities. So I cleaned dishes and set the tables, washed ingredients and chopped vegetables. I was the roamer, doing monotonous tasks that allowed me to keep mostly to myself. Eventually they ended up offering me a job in exchange for a minimum wage, meals and free board.

But even when it was clear I could cook, I never told anyone I had been a chef in my past life or that I ran a catering business before I ended up homeless. If I had they would probably have helped me to find a job in the industry, and that would have meant getting back out into the world. I'd become too accustomed to the protected life here to do that. I also worried that if I did find work out there, someone from my old life might see me and ask questions. Richard had already threatened me with what he'd do if anyone knew I wasn't tucked away in a mental institution. If it wasn't for my boys, I probably would have taken the chance to start over again, even if there was the possibility I could end up in jail. But they were all I thought about and I couldn't risk it.

Sheena places printouts of two recipes on the bench. 'They've sent in a list of everything they need for the class. We'll put the women in groups of three, so maybe you could set up four stations on the bench and one for the volunteers?'

'Sure,' I say, glancing over the list.

'Today's a trial, but if it goes well, we'll do it again. It would be great if all the women had a chance to participate.'

'It's a lovely idea.'

'That's what I thought,' says Sheena, pulling the hair that was falling loosely around her face back into a clip. 'The spots are all filled for today's session, but would you be able to stay in the kitchen? Just in case the volunteers need anything.'

'Of course, that's fine.'

'Okay, great. I better get back to it.'

I open cupboards, taking out as many mixing bowls and measuring cups as we have and space them out across the bench. I grab knives and spoons from the drawers. We only have two whisks and spatulas, so they'll have to share those.

Even though I'm meant to be new here, this place is my home now and I'm comfortable in this environment. I know where everything is kept, where everything belongs, the day-to-day running of the place down to the smallest details.

I place two frying pans on the stove and turn on the oven to warm up before heading to the communal lounge for a coffee and sandwich before the session starts at one.

Heather is sitting on the couch by the window, eating her lunch.

'Can I join you?' I ask, holding my mug and plate.

'Nora, hello. How are you doing?'

'I'm okay,' I say, sitting down next to her.

'How are you settling in?' asks Heather.

'Well, thanks. The staff are lovely.'

'They are,' she says.

It feels awkward pretending I don't know Heather, especially when I've confided so much in her over the years. She's seen me at my worst and been such a good friend. 'So how long have you been working here?' I ask her.

'Almost six years,' she says. 'My children are all grown up and my husband passed away a few years ago.'

'I'm sorry, that must be tough.'

'It is,' she says, taking a sip of her tea. 'But life goes on. I used to only work days, but I was so lonely at home by myself after my husband passed. When the job came up for the night-duty manager, I jumped at it.'

The shelter's doors close at eight in the evening, so she mostly only gets woken if there's an emergency.

'The women and kids come and go, but they feel like family while they're here,' says Heather.

I know what she means. It was only when I became involved in the day-to-day life at the shelter, being part of a community of other women, that I started to recover and feel a sense of self. But I can't tell her that, because for this Heather I've been here for less than two weeks.

'Have you been in touch with your children?' she asks.

Heather knows everything there is to know about my boys. Richard and everything he did to me was off limits, but when it came to my children, I found talking about them with her was a way to keep them present in my life – the things they would have been doing, every year they aged. I'd make cupcakes to celebrate their birthdays. Even though no one else here knew what they were for, Heather would buy candles and we'd go to my bedroom to light them and sing 'Happy Birthday', which mostly ended in tears, mine and Heather's. But back here in 2012, we haven't done that together yet. In 2012, Olly is five and Charlie is eight. I haven't missed their birthdays.

'Not yet,' I say. 'It's not safe for me to reach out right now.'

She reaches over and squeezes my hand. 'It takes time, Nora. It will all work out.'

I just nod. It's been ten years and nothing has worked out. In all this time, I haven't been able to contact my sons. I've missed out on so much and they have too.

On two occasions I went to their school. The first time was

before Richard had threatened me. I was still out of sorts, but I had to know my children were okay. I had to see them with my own eyes.

I stood at the school gates. My hair was still honey blonde and long, but I wore it up, covered with a hat. Hiding behind an SUV, I waited. The school bell rang and it felt like an eternity that I lingered, hoping for a glimpse of them. My heart raced with anticipation. I recognised a few of the mums as they walked out of the school gate with their children, friends of the boys, so I pretended to be busy looking for something in my handbag, which was almost empty. When I saw Charlie coming out of the gate, my hand reached for the side of the car next to me. I had to touch it, something tangible to hold me back from running to him. All I wanted to do in that moment was go and get my boy, to grab him and run. Of course, I'd thought about doing that, taking my kids and fleeing. But I had no passport with me, no money, no way to provide for them. And Richard would probably have every police officer in Melbourne on the hunt for me if I did. It was just a fantasy.

When I had seen Olly's figure behind Charlie, holding the hand of Patricia, the woman Richard had an affair with, I thought I would throw up. The worst part was Olly seemed happy, his oversized schoolbag on his back, eating an ice-cream she'd obviously bought for him, always a guaranteed way to win over a five-year-old. Even though I wanted to burst into tears and turn away, I couldn't draw my eyes from them. They walked to her car, a brand new navy BMW that I presumed Richard had bought for her. Olly climbed inside and then Charlie became upset about something. Patricia said something to him and Charlie finally climbed into the back seat. Then they drove away. Another woman leaving with my children, my flesh and blood.

The second time I found myself standing outside the school gates was several months later, after my altercation with Richard. That time I didn't hide behind a car; I felt safe with my new look. I had enough money from working in the kitchen to buy some cheap non-prescription glasses to add to my disguise. I stood to the side of the school entrance, keeping my distance, not wanting the boys to recognise me. They thought I was suffering from some kind of mental illness and in a special hospital. Seeing me seven months later would only unsettle them, especially if I couldn't keep them with me. However much I longed to hold them in my arms, breathe them in, their wellbeing was my main priority.

Patricia had picked them up again. When she passed by, Olly and Charlie in tow, she had glanced back, staring straight at me. After that, I was too scared to go again.

Heather and I sit quietly now while we finish our sandwiches. 'I have to get to the kitchen,' I say, getting up to take my plate and mug to the sink. 'They have some surprise workshop today.'

'Sheena hasn't stopped talking about it all week,' she says. 'She's so excited that we have professional chefs coming in.'

'Professional chefs?' I run my hands through my hair, feeling self-conscious.

'You look lovely, Nora,' she says.

'Thank you.' Although I'm not sure I would agree.

When I enter the kitchen, some of the residents are gathered around the large island bench in the centre, and two women with aprons on are facing the bench on the other side, next to the stove, sorting through ingredients. I move to stand at the back of the group of women.

A sense of unease fills me, and when the two chefs turn around, I realise why. A lump catches in my throat and my pulse races. Elle, my past self, is in the same room as me. We're standing metres apart. It's absolutely surreal that she's me and I'm her. It's difficult to comprehend that we're one and the same. But we are. I'm her future, and she has no idea what her future has in store for her.

I've spent countless hours researching time travel in an attempt to make sense of how I could be living in the past, in the same time-line as my former self. I have no idea what I'm meant to do and if it is even safe for Elle and me to be in the same room together – we share the same body and soul. I've even thought about one of Char-lie's favourite movies, *Back to the Future*, and Doc warning Marty that if he comes into contact with his old self they might both be erased from existence. But I think that had something to do with making changes that would affect his parents' falling in love and having him. That's not going to happen here. I can't change Elle's past, or anything that happened before today. And when we stood together in the bakery, there didn't seem to be any effect, so I assume we will be fine being in such close proximity to each other.

As much as I've tried to make sense of this situation, it's ulti-mately unexplainable, and it's impossible for me to know the answers. The only thing I can really do is accept what's happening. If I don't, it will do my head in and I'll achieve nothing with this chance I've been given. One thing I am certain of is that if a higher power has sent me back in time, there has to be a reason for it.

I lean against the cupboard and my eyes drift to Georgie. I can't believe she's here. It's been so long since I've seen her beautiful smiling face. Practically a lifetime ago. I shake my head, watching them both. Georgie and Elle are together. That means they're still friends. Maybe it's not too late.

Chapter 13

Elle

I can't believe it's her. She's standing at the back of the class, and when my eyes connect with hers, she looks away. I assume she remembers me. Maybe she's embarrassed because she asked me for money and I bought her food. I don't want her to feel uncomfortable so I try not to look directly at her.

After last week's session at the other shelter, we decided the cooking class would work better with a smaller group of twelve women. We're making the tacos with saucy beef and guacamole that I make most Sunday nights for dinner. It's simple and cost-effective and a meal the women will be able to make for themselves when they leave the shelter. I've also printed out copies of the recipe for them as well as one for the chocolate brownies we're making.

'Hi, everybody. My name is Elle and this is Georgie.'

Georgie waves.

'We're so excited to be here today to cook with you. Georgie and I are caterers and today we're going to show you our recipes for tacos and brownies.'

The women are working in groups today. We hope that being involved in the cooking process will be therapeutic and help take their minds off anything negative that's going on in their worlds.

I glance at Georgie for her to take over.

'We're going to prepare the guacamole first. Grab your tomatoes and dice them – it can be chunky or finely diced. Either way it will taste delicious. It's more about having the right combination of ingredients.'

The women listen and follow the steps as Georgie shows them how to prepare each ingredient. She squeezes half a lime in her fist, letting the juice run into the bowl.

'Now season with a generous amount of salt before we combine.' Georgie mixes the ingredients gently with a spoon and then tastes the guacamole. 'It's always important to taste-test – sometimes a little extra salt is all that's needed to bring out the flavour.'

'Ooh, that's delicious,' says one woman, the first to speak since we arrived.

When I called the shelter and spoke to Sheena to organise the workshop, she gave me a brief insight into what some of the women had gone through, although I'm sure she didn't scratch the surface. Coming here today, into their reality, I'll do my best to make them feel comfortable and distract them from whatever situation they're in. I know from experience that being immersed in cooking has that power. It's been medicinal for me over the years when I've needed it.

When I'm working with Georgie, or even on my own, creating

recipes, I forget about everything else going on in my life. My mind stops going at full speed and I focus on the task at hand. I'm completely present. Sometimes life can be overwhelming, between running a business, looking after children and a home, being a wife. Especially the kind of wife Richard wants. I'm not sure I fit his mould of who that person should be. Over the years I've managed to work out what things to let go and what are worth the fight, like our argument the other week after the dinner party. I wasn't going to give in and accept responsibility for something I didn't do. But when he gets like that, he's like a bull – he can't see beyond his blinders.

'Elle's going to show you how to prepare the spice mix for the beef,' says Georgie.

I pick up a spoon. 'We're going to take a teaspoon each of cumin, ground coriander and dried oregano, and half a teaspoon of dried basil and add it to the bowl.' I wait for the women to catch up before continuing. 'Then we're going to add a teaspoon of beef stock powder.' I measure it out and then pass the tin to the group of women standing to my left. When I look up, the woman at the back is watching me. Intently. As soon as she notices me looking in her direction, she looks down. I clear my throat. 'Season with salt and pepper and then add a splash of water and mix it into a paste.' Even if the women only use half these ingredients when they cook it on their own, it will still taste great. I pull back the lid on a tin of diced tomatoes and the women follow. 'Add the tomatoes and the beef mince.' I pull up my sleeves. 'Now for the fun part,' I say, working my fingers through the mince. 'Really get in there. Give it everything you've got.'

A few women laugh and they start to chat in their groups, obviously feeling more comfortable as they take turns, fingers sloshing around in their bowls of ruddy-orange mince. I wonder why the woman standing at the back isn't participating, only watching. I glance her way and smile. I hope that small gesture lets her know that it's okay. I'd love it if she joined in too, but she seems even more reserved than the other women.

'Mm, it smells great,' says an older woman.

'My kids are going to love this,' says another.

'Wait till it hits the pan,' says Georgie.

She turns on the stove and drizzles oil into a frying pan as I wash my hands at the sink. 'Come gather around,' she says.

The women move to the stove to watch her cook the meat.

They take turns cooking their mince in the frying pan under the watchful eye of Georgie. Then back at the island bench, we assemble the tacos, and they try one each. It feels so communal, like we're a group of friends coming together to cook. Except for the woman at the back. She hasn't tried a taco or moved from her spot.

Georgie and I show them how to make the brownies and the women follow along in their groups, adding ingredients to their mixing bowls and whisking until the texture is smooth. When they're baking in the oven, Georgie and I pack up the remaining ingredients and the women go to make coffee and tea in the lounge to have with their brownies. The woman I met at the shops on Glenferrie Road is at the sink cleaning the dishes. I wonder why she stayed back to clean when all the other women left.

'I can help with that,' I offer.

'I've got it covered,' she says, avoiding eye contact. But when I move back to the island bench, her eyes follow me. And not just me, she keeps looking at Georgie too.

Leaning into Georgie, I whisper, 'That's the woman I told you about, the one I bought the tuna patties for.' I motion my head in the direction of the sink. 'She stood at the back during the class.'

'Maybe she works here.'

'Or maybe she felt uncomfortable after the other day.'

'She looks kind of familiar, don't you think?'

'I guess she has one of those faces,' I say.

Georgie looks at me questioningly.

'You know what I mean, a recognisable face,' I explain, keeping my voice hushed.

Georgie shakes her head. 'Did you say hello to her?'

'I smiled.'

'Elle, you should say something to her.'

'What should I say?'

'I don't know. Did you enjoy the class? How long have you been living here?'

Of course Georgie's right. It would be rude of me not to acknowledge that we met. I venture over to the sink, although it does feel awkward. Not knowing what to do with my hands, I grab a tea towel and start drying the dishes. 'Did you enjoy the cooking class?' I ask.

'It was great,' she says, not looking at me. Her glasses are steaming up from the hot water.

'Have you been living here long?'

She's about to answer, then hesitates for a moment. 'A couple of weeks.'

The timer goes off for the brownies and I open the ovens and take out the trays, placing them on the island bench. I raise my eyebrows at Georgie and she just shrugs.

'I couldn't stay at my desk any longer,' says Sheena, the receptionist, walking into the kitchen. 'It smells amazing in here.'

'You're just in time,' says Georgie.

'Where can I find a clean knife?' I ask.

'Top drawer on the left,' answers the woman at the sink.

'Have you ladies met Nora?' asks Sheena.

'No, not properly,' I say.

'Nora, come and meet Elle and Georgie.'

She pulls off her gloves and comes over from the sink.

'Nora's a chef too,' says Sheena. 'Everyone's loving her food.'

'So you work here?' I ask.

'No,' she says, 'I live here. I'm just helping out in the kitchen.'

Georgie holds out her hand to shake Nora's. 'Lovely to meet you.'

'You too,' says Nora.

'You look so familiar. Have we met?' asks Georgie.

'I don't think so.' Nora glances at her feet. Georgie must be making her self-conscious.

'I'm Elle,' I say, extending my hand. Nora looks at my hand like it's burning coal, but after a moment of hesitation, she reaches to shake it. When her hand slots into mine, our eyes lock and an unnerving sensation pulsates through me. I can't quite put my finger on what it is, but it makes me uneasy.

Nora lets go quickly then returns to the sink, puts the gloves back on and turns on the tap.

'Ooh, can I try one?' asks Sheena, eyeing the brownies.

'They're hot, but I'll cut you a slice,' says Georgie.

Sheena takes a bite. 'These are delicious. They taste just like the ones Nora made the other day. What was your special ingredient again?' she asks Nora.

Nora mutters something under her breath.

'That's right, orange rind,' says Sheena.

'That's ours too,' I say, staring at the back of Nora's head. She continues washing the dishes like she hasn't heard a thing.

Chapter 14

Nora

I keep my head down, scrubbing the dishes, not daring to turn around. I can feel Elle's eyes on me, scorching the back of my head. I'm fairly certain she noticed me staring at her during the workshop, but how could I not? I'm taking in every inch of the woman I used to be. I want to be her again.

Although I could pass on the subdued part. Richard had a way of knocking the fun out of Elle. He made her doubt the wonderful, lovable person she was and question her worth. And that was before he robbed her of everything that mattered in her life.

But clearly I haven't been sent back to the past to pick up where I left off and become Elle again. I'm still fifty-one years old. I'm still Nora, a woman who has lived a completely different life these last ten years. It almost feels like we're two individual people, although the reality is we're one and the same. If this has happened, me being sent to the past, so I can help change the course of Elle's future, I'm guessing I won't be able to change everything that happened before today. But even though the present Elle has been stomped on, I know she's still brave inside. Richard hasn't completely crushed her yet.

The last thing I'd expected was for her to show up at the shelter today. And with Georgie. I must have had some effect on her when we met outside the bank and she bought me food for her to come here today and volunteer to run a cooking workshop. I wonder if she's planning on doing more classes. Either way, it was something I never did, so I guess me being here is changing things already. I'm surprised that Richard would allow it, though. He was always so possessive of her time. My time. If I'd wanted to volunteer my services and do workshops for women in crisis, living in shelters, he would have shut down the idea instantly. I hope he hasn't given her a hard time about coming here.

It was bizarre to hold her hand, *my* hand. It felt like I was having an otherworldly experience. Mystical. Goosebumps ran up my arms and legs and every inch of my body tingled. Elle didn't show any signs of recognition, although I overheard Georgie mentioning that I looked familiar.

It's hard to believe that of all the shelters across Melbourne, and there are quite a few, Elle and Georgie ended up here. But maybe it's all part of the grand plan, whatever it is, that's happening to me.

I'm overwhelmed to see Georgie again. I had to place my hands behind my back and grip the cupboard handles so that I wouldn't fling myself onto her. When she offered me her hand, I wanted to pull her to me and hug her. To hold on to her for dear life, to hold on to our friendship, because Richard destroyed that too.

I know he was the mastermind behind everything. I've spent every night of the last ten years lying in bed, going over everything that happened. I may not know how Richard managed to drug me, but I do know how he ruined my business, shattering my relationship with Georgie in the process. Everything was methodically planned.

It began in the weeks after Georgie brought up expanding our catering business. When Richard found out about it at the dinner party, all hell broke loose. I know now that when he said he went into the office the following day, he was really with Patricia. No wonder he was so relaxed and happy when he came home – he'd probably spent the day having sex and planning my demise.

It wasn't long after that he began showing interest in my 'little' catering business. I was so naïve. I actually thought he was coming around to the idea of the expansion, when in fact he was working out how to withdraw money from the business and make Georgie believe that it was me stealing it. I managed all the accounts, so of course I would be the only suspect. He told me about a new software program that would be so much easier to use. He offered to install it for me and set it up. In fact, he spent a whole weekend getting it working for me, transferring all our clients' accounts. I just didn't know that while he was doing it he was adjusting the revenue from each client and adding random expenses, making it look as if we were only breaking even. He had slowly been transferring the difference from the actual amounts to our personal joint account, over weeks, and I'd had no idea.

Georgie was the first to discover that the business account had no money. She was buying ingredients for the breakfast order with our business credit card and it was declined, more than once. She came straight over to my place utterly panicked, and so was I when she told me.

'We can't have nothing in the account,' she'd said, flustered.

'Of course we have money. There must be some kind of mistake.' I'd grabbed my laptop and sat down at the kitchen table,

Georgie hovering over my shoulder. I checked our bank account and she was correct, the balance was zero. 'This can't be right,' I said, pointing my finger at an amount on the screen. 'There are at least a dozen transactions made over the last few weeks to an unknown account. They all have the same trading name, but I've never heard of it.'

'It's not familiar to me either,' said Georgie.

'And it doesn't say what they're for. I always write what the expense is in case I don't recognise the trading name when I check the statements.'

'Have a look at our clients' accounts and see what invoices are outstanding,' she said.

I had opened the accounting system and scanned through the list of client invoices due. 'That doesn't look correct either,' I said, pointing to a recently billed amount. We'd undercharged them. 'For that fee we wouldn't have made a profit.' I could feel the colour drain from my face as I checked every single item. I then proceeded to run through the spreadsheet of expenses for the last few months.

'What is it? What's happening?' Georgie asked.

'Just give me a minute.'

I leant back in the chair, dazed, my mind a whirlwind. 'This isn't right. None of this can be right.' I ran my hands through my hair. 'The invoices are too low and there are expense items I don't recognise.' My hands were shaking, my throat felt thick.

'We have to go to the bank and let them know what's going on,' said Georgie, frantically getting up from the chair.

'Let's go.' I grabbed my handbag and car keys.

Georgie had been silent on the drive to the bank, picking at her fingernails, which she did when she was uptight. I parked the car and we sprinted towards the bank.

'We need to speak with the manager,' I said, puffing to the clerk. 'It's urgent – our business account has been emptied.'

Ten minutes later we were in a private meeting room with the bank manager. He confirmed that the funds in our account were zero.

'I'll lodge a transaction dispute and the bank will investigate where the funds have gone,' he'd said.

'How long will that take?' asked Georgie, her arms crossed against her chest.

'It could be up to two weeks.'

'Two weeks! We can't run our business with no funds!' Georgie was furious.

'If our system was hacked, will the money go back into our account?' I asked, my knee bopping up and down like I was bouncing a ball on it.

'It depends. Let's get the process started and trace where the funds have gone,' said the manager.

Both Georgie and I let out an audible sigh.

The following two weeks were excruciating while we waited to hear back from the bank. I had spent the time meticulously matching the paper copies of every invoice sent to clients as well as the physical copies of our expense receipts, that I stored in a manilla folder, with the amounts on our system. And when I arrived at the same result, that they didn't equate, I repeated the process, like I was expecting it to magically change. Richard was of no help. He didn't seem to care that our system had been hacked, which was odd considering he'd invested so much time setting it up. Although, surprisingly, he did offer to loan us the money to cover our business costs until we heard back from the bank.

Georgie didn't seem herself either. She was eerily quiet during our mornings spent cooking for client orders. She knew that Richard had changed over our system and she'd voiced that Tye didn't think it was a coincidence. I agreed that the timing of us being hacked and the new system being installed was strange, but I suggested it may have happened when all our information was being transferred.

I wasn't shocked that Tye would question it. He tolerated Richard and was amicable for Georgie's sake and mine, but Tye had been wary of Richard from the moment I'd started dating him. I knew that because Georgie had told me back then that Tye thought Richard was stuck-up and pompous. After I'd married Richard, Georgie stopped relaying Tye's feelings, but I could tell there was often tension between the two men. Richard had a tendency to gloat about his business dealings at the same time as being cagey about the details.

When the call finally came from the bank, that the money had been traced from Notch's bank account to my joint account with Richard, Georgie didn't seem surprised at all. Me, I was completely knocked for six. Not to mention devastated. I didn't blame her for accusing me and Richard. The accounts were my responsibility and I had access to everything. I couldn't explain how the money ended up in our personal bank account, and as soon as I found out, I transferred it back. Richard seemed just as stunned at the discovery that the money was in our account as I was.

I thought after the money was returned that things would go back to normal. But then the call had come the evening the money was transferred back to our business account.

'Elle, it's Tye.'

'Hi,' I said, surprised that Tye was calling me. My first thought was that there'd been a problem with the transfer. I adjusted the pillows behind my head and rested the book I'd been reading over my lap. Richard was working late and the boys were already tucked in for the night. 'Is everything alright?'

'No, Elle, it's not.'

I sat up straighter, my chest tightening. 'The transfer went through, didn't it?'

'It did. The thing is – and please know how hard it was for me to make this decision – but I don't want Georgie working with you anymore.'

My mouth fell open. 'But ... but we run a business together, we have clients and orders to fill.' I held on to the force of tears welling, waiting to burst.

'I know, and this is so hard for us to do, but it needs to be done.'

'But I didn't do anything! Tye, you have to believe me,' I had begged. 'The system was hacked, it's not my fault.'

'You can't really believe that, can you, Elle? The accounts were falsified, and the money was transferred to your personal account.'

I felt like I was going to throw up. 'I get that the evidence points to me, but you have to believe that I had nothing to do with it.'

'But you and Richard changed the accounting system just days before it happened.'

'Tye, please, Richard would never do such a thing.' The amount of money that had been in our Notch account was like small change to Richard. Of course I couldn't say that to Tye, but there was no reason for Richard to take the money.

'Look, I've contacted our lawyer—'

'Why do you need a lawyer?' I bolted out of bed, pacing our bedroom in my nightie, barely able to breathe.

'To draw up papers to dissolve the business.'

'Tye, I'm begging you, please, don't do this.' My livelihood was at stake.

'I'm just doing what's best for Georgie. I don't trust Richard, which means I can't trust you. I don't know how he convinced you to do this, but it's over now.'

'Tye, I'm not behind this! Neither of us are!' I sat down on the edge of our bed, not knowing what else to say to convince him.

'There's one more thing, Elle.'

More? What more could there possibly be?

'I've asked Georgie not to have contact with you.'

'What? You can't do that!' Now I was enraged. 'There's no way Georgie will do that!'

'Georgie agrees it will be easier this way.'

Every word he uttered after that was like a thick, grey fog.

I had received the papers within days. When I tried to call Georgie she would reply with a message to please not contact her. And then it was too late.

I can't let all that happen to Elle. I pull off the gloves as Sheena is thanking Elle and Georgie for coming in.

'This has been wonderful,' says Sheena. 'Such a boost for morale.'

'It's been a pleasure,' says Georgie.

'We'd love to have you back,' says Sheena. 'Assuming it's not too much trouble.'

Elle looks to Georgie like she's checking with her.

'Sure,' says Georgie. 'We'll check our schedules and work out a time.'

'Fantastic,' says Sheena, clapping her hands together. 'Let me walk you out.'

Elle turns to me. 'Bye,' she says. 'Nice to meet you.'

'Bye,' I say, lifting my hand to wave then feeling like an idiot for waving to myself.

'Bye,' says Georgie. Her eyes linger on me for a moment.

I smile at her, hoping for some kind of recognition. How could she not know my smile?

She tilts her head slightly to the side then looks over at Elle and back at me. 'See you next time,' she says, then walks out the kitchen door.

She'll be seeing me before then.

Chapter 15

Elle

The moment we step out of the shelter door, the refuge becomes lost among the buildings, as if it doesn't exist. There's no signage other than the street number above the doorway. As we walk to my car, pleased as I am with how the session went today, I can't help but think about the challenges these women must go through, the courage it must have taken to have fled their previous lives. It makes my problems seem trivial.

'So what do you think?' I ask Georgie, pulling on my seatbelt. 'I know you planned on only coming to the first couple of sessions, but I'd love to do this with you.'

'I'm in,' she says. 'They really loved it.'

'They did, didn't they?' It took a while for the women to warm up, but once they were immersed in it, they seemed to relax and feel comfortable. I'm so relieved, especially after last week's session. 'Even if we run them every other week, I think it's doable,' I say.

'Definitely. Maybe we could organise two or three shelters to rotate between.'

'Great idea.' We stop at a red light and I look over at Georgie. 'I still can't believe the woman I met was there. What are the odds?'

'Probably high,' she says.

'I'm glad she has somewhere to live and she's not sleeping on the streets. It's so awful, isn't it?'

'It is,' says Georgie.

'She seemed pretty uncomfortable. Although it sounds like she's new there, so maybe she's getting used to living at a shelter.'

'I'm sure I've met her somewhere. She looked so familiar. It was like I was having deja vu or something,' says Georgie.

'Well, Sheena did say she was a chef. Maybe we've met her at an industry event before she ended up at the shelter.'

'Maybe.' Georgie stares out the passenger window.

'I haven't told Richard yet,' I say.

She turns to face me, her eyebrows raised. 'Why not?'

'He won't want me taking on anything else.'

'How do you know if you don't tell him?'

My fingers tap on the steering wheel. 'I just do.' Of course Georgie sees how Richard can be, but she doesn't know the half of it, what he's like behind closed doors.

'Elle, you're volunteering your time to help others, how can he not be all for it? Tye thinks what we're doing is great.'

'Let's not compare Tye to Richard. Tye thinks anything you do is fantastic. Anyway, I am planning to tell him, I'm just waiting until I'm in a routine of it.' I don't mention that I'm too scared to talk to him about it because I'm already anticipating his reaction. Especially after the way he responded the other week when dinner was late. Georgie wouldn't understand. She'd tell me to do what I want to do and to stand up for myself, but she doesn't understand the ramifications if I do. The truth is that I don't fully know them either. I always end up doing as Richard asks. It's certainly better for my family if I keep the peace.

'Well, I know it's only a small thing, but it feels good to give back and do something to help. How could Richard argue with that?'

As much as I hope Georgie is correct, I'm not so sure Richard will see it that way.

'Let's work out our calendars for next month and we'll schedule a few workshops in,' she says.

'Thanks, George. I think this is going to be great.'

I drop Georgie home and drive to school to pick up the boys. I walk into the building and down the hallway to the classroom set up for after-school care. Looking through the window set into the door, Olly is sitting on the carpet playing a game with another child, but I can't see Charlie. The teacher is at her desk reading a book, a half-full platter of cut-up fruit in front of her.

'Mum,' says Charlie from behind me.

'Hi, sweetheart,' I say, running my hand over the top of his head before planting a kiss on it. 'Where were you?'

'In the bathroom. Can we go now?' he asks, opening the door to the classroom.

'Sure.' I follow him into the room. He goes to grab his bag. 'Hello,' I say to the teacher, a different one to last week. 'I'm Olly and Charlie's mum.'

'Hello,' she says, glancing up from her book at the same time as Olly runs to me.

'Hi, mate.' He wraps his arms around my legs and I bend down to hug him. 'Go grab your school bag.'

Olly hands me his bag and takes my hand. 'Thank you,' I say to the teacher.

She nods and continues to read.

We walk out of the building and through the school grounds. Freshly mowed grass flanks the walkway leading to the gate.

'How was aftercare?' I ask the boys on the drive home.

'Fine,' says Charlie.

'Good,' says Olly.

I glance up at the rear-view mirror. They both seem tired and guilt washes over me, but there's no alternative if I want to do this. My mother lives in a home, my father died last year and both of Richard's parents have passed away.

When we arrive home, the boys make a run for the couch, arguing over what television show to watch.

'Boys, work it out!' I call from the kitchen. After last week when I fell asleep on the couch, I don't join them. Instead, I make myself a cup of tea and start preparing dinner.

By the time Richard gets home, the boys have eaten and I'm upstairs watching Olly in the bath. He's rubbing the soap over the side, cleaning it.

'Don't forget your arms,' I tell him.

Richard comes to the bathroom and stands at the door, already changed out of his suit into jeans and a shirt.

'Daddy!' Olly squeals.

'How was your day?' I ask.

'Busy,' he says. 'Before I forget, I have a work dinner tomorrow night.'

'Okay. Dinner will be ready soon. I'll just finish up here.'

'Dad, will you play snakes and ladders with me?' asks Olly.

'Maybe later,' says Richard, turning to go downstairs.

Olly looks up at me, his eyebrows scrunched together, his mouth pouting, because he knows 'maybe later' means no.

'Daddy's just tired. Come on, time to get out.' I wrap the towel around him and he walks off, sulking to his bedroom. I pull out the plug and hang the bathmat over the towel rail.

When I get downstairs, Richard is standing in the kitchen nursing a Scotch.

'Won't be long,' I say, checking on the herb roasted chicken in the oven then pouring dressing over the salad. I can feel Richard's gaze on me. I look up and his eyes are piercing. 'Everything okay?'

Charlie and Olly run into the room in their pyjamas and head straight for the couch.

'Boys, no TV – play a game,' I call out.

They moan about it, but Charlie goes to the cupboard and retrieves a game.

'When were you going to tell me?' asks Richard.

I open the drawer and grab knives and forks, and then move to the cupboard and take out two plates. 'Tell you what?' I have no idea what he's talking about, but whatever it is, I can hear in his voice that it's not good.

He laughs. 'You always act so innocent, Elle. But when will you learn not to go behind my back?'

I breathe out wearily; these games are exhausting. 'Richard, I don't know what you're referring to.'

He moves to the other end of the kitchen, near the fridge and picks up my phone from where it's charging on the bench. 'Check your phone, Elle. There's a message from Georgie.'

'Why were you looking at my messages?' I take the phone from him, drawing in slow, steady breaths. If I don't, I'm sure to say something I might regret.

'The screen flashed with a message when I walked past. I saw it was from Georgie, thought it might be work-related. But it's not, is it?'

I read the message from Georgie. She's sent me some possible dates for the next few cooking workshops. I stiffen, avoiding his gaze.

'What cooking workshops is she talking about?'

'We just ran a couple of cooking classes at a shelter for women.'

'You what?'

I repeat myself. 'We ran cooking classes at a—' But he cuts me off.

'I heard you,' he scoffs. 'Do you really think a cooking class is going to help them? It's just a waste of your time.'

How can he think that? My blood boils through my veins, but I remain composed.

'And when did you do this little activity to make yourself feel better?'

'Richard, it's not like that at all.'

He bangs his fist on the bench. 'When?'

'One this afternoon and one last week.' I glance over at the boys. Charlie is watching us. 'I'll come play soon, boys,' I call out, both to reassure Charlie that I'm okay and to remind my husband that the kids are only a few metres away.

'And where were our children when you were doing this?'

A lump catches in the swell of my throat. I push it down. 'The boys went to aftercare.'

His jaw drops and his eyes grow dark.

'Richard, they were fine. They had fun.'

'You're out of control, Elle! First you lie about the business expansion and now this!' His voice has climbed an octave.

'Richard, the boys,' I hiss under my breath.

He leans towards me, lowering his voice slightly. 'When were you going to run this past me?'

'I was just waiting to make sure it was something I wanted to keep doing and that it fit in with everything.' I put my phone back down and grab the oven mitts from the bench. I'm about to take out the chicken when Richard grabs my arm. My heart is pounding so forcefully against the walls of my chest, I think I can hear it.

'Don't walk away from me,' he barks, pulling me closer.

'It's really not a big deal,' I say, but my voice is threaded with anxiety.

'You're so selfish, Elle. Always putting your career, and now this, before your family. Before your children, before me.'

'That's not true,' I say. 'You know the kids and you come first.'

'Well, start acting like it,' he says. He releases my arm, pushing it away like I have some contagious disease. 'Tell Georgie you can't do it.'

My heart sinks.

'I'll be in my study,' he says, walking off.

'What about dinner?'

'I'll eat later.'

At the sound of his study door slamming, I shudder. As much as I want to continue running these workshops with Georgie, I can't now. My boys are all that matter and I want them to grow up in a peaceful home, not one with parents who fight with each other.

I pick up my phone and reread Georgie's message, trying to come up with a possible reason for why I can't do the workshop that's not related to Richard. It's only then that I remember that I switched my phone off when I put it in the charger after we came home because it was driving me mad, beeping with messages. I sometimes do that when I need a few hours of peace and quiet, or uninterrupted time with the boys. Richard couldn't have seen a message flashing on my phone because it was off.

Chills run down my spine. Richard has the password to my phone. And he checks my messages.

Chapter 16

Nora

There are ten women in the group therapy session that Mary is running. I hadn't intended to join, but Mary insisted. It was all part of the healing process, she told me, which of course I already knew. I'd attended sessions once a week the first year I was here, as well as one-on-one counselling sessions with Mary. Mostly I just sat there and listened to others speak about the path that ultimately led them to the shelter. At the time I was so confused by how I'd even ended up here.

Janelle rubs the feeling stone between her fingers. 'I couldn't let my girls see me like that again,' she says. 'I didn't want them to think they had to take care of me.' Janelle's been here for six weeks with her two young daughters. Her husband was physically violent and she fled with her girls. It took being knocked unconscious and waking up to the face of her seven-year-old daughter placing a washcloth over her forehead for her to realise she had to leave. She wipes at her eyes with the back of her fingers and pauses for a moment.

'It's okay,' says Mary, 'take your time.'

'It's still so raw.' Janelle sniffs, her eyes track to the woman next to her and then she glances to each of us in the circle.

'You're so brave,' I say, when her eyes connect with mine.

'I don't feel it,' says Janelle.

'You are. You took your girls and ran.' I never would have spoken up ten years ago, but for some reason I can't hold onto my words any longer. 'I left my boys behind.' I know it was because I had no time to plan my escape, Richard was having me institution-alised that afternoon. If I'd taken the boys and fled, I wouldn't have been able to care for them; I was feeling so unwell at the time. My only option in the moment had been to save myself. But still, I felt I should have done something more.

'I'm so sorry they're not with you,' says Janelle.

'Thank you,' I say.

Mary leans forward, resting her elbows on her knees, hands entwined. 'I think it's a really important reminder for all of us that each of you have endured difficult situations with different circum-stances. Whether you were dealing with physical abuse or mental abuse, which can be just as destructive, you could only do what was best for you at that time. Sometimes, if children aren't at risk at home with another caregiver, it can be easier for them to adjust to the situation if they remain at home.'

It's like Mary can read my thoughts. She looks over at me and I give her a small nod in return for her words of kindness, although it doesn't assuage my guilt. The sad part is that when I was living it, I had no idea that Richard's controlling nature was a form of mental abuse. I brushed it away as a low part of our relationship until Mary enlightened me, in very similar words, all those years ago. And when I found out several months later, direct from Richard's mouth, that he'd actually been drugging me, causing harm to my body, well, then it was clear as day that there was physical abuse too.

The day after the dissolution of my business, I felt unwell. My head had been hazy, like I had brain fog. Despite Tye's request, I'd been phoning Georgie all morning in an attempt to explain myself, but she hadn't answered any of my calls. I couldn't let our friendship come to an end for something I didn't do. She had to know in her heart that I would never betray her trust. I had to make her believe me.

I had been sitting at the kitchen table, my laptop open, scrolling through our expenses from the last few months for the umpteenth time, hoping that something would jump out at me that I hadn't seen before and everything would suddenly make sense. My phone beeped on the kitchen bench. I jumped up to go and get it and was so disoriented that I walked to the oven instead of the bench. I did an about turn and picked up my phone, my free hand holding on to the bench to steady myself.

The message was from Georgie: *I'll cover this week's orders and send a letter to all our clients.* I assumed she meant she would start up her own catering business, with our clients, and the letter would just be a formality to let them know there was a change of ownership.

I shook my head, my lips pressed together, and placed the phone back on the bench when it beeped again with another message from her. A spear went through my heart as I read the words: *I'd really appreciate it if you stopped contacting me. There's nothing you can say to make us change our minds.*

How could Georgie do this? How could she not believe me? Tears streamed down my cheeks, an ache taking over every fibre of my body. Taking one step at a time, I had climbed the staircase like I was ascending a steep hill, pulled back the covers of my bed and got in, succumbing to the tears and exhaustion.

Two hours later I woke disoriented and sat up panicked: I'd missed school pick-up. Glancing at my watch I saw it was only two o'clock and my head fell back on the pillow. I closed my eyes and could literally see all of our business expense amounts, like a screenshot imprinted in my brain. Maybe that was what was causing the dizziness. I'd barely left my computer all morning because I just knew the answer that would explain everything was there somewhere. I just had to search a bit harder and it would reveal itself.

I still had an hour before pick-up to solve the puzzle of how the business money ended up in our personal bank account. I knew I had nothing to do with the fraudulent transactions, which meant it could only have been a hacker ... or Richard. Pulling myself out of bed, I had trudged back downstairs, determined to prove to Georgie and Tye that it wasn't me and to prove to myself that it wasn't Richard.

My mouth felt parched. I filled a glass of water and guzzled it down, grabbing a packet of Tiny Teddies from the pantry for a hit of energy. Planting myself back in front of the computer, I went through our accounts one last time, clinging to the speck of hope left in me that there was a simple explanation, and everything could go back to how it was. Of course, I couldn't dismiss the fact that Richard had access to all our information when he was installing the new system. He could have changed all the amounts then. But the bank statement showed that there had been payments being made from the business account for several weeks, which made me doubt that it was Richard because if it was, then that would mean that he'd had access to my computer for some time now. It was also difficult to believe that my husband, the man I shared my life with, had a family with, could be involved in this and commit fraud. There was absolutely no possible reason for him to do what Georgie and Tye were accusing us of.

By the time I'd collected the boys from school, my head was pounding. I took two paracetamol when we came home, and two ibuprofen an hour later when it still hadn't settled. Richard was out at another work dinner, and after I put the boys to bed, I sat on the couch waiting for him.

When I heard the front door open, my heart thumped against my chest. Richard came in and collapsed on the couch near me.

'I'm exhausted,' he'd said.

His breath stunk of Scotch, which was surprising considering he'd been at a work dinner. When I'd accompanied Richard on dinners in the past, he barely drank so he could be switched on for clients.

'How was dinner?'

'You know, same same. Wining and dining clients is never fun. Boys asleep?'

'Yes, for a couple of hours already.' It was after ten.

'Good. I think I might head up.' He'd pushed himself off the couch.

It was now or never – I had to know the truth and there was only one way to find out. 'Richard ...'

He turned around and looked down at me.

'We need to talk.' I braced myself, knowing full well his reaction wouldn't be pretty, but I couldn't let this one go. My business was over, my friendship with Georgie, over.

'Can't it wait until tomorrow?'

'No, we need to do this now.'

'Do what exactly?' He sat back down, seeming to sober up quickly.

'It's about the money going out of my business account and into our joint account.'

'Elle, when are you going to let it go? You should be grateful Georgie hasn't filed a complaint. You know you could go to jail for fraud.'

My mouth gaped at him. 'You know full well I didn't transfer that money!'

'Lower your voice, you'll wake the boys.'

'You're the one who updated our system. You had access to all our files.'

'Are you seriously accusing me?' He stood up from the couch.

'Yes!' I stood too, my hands clenched by my side.

'You ungrateful bitch. I told you to transfer the money back to the business straight away. Why the fuck would I take the money and give it back? *And* give you a loan?'

He looked at me like a lion eyeing its prey. But I'd started the conversation and I intended to get to the bottom of it. Richard had gone too far this time.

'That's what I'm asking you. Why would you do that?'

'For that amount of money? I wouldn't waste my time.'

I couldn't argue with that.

'Get your act together, Elle, and stop behaving like a crazy person. You're the only one to blame here. If you want to steal from your own business, go right ahead, it doesn't have anything to do with me. And as far as Georgie's concerned, I'm quite happy not to have her invading our space half the day.'

'You're not even here when she is.'

'But I know she's been here. You two are too close. It's not healthy.'

'That's absurd.'

'Elle, I'm warning you. This discussion is over. I don't want to hear about it again.' He'd stormed out, leaving me standing there shaking from head to toe.

I slept in Olly's bed that night.

The following day, my symptoms had gone downhill rapidly.

Now I know why. Richard made his intentions pretty clear, although at the time I couldn't see it. He didn't want Georgie in my life, and with her gone, I had no support system left.

After the women have left the group session, I help Mary stack the chairs.

'How are you settling in, Nora?' she asks.

'Good, thanks,' I say, placing the last chair against the wall.

'It was lovely what you said to Janelle earlier,' says Mary. 'A big part of the healing process is knowing you're not alone and having other women to support you. You did that for Janelle today, and for all the women in the room.'

I nod, giving Mary a slight smile.

'There's no rush, you know?'

My eyebrows raise, unsure what she's referring to.

'To share your story,' she says. 'But I hope you'll feel comfortable to in the next week or so. It's an important stage to go through.'

I know she's right, but I don't want to have to go through my past again, especially now that I'm so focused on rewriting it.

'And my door is always open, even for an unscheduled chat.'

'Thank you,' I say. When I had a private consult with Mary, when I arrived here for the second time, I was so thrown with what was happening to me, the staff behaving like they didn't know me, discovering that I was in fact back in 2012, I couldn't think straight, let alone hold a conversation. And when I eventually realised what was happening, I only had one agenda and was focused on that. I'm quite certain that the reason I've been sent back to the past isn't to spend my time in more therapy sessions. Devoting hours discussing Richard's actions or practising techniques to let go of all that happened isn't going to help Elle.

'Take care of yourself, Nora,' says Mary, before heading back to her office.

That's what I intend to do. I glance down at my clothing then head to the shared cupboard in the hall and rummage through it to find something to wear that will make me look even more familiar to Georgie. I grab a pair of light blue denim jeans and a pale blue sweater that's a size too small.

'Do you need any help?'

I startle at the sound of Heather's voice and turn around, clothing clutched to my chest. I feel like I've been caught stealing. The first time I took clothes from the cupboard all those years ago, Heather assisted me. I would never have felt confident enough to rummage through the clothing myself. But this time around, everything is so familiar to me. 'Sorry, I didn't see you there. I'm going to meet an old friend and I wanted to look nice.'

She glances at the clothing in my hand then reaches down to the second shelf and pulls out an azure scarf. 'This will go perfectly with your eyes.'

'How did you know that was in there?'

'I know where everything is in this place.' She winks and takes my hand. 'Come with me.' In her room, she sits me down at the small round table near the window. There's a mini fridge, toaster and kettle, and a sink to wash up in; her room mirrors the one I used to sleep in. Heather opens her cupboard and takes out a make-up bag. She moves the other chair so she's sitting opposite me. Then she gets to work.

By the time I find myself standing outside Georgie's house, I'm feeling more like myself than I have in a long time.

Chapter 17

Nora

My hand trembles as I reach for the doorbell. Georgie's car is in the driveway so I assume she's home. I can't believe how nervous I am. It's Georgie. But so much time has passed.

Taking a deep breath, I press the bell and twist the beaded bracelet on my wrist, a reminder of why I'm here and everything that's at stake. My family.

Footsteps approach the door. Georgie opens it and I can see that she's surprised to find me on the other side.

'Hi,' she says. 'It's Nora, right?'

'Yes,' I say. It's a good sign she remembers my name from yesterday but all I can do is stand there staring at her, mute. I should have prepared something to say, at least to get me through the front door, but I wanted the conversation to seem natural. Now I'm thinking that was a mistake. 'I don't mean to intrude, but I need to speak with you.'

She's looking at me as intently as I'm looking at her, like she's trying to work out why I'm here.

'How did you know where I live?' she asks, her eyes scanning the street.

'Well, that's what I wanted to talk to you about.'

Her eyebrows scrunch up.

'May I come in?'

She's hesitant.

'Please, Georgie, I won't stay long.'

Maybe it's something in my voice, the way I say her name, but her features soften and she moves to the side, allowing me to enter. I wait for her to take the lead and follow her to the living room. I know her house back to front, but I'm conscious of not being too familiar and scaring her away.

'Can I get you a coffee, tea?' she asks.

'A tea would be great, thank you.' A coffee will only make me more jittery than I already am.

She gestures towards the sofa for me to sit down. I watch her push through the swinging door to the kitchen and hear the kettle being filled, the clatter of teacups, the opening of a jar. Knowing Georgie, she'll come out carrying a tray with a teapot, cups and saucers, and a plate of homemade shortbread. She's very proper like that. Her parents are English and she lived in London until she was eight, so serving real tea with actual tea leaves that you brew in a pot is second nature to her.

Georgie returns with the tray and sits in an armchair. She gives the teapot a little swirl and then pours through a strainer into a cup.

'Sugar, milk?' she asks.

'Just a teaspoon of milk, please.'

The teapot stops mid pour and she looks at me. 'That is odd, the only other person I know who asks for a teaspoon of milk is Elle. Most people would say a drop or a dash.'

I just smile and take the teacup from her. It tastes just how I remembered Georgie's tea. 'This is good,' I say, unwinding a little. 'So much better than a tea bag.'

She holds out the plate of biscuits, and as much as I want to get to the heart of why I'm here, I can't resist. Georgie's shortbreads are my favourite.

'Thank you.' I take a bite – heaven. My eyes instinctively close, and when I open them, she's staring at me.

'Now that really is weird. Elle does that too when she eats the first mouthful of my shortbread.'

'Does what?' I ask, feigning ignorance.

'She closes her eyes and gets this dreamy look on her face.'

I clear my throat and place the biscuit on the side of the saucer. 'They're delicious.'

She takes a bite of one. 'You really do look very familiar, Nora. Have we met before?'

I take off my non-prescription glasses, my cloak of armour, and look at her. 'We have met, Georgie. In another lifetime.'

'I'm not sure I follow.' She looks confused and leans forward slightly to place her teacup and saucer on the wooden coffee table, then leans back.

I'm worried I've made her nervous. I may not have as much time with her as I'd like. 'I know you pick at your fingernails when you're nervous.' She looks down at her hands; she is doing it right now. 'I know your husband is Tye, you started dating in high school and you've been married for sixteen years. Your daughter, Holly, is ten and your son, Max, is seven.'

Her eyebrows furrow as I speak.

'You and Elle have been running the catering business for almost four years.' I talk quickly. Georgie's lips are now pressed together, and I'm concerned she's about to ask me to leave so I speak even faster. 'Your parents are divorced, your dad moved back to England when you were fifteen, you're very close with your mum, she lives a few blocks away and helps with your kids after school so you can work. You run the PR and marketing side of the business, Elle manages the admin and accounts.'

She holds up her hand. 'Stop! I've heard enough. Who are you? Have you been researching me?' she asks, an edge of hysteria in her voice.

'No! Not at all. Georgie, can't you see who I am? Why I'm so familiar to you?' I don't think before I say it. 'It's me, Elle, ten years from now.'

She stands. 'Look, I don't know who you are or what you're trying to do, but I think you should leave.'

I have to think of something that will convince her. My brain goes into overdrive. I know Richard isn't drugging Elle yet; I saw her yesterday and she looked well, healthy. Instinctively I stand, my fingers pointing at her as my words come out in a jumble. 'You just put a proposal together for the expansion of the business. Elle didn't tell Richard, but he found out about it from Tye at the dinner party.' Yes, the dinner party – that would be a recent event for her.

'How do you know that? Are you a spy?'

I shake my head. If the moment wasn't so tense I'd laugh at the absurdity of her question. 'You served steamed prawn dim sum ... ah ...' I try to jog my memory. 'Vegetable san choy bow and duck spring rolls for entrée.' I say it like I've just won the lottery. 'Richard made a fuss about me eating too much and ignored me when I asked him to pass me a spring roll. So you' – I point again –

'picked up the platter, went around to everyone at the table and offered them a spring roll.'

The colour drains from Georgie's face. She looks like she's seen a ghost and sits back down but stays on the edge of the seat.

'You were brilliant,' I say, getting right into it now. 'You said, "Elle, you have to try these, I was thinking of adding it to the menu." Then you gave me a heaped dollop of hoisin sauce and sat down.'

'I ... how could you possibly know all this?'

'You'd added an unusual ingredient.'

Her mouth opens then closes, as though she's lost for words. For Georgie this all just happened recently.

'Cinnamon. It was cinnamon.' I sit down, relieved. How could she not believe me now?

She leans back into the armchair, fingers pressing at her temple like a headache is coming on, and casts her eyes to her lap. When she looks up, she says, 'You're right, Nora, that all happened. I have no idea how you know all that but I assume Elle or one of the other guests relayed it to you. But what is it that you want?'

I sigh, I haven't got anywhere. 'George, don't you recognise me? I know I've changed a lot, I've been living at a shelter for the last ten years, but you must be able to see that it's me.'

Please know that it's me.

'I admit that you do look a bit like Elle, but obviously Elle is forty-one and she lives in her home with her husband and children.'

'Richard set me up. He drugged me and I had to run.'

'Elle wouldn't leave her kids. There's also the fact that what you're saying is, well, it's impossible, insane.'

'Elle doesn't have a choice but to leave,' I say. I don't know why that's the first thing I think to say but I have to defend myself.

'Richard drugs her, he makes out like she's an unfit mother and she runs because he's about to lock her away in a mental institution.'

'That's quite a story,' she says. 'And I admit I'm not a fan of Richard, but I can't imagine him doing that to Elle.'

I realise I'm not going to be able to convince her. But I can still try to protect Elle by warning Georgie. At least then she might think twice before leaving Elle out to dry. 'Look, I get it, if someone told me they were from the future, I'd probably laugh in their face. I don't know why this is happening either, but I have to believe that someone up there' – my eyes look up – 'is giving me a second chance to save myself. To save Elle. If you don't believe that I'm her, at least let me tell you how Richard steals money from the business to make it look like it was Elle.'

'He what?'

'He destroys your business partnership and in the process your friendship with Elle.'

'I'm listening,' she says. 'I must be mad, but I'm listening.'

I tell her what's about to happen in the next week. Every single detail so that when it does, she might believe me, but more importantly so that she believes Elle when she tells her that she didn't do it. 'Please, Georgie, even if you think this isn't going to happen, when it does, please believe her.' I'm begging. 'You didn't last time, you didn't answer her messages or calls, you didn't even let her explain. I haven't seen or spoken to you in ten years.'

'I would never do that,' she says. 'Elle's one of my closest friends.'

'You do. Just know this time that it's Richard. It's all Richard.'

'So he's behind this whole thing you say is going to happen?'

I take a deep breath and bite my lower lip. 'He's just getting started.' I stand up to go, but before I leave, I say, 'Just don't forget about her.' My voice is choked because that's exactly what happened last time. I look down at Georgie, I can see she's too shocked to get up. 'I'll let myself out.'

I walk to the bus stop and pace the pavement while I wait. This has to work. Even if Georgie hasn't believed a word I've said, this is all going to pan out just as I told her it would. Every single detail. I just pray that Georgie changes the outcome.

Chapter 18

Elle

When I wake up on Saturday morning, Richard is still asleep. I change into a tracksuit, turn our door handle until the latch goes in and gently close it behind me. I do the same to Charlie's door so he can sleep in too. Passing Olly's bedroom, his bed is empty. I find him sitting on the rug in front of the coffee table watching television, spooning cereal into his mouth. The cereal box is open on the bench along with the milk and some splatters of each that I assume have missed the bowl. I cap the milk and place it back in the fridge.

'Good morning, sweetheart. How did you sleep?' There's another trail of spilt milk on the floor leading to the coffee table. I bend to kiss the top of his head.

'Look, Mummy – I made breakfast by myself.'

'Good job.' I grab the remote from the couch and turn the sound down then open the curtains. It's meant to rain later, but right now it's clear outside and I'm desperate for some fresh air. I feel like I've been cooped inside for days. Maybe it has something to do with the silent treatment from Richard. He didn't say a word to me for days after he read the message from Georgie. Yesterday he spoke to me, but he was removed. 'Will you come with Mummy for a walk after you finish your cereal?'

He looks up at me. 'Can I play on your phone?'

'Yes.' It's a fair trade. Olly's happy to sit in the stroller if I let him play games on my phone. Richard thinks it's ridiculous putting a five-year-old in a stroller, but I can't leave Olly alone, so the alternative is not to go. I head upstairs to his bedroom and grab some clothes for him. While he dresses, I fetch my runners from the laundry.

'Come on, mate, let's go.'

He climbs into the stroller, my phone in his hand, and as soon as we step out of the front door, the crisp air engulfs me. As we walk along the path, I'm drawing it in as if I have no air supply, then releasing it in huge bursts. I have no control over my breathing, and after it does this several times, it finds a natural rhythm and returns to normal. I've been so full of tension since I found out Richard reads my phone messages. What if he checks my calendar diary too? I know that he's my husband, but it feels like a complete invasion of privacy.

Every time a thought comes in about Richard's reaction to the cooking workshops, I try to think of something else in my life, something that's positive to overpower that thought. It's an effort. The thoughts keep creeping back in, but after we've been walking for almost half an hour I seem to have won over my mind. Now it feels empty, and in turn I'm more present and can see everything around me so clearly.

I stop and pick up an autumn leaf from the grass. 'Look at this pretty leaf,' I say to Olly. He glances, but isn't interested, too busy with my phone. 'Do you want to hop out and collect acorns?' The grass next to the footpath is scattered with them.

Olly considers this for a moment then climbs out of the stroller, leaving my phone on the seat. He picks up acorns and folds the bottom of his sweater to hold them. I help him gather them too, and when his top is full, I hold it up for him while he gets back into the stroller.

'Do you want to put them in a jar when we get home?' I ask, as we continue to walk.

'I have to count them first,' he says.

'Maybe we can make a guessing game, and Charlie and Dad have to guess how many acorns are in the jar.'

'Can we?'

'Sure.'

'Can the winner get a prize?'

'I can make the winner pancakes for breakfast.'

He turns his head to look up at me, a huge smile on his face.

'You know you can't be the winner, right? You'll know how many acorns are in the jar.'

I can see him processing this. 'Then make it the winner and the game maker get pancakes.'

I ruffle the top of his head. 'Sounds like a plan, buddy.'

When we get home, Richard and Charlie are sitting at the table eating breakfast. The newspaper is open in front of Richard, a slice of toast in one hand, his phone in the other as he reads something on it. Charlie is shovelling in cereal, presumably Coco Pops, and watching the television.

Olly runs to them, holding his sweater to keep in the acorns. 'Look what I got.' He climbs up on the chair, lifts his top so that the sweater rests on the table and then he lets the acorns loose.

'You're making a mess,' says Charlie as acorns fall to the floor.

Richard barely looks up.

Olly picks up the ones that have dropped, placing them on the table. 'Mum, can you get me a jar?'

'Sure.' I grab an empty jar from the pantry and take it to the table. Olly is explaining to Richard and Charlie the game he's making. I can tell Richard's only half listening.

'Do you have a minute?' asks Richard. 'I want to show you something.'

Dread fills me, but I say yes. I have no idea what I could possibly have done now.

I follow Richard to the study and sit on the couch next to his desk. Richard sits in the brown leather desk chair. 'We've been trialling this new software program at work and the staff in accounts say it's really easy to use.' He opens his laptop and types. 'I thought it might be good for your business. It will probably save you time as well.'

This I hadn't expected. I try to hide my shock.

'Come and have a look.'

I get up and move to his side of the desk, leaning over his shoulder as he shows me the program.

'Do I just buy and download it?' I ask.

'I can do that for you. If you want.'

'That would be great. Thank you.' I genuinely mean it. Richard rarely takes an interest in my work.

'I can set it up for you too.'

'Are you sure? Won't that take time?' I'm perplexed that he would do that for me.

'I don't have much on this weekend. I'll find time.'

'That would be amazing, thank you. What do I need to give you?'

'Just bring me your laptop and show me where everything is and I can take it from there.'

'I'll go grab it.' I stop at the door to his study and turn around. 'I really do appreciate this.' I smile at him and then retrieve my laptop from the kitchen.

Richard spends most of the day setting up the system and I take the boys to the park and then to visit Mum to keep them busy. By late afternoon, Richard's finished. He seems so excited as he takes my hand, guiding me towards his office. I haven't seen him like this for a while. He sits me in his desk chair and kneels next to me as he runs through the program, explaining how it all works.

'This is great,' I say, although it doesn't look too dissimilar to our current program. But I don't want to disappoint him or seem ungrateful seeing he's gone to so much effort setting it up for me.

'I have a few more things to put on, but I'm almost done.'

'Take your time. I'll make us a nice dinner.'

We don't have plans tonight so I cook us something special. The boys are fed early, and after they go to bed, I open a bottle of red wine to let it breathe. I coat the lamb fillet that's sizzling away with the juices in the pan, adding a knob of butter. Thin slices of eggplant, red peppers and zucchini are roasting in the oven. When the lamb is cooked I place it on a chopping board to rest, then assemble rocket leaves and the vegetables on an oval platter and drizzle it with a balsamic glaze and extra virgin olive oil before scattering olives and crumbled feta over the top. While the meat is resting, I set the table, light a candle in the centre and pour us each a glass of wine. Pressing my finger to the centre of the meat, it feels tender and ready to be sliced. I place the thin strips on top of the salad then text Richard that dinner is ready before taking the platter to the table.

I'm overwhelmed that Richard has been working all day to set up this new software program for me. He must have spent at least six or seven hours in the study. He does that sometimes, surprises me. Usually it's after we've had an altercation that he goes and does something nice. Often he sends flowers, other times it's a dinner out at a fancy restaurant, just the two of us. One time he organised a surprise weekend away. But this feels different. He's given up his time for me, and that feels like so much more than anything he could buy me.

'It smells delicious in here,' he says, coming into the kitchen.

We both sit down at the table, opposite each other. He picks up his wineglass and I follow.

'A toast,' he says. 'To good things to come.' He clinks my glass with his, looks into my eyes and we each take a sip, before eating our dinner.

Chapter 19

Elle

Georgie calls me from the grocer on Monday afternoon. I've just arrived home from picking up the shopping for tomorrow's menu and she's buying ingredients for the breakfast order. She tells me our business debit card has been declined.

'I just used it half an hour ago and it worked. I'll wait while you try it again,' I say.

'I already have, three times, and it's showing up as declined.'

'That can't be right. Use your credit card and I'll reimburse you later. I'll call the bank.'

She pauses on the other end. 'The thing is, I checked our bank account and the balance is zero.'

'What? Wait a sec.' I open my laptop where it sits on the kitchen table. 'Let me check.' I enter my password and open our business bank account. Georgie's right. The balance is zero. I stare at the screen in disbelief, panic rising in my chest. It can't be possible that we don't have funds in our account.

'Elle, are you there?'

'Yes. You're right, it's empty.'

'I'll come to your place now. I'm sure it's just some kind of error,' says Georgie.

'Okay,' I say, hanging up the phone, surprised she doesn't sound as frantic as I'm feeling right now. I pace the living area waiting for her, and as soon as I hear her car pull up, I run to the front door to open it.

'What are we going to do?' I ask, reaching for her arm and pulling her inside.

'I'm sure the bank will sort it out,' she says. 'Did you go through the transactions on the bank statement?'

'No,' I admit. I was too afraid to do it on my own. What if this isn't a mistake and our account, in fact, has zero funds?

We sit down together in front of the computer and scroll through the bank transactions over the last few weeks. There are at least a dozen unfamiliar payments going out that I don't recall making. I always include what the expense payment is for so I can easily reconcile it with our accounts, but these ones don't list the item and I don't recognise the trading name of where it's been paid to.

'Can you bring up the accounts on our system?' asks Georgie.

I click on the new software. 'Richard put a new system in on the weekend,' I say, focusing on the computer screen as I scroll through our clients' accounts. 'But it's pretty similar to the old one.'

I check the revenue coming in for the last few weeks. 'That's odd. The amounts look like a lot less than what we charge. I'll have to check them against the invoices, but with these amounts we'd only break even.'

I scan the expense amounts. Each one has the date, where

the purchase was made and what for. They're all for the usual places where we shop for ingredients and other supplies. There are also amounts we allocate for monthly payments for electricity and gas, for working from home. Georgie and I haven't allocated ourselves a salary, we only take our earnings from profit, but Sarah's salary is listed too. But then I notice some unfamiliar expenses.

'I have no idea what these ones are for,' I say, pointing to them.

'I'll grab the folder of receipts,' says Georgie, getting up to go to the drawer in the entertainment unit under the television where I keep work files. She hands it to me and I crosscheck physical receipts from the last few weeks with the ones listed in the system. I can't find receipts for the expenses I don't recognise.

I look over at Georgie and her fists, resting on the table, are clenched. The accounts are my responsibility. 'George, do you think we've been hacked?'

'I don't know,' she says. She seems agitated but still much calmer than me. My insides feel like there's a mouse gnawing away in there.

'Let's go to the bank,' I say getting up. 'They'll be able to trace where the payments have gone to.'

She grabs my hand to pull me back down. 'I already called the bank on my way here. They're tracing it for us, but they said it could take a couple of weeks.'

'A couple of weeks? What are we meant to do in the meantime? We have no money to buy ingredients with.' I'm stressed beyond belief. We can't run our business with no funds.

'We can use our personal money while we're waiting,' she suggests.

I exhale in frustration. It's not ideal, and Richard won't be happy about it, but we have no other choice. 'Okay,' I say, ruffling through the pile of receipts. 'I'm going to check these again.'

'I'll make us a tea.' Georgie goes to the kitchen.

I've re-checked every single receipt and still can't find the missing ones. The unknown expenses on the software system aren't listed in our bank statement either, so I assume they've been tampered with on my computer and not from the bank's end. I close the manila folder and return it to the drawer, taking out the folder I keep with hard copies of invoices that I send to clients. I'm pedantic like that. I like to keep physical copies of everything for when I do our business tax return.

I reconcile the invoices with the amounts listed on the system and there are months of invoices we've billed that don't match the physical copies. At least when I check payments into our bank account from clients, they are the correct amounts. The unknown expenses on the software system aren't listed in our bank statement either, so I assume they've been tampered with on my computer and not from the bank end.

But what I can't work out is that the system doesn't list the payments that are showing up in our bank account made to an unknown account. They're all to the same trading name, with no description, and for the same amounts. I have no idea what they're for, but I assume that when I add up those amounts they'll equal the difference between the correct invoices and what the system says has been invoiced plus the extra expenses.

All I can think is that we must have been hacked. How will we be able to keep the business running in the long term? We'll have to apply for a bank loan, something Richard forbade me from doing when we started out.

It's two gruelling weeks until Georgie hears back from the bank. She comes over after school pick-up, and while our kids play outside in the cubbyhouse, we sit down at the kitchen table and she fills me in. The money has been traced to my personal joint account with Richard.

'What?' I push back my chair and pace the length of the table. Heat flushes through my body and I'm sure smoke must be coming out of my ears. This cannot be happening. I come to a stop next to her seat and drop to my knees, latching on to her hand. 'Georgie, you have to believe me, I would never, ever take your money.' My breathing becomes heavy. Georgie's not saying anything. 'I'll call the bank right now and tell them to put it back in the account, every cent.'

'Of course I know you didn't do it,' she says. With her free hand she picks up her glass and takes a sip of water. 'And I know the money will go back into our account.

'How can you be so calm?'

'Because it will be sorted out.'

'But you must think I'm to blame, that I did this!'

'Not at all – it didn't even cross my mind until you mentioned it right now. I know you aren't capable of something like this.'

I stand, returning to my pacing. 'But I'm responsible for the admin and accounts. The money was transferred to my account!'

She laughs. 'You sound like you're trying to convince me that you did it.' She gets up from the chair and comes to stand in front of me. 'Elle, I know without a doubt that this wasn't your doing. We must have been hacked.'

'But how can you know, how can you be so trusting?'

'Because I know you and I trust you with my life.' She wraps her arms around me, squeezing me tight.

'I trust you with my life too,' I say, wrapping my arms around her too. I feel her body shake in my arms. She's crying. 'Hey, are you okay?'

'I'm fine,' she says, swiping under her eyes with her fingertips. 'I'm just so lucky to have a friend like you.' She takes my hands in hers. 'No matter what life throws at us, we'll get through it together. I'm always here for you, Elle. Always.'

'I know. I'm always here for you too.'

We sit back down at the table. The kids are squealing in the backyard.

'I can't believe we were hacked,' I say. 'I always do the security updates on my computer. I'll have to ask Richard if there's an anti-hacking system we should install.'

'Good idea,' says Georgie. 'Kids, let's go!' she hollers over her shoulder.

Chapter 20

Nora

Heather knocks on the open door to the shared bedroom. I spent the morning with Mum and she wasn't having a good day. I'd forgotten how draining that could be, so I lay down when I came back to the shelter and must have fallen asleep.

'Hi,' I say.

'Sorry to wake you, but Sheena said there's someone here to see you.'

My body clenches; immediately, I assume it's Richard. But then I remember it's 2012 and Richard doesn't know that I live here. In fact, he doesn't even know this version of Elle exists yet or that this is where she ends up. My muscles relax again. 'Thanks,' I say to Heather. 'I'll be there in a minute.'

I take a sip of water from the glass next to my bed and my hands reflexively check my face. My skin is dry and I can feel the deep wrinkle lines. I'm sure I wouldn't have aged so quickly if my life hadn't taken such an unexpected turn. It wasn't even that I took more care of myself when I lived at home, although I did at least have a daily skincare routine. I'm sure it was the constant stress of the situation I found myself in and the anger at losing my children, career and home that aged me. I've been filled with so much resentment and rage towards Richard, I can feel it in every bone in my body, every cell and fibre of my being. I'm sure it's the reason I look a dozen years older than I am.

I walk to the reception area. 'Hey, Sheena. Heather said there's someone here to see me?'

Sheena motions her head in the direction of the chair where Georgie sits picking at her fingernails. She stands up when she sees me. Even from here I can see her eyes are puffy and red. It's been two weeks since I went to meet with her, so I assume the events I warned her about have happened. I glance back at Sheena. She's probably wondering why Georgie's here for me seeing she introduced us a few weeks ago at the workshop. I open my mouth to give her some kind of explanation, but she says, 'Mary's left for the day. You can use her office if you like.'

'Thank you.'

I gesture with my hand to Georgie and she follows me in silence. I open the door to Mary's office and close it after her. Georgie sits down at the table, like her body is too heavy to hold up. I take the chair beside her and wait for her to tell me why she's here, although by the look on her face, I already know.

'It happened,' she says. 'Everything you said would happen happened.'

I nod. I'm relieved my presence here hasn't changed those events, at least. I need Georgie on my side. When I speak to Elle, I have no doubt she'll react the same way Georgie did when I went to see her. But she trusts Georgie, so hopefully she'll listen to her.

Even if this is the only thing I do for Elle – for me – it's worth it, because I'm pretty sure I've just saved her friendship with Georgie, and no matter what else happens, she's going to need her more than ever.

'Do you have premonitions?' she asks. 'How do you know the future?'

I tense and then breathe out slowly. I presumed she believed me, that I am who I say I am, but she doesn't. Instead, she's trying to rationalise something that can't be made sense of. 'I know Elle's future because I've lived it. I am her, Georgie. I'm Elle.'

'But ... but how can this happen?'

'I have no idea. I really don't.'

'You must have done something. Something must have happened for you to go back to the past.'

I close my eyes and picture the day I met Elle on the shopping strip. My eyes flick open. The time capsule. That must be it.

'I went back to my old house,' I tell Georgie. 'It was up for sale.'

'Richard's selling the house?'

'He sold it years ago. The current owners are selling it – in 2022. I went back because the summer before I left, I buried a treasure with Charlie and Olly in the backyard. We made a time capsule, and it was the only tangible piece of them I had left. I thought it would be safe to go back now because it wasn't Richard's house anymore. It was buried behind the cubbyhouse and I dug it up. Then I walked down the street and there was Elle.' I fill her in on our encounter.

'This is all so surreal. But how did you end up here?' She looks around the room. 'You live at a shelter.'

'I do. It's a long story,' I say.

'I have time,' says Georgie. 'Please, Nora, I want to know every-thing that happened to you.'

'Okay,' I say, taking a breath, not really knowing where to even begin. So much happened in such a short space of time. Some of it I remember clearly and some of it is muddled. 'Before I left home, I'd been unwell for at least five weeks. I could barely function and I was at a loss as to what was wrong with me. Richard had come clean about his affair several weeks earlier.'

'Affair?' Georgie raises an eyebrow, then her lips purse.

I nod. Deep down I'd had an inkling there'd been someone else for a while. He'd been behaving so differently. When we'd had arguments, he got over them quickly, which was unusual in itself, probably because he had another woman fulfilling his needs, which basically meant building up his ego.

'The sad part was that I would have forgiven him for the affair if he'd ended it. For our family. But that wasn't what Richard wanted. He wanted a divorce.' Of course, when he told me that he wanted to end our marriage, I was ready to throw him out. As foggy as my mind had become, that was one thing I was clear on. 'Richard insisted that we live together for a while for the sake of the boys. He said it would be easier for them to adjust to our situation if they had both parents living under the same roof. We could lead separate lives, but still be a family.'

'Meaning he could have a guilt-free affair and you could continue looking after the boys and the house,' says Georgie.

'Something like that.'

'Unbelievable,' she says.

My thoughts exactly. 'I was too exhausted to put up a fight. I was at a point where I just didn't care. I had no one to turn to. You weren't speaking to me, and more often than not my mum didn't even know who I was.'

And the truth was, I was only half-lucid most of the time. I had fallen into a heap, even more so than after the business fiasco. I would spend most of the day in bed. I had no energy, and any strength I did have I saved for the boys.

'Richard organised a nanny to take the boys to school and back because he was worried about me driving them. She stayed in the afternoons to make dinner for them.'

She was older than me, in her late forties, with rich dark brown hair and striking green eyes. I couldn't believe that me being unwell was what it took for Richard to allow a nanny to help with the boys. That and an impending divorce looming over us. I only found out the night before I left who she really was, but I refrain from telling Georgie that part yet. I can see she's already finding all this distressing enough.

'The day I left, the boys were at school and I'd just come home from a walk around the block.' I thought if I got my body moving it might clear my head, but I felt off balance, so I went back home. 'When I came inside, there was a suitcase by the door. My initial thought was that Richard was finally leaving.'

As relieved as it made me, I remember feeling anxious too. I didn't feel capable of looking after the boys by myself while I was in this state. The doctors didn't know what was wrong with me and my symptoms were becoming worse by the day.

Georgie listens patiently. I notice she's practically tearing at the tips of her nails.

'I could hear Richard talking on the phone in the kitchen so I stayed in the entrance and waited. Obviously I didn't trust him, not after everything that had happened. And it was unusual for him to be home during a workday. I thought he'd gone to work that morning, but I couldn't be certain.' I look down to the floor, the memories still stinging after all this time. 'He was saying something like, "I'm taking her later today. I'll give her a chance to say goodbye to the boys."'

'Was he talking about you?' she asks.

I nod, close my eyes and see myself creeping down the hall to hear him better, then sliding down the wall. Just thinking about that moment makes my heart beat so fast I think it might combust.

'He was saying that it's all organised, and that it was a shame that it's come to this but he had no choice.' I open my eyes and look at Georgie. 'He said I was unfit to look after the boys, that I was a danger to myself.'

'Who was Richard speaking to? The other woman?'

'His lawyer. He'd organised a restraining order.'

'What the ...' Georgie looks furious. 'Against you? What on earth for?'

'He said I tried to attack him. That I was a physical threat to the boys and him, and to myself.'

'That's absurd!'

'I know.'

'So what did you do?' asks Georgie.

'I confronted him. I walked into the living room and asked him who he was talking to and if he was leaving.'

'What did he say?'

'He told me he was speaking to his lawyer and that he wasn't leaving, I was. He said I wasn't a well woman. I told him I was okay, that my ill health was from all the stress of everything that had happened over the last month. That it was all too much.'

'Of course it was. It would be a lot for anyone,' says Georgie.

'Richard said I couldn't function or take care of my children. Which was true, I was really struggling, although I didn't tell him that.'

My symptoms did seem to come and go that first week they started. It was around the time Richard had suggested we go away for the weekend to Daylesford. He thought the fresh air and a rest would clear my head after I'd lost the business. And it did until the last day, when he told me he was leaving me for Patricia. Back home my symptoms started up again. I was certain it was just my body reacting to my life being turned upside down.

I choke back tears as I remember our encounter. 'Richard had been consulting with my doctor without my knowledge.'

'Is that even legal?' asks Georgie.

'Apparently. If I was a danger to myself and he was my next of kin, he could speak to him. He said my dad was dead, my mother incompetent and that he still cared about me and was just trying to do what was best for my wellbeing.'

'Do what exactly?' asks Georgie, her eyes glistening.

'Put me in a mental hospital. Nothing less than the best place in the state for his wife. And of course, when I was better, if I got better, he'd kindly help me get back on my feet. I only found out a couple of months later that he was drugging me to keep me unwell.'

Georgie's eyes look like they're going to pop from their sockets. 'You can't be serious!'

'I am.'

Georgie swallows. 'I ... I just can't wrap my head around any of this. How could he do this to you?'

'I've tortured myself over the years trying to look for reasons and signs that I might have missed, when everything in my marriage began to go wrong or if it had always been that way.'

'Well, if you ask me, Richard was always controlling. Tye never really liked him. Even when you started dating, he didn't think Richard was right for you, and it wasn't just the age difference. Tye thought he was arrogant. And don't think I didn't notice the way he commented on what you ate, or the times I arrived early for work and he'd criticise the outfit you had on. I don't know how you put up with it for so long.'

'I guess I just weighed the good with the bad and thought I came out okay.' I understood that a marriage had ups and downs, and when things went downhill, I told myself to hold on, it was just a low, a rough patch, and we'd climb back up.

'You must have been terrified. I don't know what I would do if someone tried to have me committed,' says Georgie, her voice full of wrath. I can tell she's feeling every bit of this, and not for Elle but for me.

'I lost it.'

When Richard told me, I thought I would literally explode like a bomb. The glint in his eyes and the smirk on his face repulsed me, he was clearly relishing the moment. 'I guess I figured if Richard was already making claims to his lawyer that I was a danger to everyone around me, including myself, then what did it matter if I attacked him. I mustered every last ounce of energy and lunged at him, but I didn't make a dent. My body was too weak, and he was too strong for me. Somehow Richard had managed to get my doctor to sign off on having me committed, or at least that's what he told me. For all I know he could have written the doctor's referral himself. He said I could either go willingly or he'd drag me there.'

The look in his eyes is imprinted in my mind forever, his dilated pupils so dark, I was sure he meant every word. It didn't matter what I said. Richard's mind was made up and he was on a mission to destroy me.

'He told me I could say goodbye to Charlie and Olly after school,' I continue.

'The bastard. What did you do?'

'Richard went to his study and I went upstairs to lie down.'

I had slammed my bedroom door after me and fallen on the bed in a heap, my chest so constricted I could barely breathe. But there was no time to feel sorry for myself, in a few hours Richard would have the pleasure of locking me up in a mental institution. He wasn't going into work, he was staying in his study, guarding me.

'I was distraught, but I managed to pack a few things.'

I opened my closet, grabbed a backpack from the shelf and stuffed it with some undies and socks, two spare t-shirts, and a jacket. But my handbag was downstairs and I realised Richard had probably packed it in the suitcase. In that moment, my hands fell to my sides in surrender, the backpack dropping to the carpet. How far could I get without money? I looked to the closet and opened Richard's cupboards. His pants were folded over hangers, lined up neatly across the bottom rack. Adrenaline had coursed through me, giving a newfound energy. My hands were frantic as they checked every single one of Richard's pants pockets for money, but they were empty. Then I saw his gym bag on the floor next to the armchair by the window. I rummaged through it and in the side found a fifty-dollar note next to his gym membership card. I stuffed it in my pocket and ran to the bathroom, grabbed my toothbrush and toothpaste, and turned on the shower. Our house was renovated, but old, and you could hear all the upstairs plumbing downstairs. I prayed Richard would think I was in the shower. I threw the backpack over my shoulder and crept past the boys' room. My heart felt like lead.

'There was no time to say goodbye to the boys. I couldn't explain to them what was happening and that I'd be back for them soon. It seemed like this would be my only chance to escape, so there was no choice but to go,' I tell Georgie, holding on to my tears. At the time, my plan was to come back for them. Hire my own lawyer. Richard wouldn't get away with it.

My head was pounding and I felt dizzy again as I tiptoed down the stairs, but there was no time to stop. Holding on to the banister, I could hear Richard's voice from the study, talking on the phone.

Georgie is gaping at me, waiting to hear what I did next.

'I went out the back door in the laundry and down the side of the house. And then with everything I had left in me, I ran.'

'I just can't believe he did that to you,' says Georgie, shaking her head. 'Even for Richard, that's pure evil.'

I'm quiet; there's nothing left to say. This is the first time I've told anyone the full story of what happened to me. Although it feels good to share it, not to be carrying the burden alone anymore, it's also utterly draining. Reliving the day I left is just too much.

'Did you come to me then?'

I shake my head. 'No, you weren't speaking to me.'

'But I would have been there for you. I would have kept you safe.' She sits up straighter. 'Nora, there's no way I would have abandoned Elle.'

'I hadn't had any contact with you for over a month.' I look away. 'I couldn't risk it if you sent me away. And, to be honest, your house was probably the first place Richard would have looked for me. I had to get away from him.'

'But did you try to find me later, once you were settled? I mean,

Nora, you said it's been ten years.' Desperation and disbelief thread her voice.

'No.' I don't mean to make her feel guilty by telling her everything. I just need Georgie to understand what Richard is capable of, the extent that he goes to, so that the Georgie of today doesn't do the same as the person she is in my time. The only chance I have at preventing this from happening to Elle this time around is for Georgie to be on her side. Wholeheartedly.

'Then how do you know I wasn't searching for you? If I'd known Richard put you in a mental institution, I would have come looking for you. I would have tried, I know I would have.'

'Georgie, you can't blame yourself for me ending up here. This was all Richard's doing. He's a sick, sick man. He even involved the police so they'd be on his side if I tried to fight back.'

I don't want her to blame herself, but I can't deny that part of me hasn't thought about it over the years, that if she hadn't reacted the way she did, if she and Tye had believed me about the money, then maybe the outcome would have changed for me somehow.

'There's something else you need to know,' I say.

Her mouth drops open. 'More?'

'Richard found me here later,' I tell her. 'He knows where I live.'

'But you're safe now? The Richard of my time doesn't know you live here, right?'

'Yes, I'm safe for now. But Elle isn't.'

'We have to stop him. Nora, we have to – I can't let that happen to Elle.'

'We will. This time she has you.'

'She does. I still can't believe this is really happening, but I'll do whatever you tell me to do.'

That is a relief to hear, although I'm not actually sure what my next move is.

'Thanks for coming in,' I say, getting up. I'm sure she has other things to do today and I need to think of a plan. If my timing is correct, Richard starts to drug Elle soon.

Georgie stands up in front of me. Her hand trembles as she reaches with her fingers to touch my cheek, then my hair. 'How did I not know these eyes?'

I swallow, so relieved she not only recognises me but accepts that it is me. 'I can't tell you how much I've missed having you in my life.' My voice croaks, my eyes well. 'I thought I'd lost you forever.'

She pulls me into her embrace. 'You'll never lose me. I'm always here for you.'

I let her hold me briefly then pull away, wiping my nose. I know she means well, but the truth is she wasn't always there for me, and my heart still aches with the pain of losing her. I can't go through that again. Georgie gave up on me once, so there's a chance she might do it again. And the fact is I'm not Elle anymore, I'm Nora. I've become a different woman.

'How will you reach me?' she asks before leaving.

'I have your number, and if you need me, call the shelter. Just keep an eye on her until I contact you.'

'I will. I promise.'

I nod.

I'm sure she can also feel the shift in the room. There's tension in the air, but I can't help it. She forgot about me and I've been living in a shelter for women for ten years. Ten years that she hasn't been in my life. It was her choice not to believe me and subsequently end our business and friendship. I know she can't conceive of the idea that she would do that, but she did. She doesn't know the person I am anymore, and the connection that we once shared has become untethered. As much as I love her, everything has changed. I just hope Elle doesn't have to go through that the way I did.

I guess I'm not the only one who may be getting a second chance. Georgie is too.

Chapter 21

Elle

I'm making the boys' lunches when Richard comes into the kitchen, dressed in his gym clothes.

'How was your dinner?' I ask him as he opens the refrigerator and takes out ingredients for his smoothie.

'It went well,' he says. 'Have you heard back from the bank?'

He was home late last night, so I haven't had a chance to fill him in. 'You won't believe where the money was traced to. Our bank account! How weird is that?'

Richard fills the blender with a lemon wedge, avocado, kale, celery and two heaped tablespoons of vanilla-flavoured protein powder. 'Are they investigating it further?'

'No, there's no need, I've transferred the money back to Notch's account.'

He moves around me to the sink to add water to the ingredients. 'What did Georgie have to say? I can't imagine her being happy that the business money was transferred to your personal account.'

'She was fine about it. Actually, I was more frantic than she was, but she agrees the new system must have been hacked. Will you check it for me later?' I place the vegemite sandwiches in containers and wash an apple for Charlie and grapes for Olly.

'When I get time.' He places the blender jug on the base, his hand hovering over the button. 'I'm surprised she didn't think you had something to do with it.'

'Me? Why would she think that?'

'You manage the admin. The money ended up in your bank account.'

My eyes narrow. 'What are you suggesting?'

'Nothing,' he says. 'It's great it all worked out.' He flicks the switch on the blender and the whirring noise ends our conversation.

I go upstairs to wake Charlie for school. On my way back down, I pass Richard on the staircase carrying his thick smoothie. It looks like mud.

'I left yours on the bench,' he says.

'Thanks.'

Olly's still watching television when I get back downstairs. 'Olly, go get dressed for school. We'll be late.'

He jumps off the couch and runs upstairs. My smoothie sits on the bench. I can't stomach it this early in the morning and put it in the fridge for later.

By the time Georgie arrives at nine o'clock, the kitchen bench is already covered with ingredients.

'Good morning,' she says.

'Hi. Sorry, I haven't had a chance to get anything in the oven yet,' I say.

'That's fine. We have plenty of time.'

I massage my hands with soap and run them under the tap.

Georgie gets straight to work, finely slicing the spring onions. 'Did you speak to Richard about the new accounts system?'

'Only briefly.'

'Did he have any suggestions so it doesn't happen again?' asks Georgie.

'He said he'd have a look at it later.' Not quite his words, but it will do.

'It is weird that we got hacked at the same time that he changed over our system.'

My hand freezes over the peak of the iceberg lettuce. This morning Richard implied that I had something to do with the money ending up in our account, and now Georgie is questioning if we were actually hacked.

'In four years we've never had a problem, and then Richard transfers all of our information into a new program and it's tampered with. I'm not sure that it's a coincidence.'

I don't know what to say. It's true Richard had access to all of our files, but there's no way he would have adjusted the figures.

'And the money did go into your joint account,' she continues.

'Georgie, Richard wouldn't take money from you, he just wouldn't. He was relieved it's been transferred back. And he gave us a loan to keep us going in the meantime, remember?' I reach out and rest my hand on her arm. 'I'll ask him to check the system as soon as he gets home. I promise.'

'Okay,' she says.

Georgie's quiet as we work and the silence feels uncomfortable, so I put on some music.

When the food is packed, ready for pick-up and we're cleaning the dishes, Georgie asks, 'Did you organise some new dates for the cooking workshops?'

The workshops. With everything that's happened, I completely forgot to get back to Georgie about it. Richard forbade me from doing them, but I can't tell her that. 'Actually, I've been thinking maybe now's not the right time to be doing them. I'm so busy as it is.'

'We can just do them once a month, that was the plan right? If it was too much we'd just do an occasional class?'

'I know, but ...' I dry the frying pan, avoiding eye contact with Georgie.

'And now that I'm fully on board, that will lighten the workload for you. We can take turns planning the recipes.'

Why is Georgie pushing this? She wasn't even sure she'd commit to it. 'Maybe next year,' I say.

She turns off the tap and pulls the gloves from her hands. 'It's Richard, isn't it? He doesn't want you to do the workshops so you're giving it up.'

I can't lie to her, but I can lessen the truth. 'I'll admit he didn't love the idea, but it was my decision.'

'Just like not going ahead with the business expansion was your decision?'

'Georgie ...'

'Elle, can't you see? You're letting him control your life!'

'I can't believe you just said that.' I'm shocked by Georgie's outburst. I run a wisp of hair that's fallen from my ponytail behind my ear. 'I don't let him control me,' I say.

'Of course you do! He controls how big our business can be, he controls whether you can do something charitable, he controls what you bloody eat!'

My mouth hangs open. Over the years, Georgie has made comments here and there about Richard, and I know she's not mad about him, but she's never been so outraged to say anything like this. 'You're speaking about my husband,' I say.

Her hands grip the kitchen bench and she drops her head. 'I know, I'm sorry. I'm worried about you, that's all.' She looks up at me and her eyes are glistening.

'Is this about the money?' I ask.

'No,' she says, shaking her head. She takes my hands in hers. 'Elle, you need to stand up to him.'

I pull my hands away. 'It's my marriage, Georgie, not yours.' I'm infuriated she's doing this, criticising us. 'Maybe you should leave.'

I can see the shock in her expression.

She sighs. 'If that's what you want.'

'It is.'

She picks up her handbag. 'I'll see you tomorrow.'

Georgie opens the front door just as the doorbell rings.

'Hi,' Sarah says to her.

'Bye,' says Georgie.

Sarah walks into the kitchen. 'It smells amazing in here. Everything ready to go?'

I nod and help her carry the boxes to her car. I close the front door when Sarah leaves and lean my head against it. The truth is that every word Georgie said was one hundred percent true. Richard controls my life and I let him do it. But the thing is, I'm afraid of what he'll do if I don't.

I just couldn't tell Georgie that.

Chapter 22

Nora

I'm helping Lloyd prepare dinner when Sheena comes in.

'A package came for you,' she says to me. She looks as surprised as I am. In the ten years I've lived at the shelter, I've never received so much as an envelope of mail, let alone a package.

'Thank you,' I say, taking it from her and placing it on the kitchen bench.

She leaves the kitchen and Lloyd, standing over the hot stove, wipes his forehead with the back of his arm. 'Go on,' he says. 'You might as well take a break, otherwise you'll be staring at that box all afternoon.'

'Thanks.' I pick up the parcel, feeling like a curious kid eyeing presents under a Christmas tree. Who would be sending me a package? Not many people even know I exist in this time, and the ones who do have known me less than a month. I take it to my bedroom, close the door and sit on the bed to open it.

It's a disposable phone. They call them burner phones now, in

2022. Many of the women at the shelter use them in my time. It's an inexpensive mobile phone with basic features so you can contact relatives or emergency services and still remain anonymous. I turn it on and it rings in my hand, the screen flashing with Georgie's number. I answer it.

'Nora,' she says.

'Hi. I just got the phone.' Well, obviously.

'I dropped it off but I had the kids in the car so I couldn't come in. We just stopped at a park on the way home so I could speak to you.' Her voice sounds a little frazzled.

'Is everything alright?'

'Yes. Well, no ...'

'What happened?'

I listen as she relays her morning with Elle up to the part where Elle asked her to leave.

My breath draws in then releases. 'Georgie, you can't leave her angry with you. This is exactly what Richard wants. Whatever you have to do to make amends, do it.' I know I sound firm, but my whole world is at stake here.

'I will,' she says. 'I just panicked and thought you should know.'

'Thank you, I appreciate it.' I try to think of the next move. 'How did she seem? Was she behaving any differently or complaining of not feeling well?'

'No, she was fine.'

'That's good. Maybe we've delayed Richard's plans.'

'Look, I have to go,' says Georgie. 'The kids are getting restless. But use the phone to contact me whenever you need and I'll call you with any updates.'

'Okay, thank you,' I say.

I'm still holding the mobile phone in my hand, processing

everything Georgie just told me. When I listened to her relay the argument with Elle, an eerie feeling washed over me. The past is still happening, but in a different way. The events leading up to it were different, but the outcome is the same: Elle and Georgie aren't talking. What if I can't change the past and my destiny is predetermined? What if no matter what I do now to alter it, the result will be the same? But I have to at least try. There has to be a reason for this, a reason why I'm here.

I realise that Georgie warning Elle isn't going to be enough. It may also cause a rift in their friendship, and I can't let that happen again.

There's also the fact that Elle defended Richard. Despite the way he treats her, she still stood up for him. From what Georgie says, she hasn't even doubted him in relation to the business accounts being tampered with and the transfer of the money. I certainly did last time around. I knew it was his doing, but then he started drugging me the day after I questioned him. Maybe Elle didn't doubt him this time because everything was resolved so smoothly. This time she didn't have Georgie accusing her of fraud.

Elle is going to have to hear everything Richard does to her, and she's going to have to hear it from me. But knowing Elle the way I do, I'm going to have to earn her trust if she's ever going to believe me. Richard won't let Elle continue with the cooking workshops, which means she has no reason to come to the shelter. I need to see her and soon, but I can't just rock up on her doorstep. I'm going to have to come up with another way.

It's before visiting hours, which start at nine, when I arrive at Mum's, so I walk a few blocks, my mind still careening at full speed as I try to come up with a plan. Honestly, I can't think of anything other than knocking on Elle's front door when Richard leaves for the office. Maybe it would work if Georgie were there too because she'll back me up. If Georgie believes me, surely Elle will too. But the thought of going back to that house when Richard is still living there makes me feel nauseous. The thought of smelling his after-shave, the scent so strong that it fills every room of the house that he walks into, causes bile to rise in my throat.

I check my watch, it's close to nine, so I walk back to the home. 'Good morning,' I say to the nurse behind the reception desk.

'Good morning,' she says.

'How's Rosalind today?' I ask.

'She's sleeping. She had a restless night.'

'Is she okay?'

'She's fine now. We gave her something to sleep, so she might be out for a while.'

'Okay.' I've seen Mum every day since I've been here, and even though she's not always lucid, she's been getting to know the person I am now, Nora. 'Thanks for letting me know.'

'Do you want to come back later? I can call you when she wakes?'

'No, I think I'll go sit with her for a while.'

Mum's lying on her back in bed. The curtains are open and the natural light warms her face, giving it some colour. She looks so peaceful. I move to the other side of her bed and pull a chair close to her. My hand strokes hers.

Mum always thought Richard wasn't good enough for me. Somehow she knew what I couldn't see.

'Hi, Mum,' I say, my voice quiet. 'I wish I could talk to you about everything that's happening in my life. You'd probably know exactly what I should do. Your instincts were better than mine about Richard, but I guess when you're in love it's difficult to see without rose-coloured glasses.'

I did love Richard in the beginning. I think he loved me too, in his own way. It's just that his ego was too big to ever truly love someone other than himself. But in the beginning, when he was courting me, there was a flow of romantic gestures and sweet text messages. Sometimes he'd show up at my doorstep with a bunch of flowers and ask me to go for a walk, or he'd buy something because it reminded him of me. It was a whirlwind, really. He swept me off my feet, and when he proposed eight months later, I said yes.

My mum thought it was too soon.

'You're getting married? You've only known him for a few months,' she'd said, sitting at their round kitchen table with Dad and me.

'Mum, it's been eight months. I know everything I need to know.'

'Well, I don't. We've only meet him a few times.'

That was true. She'd met him briefly at my place, and both times he was on his way out as my parents were arriving. The reality was they'd only spent one evening in his company when the four of us had gone out for dinner. Mum hadn't been shy to voice her opinion, the next day, that she thought he wasn't right for me.

Mum had turned to Dad for help. 'Stuart, say something.'

'If Elle's happy then I'm happy for her,' said my dad.

She practically scowled. 'But why the rush?' she had asked me.

'There is no rush. I want to marry him.'

'But he's so much older than you, darling. It may not feel like it now, but twelve years is a big age difference. You're still so young.'

'Mum, I'm almost thirty!'

She relented, but she'd persisted with her argument for most of the engagement period. Even though she accepted Richard after we were married, I was sure Mum never really cared for him.

It's hard to imagine that such a force of nature, such a strong woman like Mum, could end up so very frail. I rest my head on my hand that touches her arm and look up at her. 'I know you'd be telling me a man like Richard isn't capable of love. I know that now. And if I told you everything he was doing before it even got really bad, you would have told me to leave him and move on. But I just couldn't. You'd probably think this predicament I'm in now was wonderful. In fact, I can imagine you telling me to use this second chance, to beat him at his own game.' I let out a small laugh. 'You'd probably tell me to do to him what he did to me.'

I bolt upright. That's exactly what she would tell me.

'Mum, you're brilliant.' That's what I have to do. To change my fate, I have to change Richard's too. It's the only way I'll ever truly be free of him.

Now I just have to work out how to persuade Elle to do that. I'm going to have to convince her like I did Georgie. There's no alternative but to go to her home, tell her all the information I know about her and then warn her about something that's going to happen, and when it does, hopefully she'll believe me.

I glance down at Mum. 'I miss this,' I say, resting my head back down. I breathe in her familiar scent and close my eyes.

Moments later, I feel her presence without moving my head. My eyes shoot open and I glance at Mum. She's still asleep, which is a relief. It would be distressing for her to witness this.

'Who are you?' Her voice is uptight.

I lift my head off Mum's arm and sit back in the chair.

'Hello, Elle,' I say.

Chapter 23

Elle

There's a woman in Mum's room, her head lying on my mothers' arm. I ask her who she is, and when she lifts her head to look at me and says hello, I'm bewildered. It's the woman from the shelter where Georgie and I did the workshop. The same woman I met shopping, near my home, and bought food for. Now she's in my mother's room. What on earth is she doing here with my mum?

I think back to our first encounter, the way she was watching me with such intensity outside the bank when I was withdrawing money. And then again at the shelter I could feel her eyes on me, but every time I caught them she looked away. Now she's at the home where my mother lives, holding her hand. Is she stalking me?

'What are you doing?' I ask.

'Visiting your mum,' she says.

'Who are you?' I ask, stepping further into the room to stand on the other side of Mum's bed.

'Nora. We met at the shelter, remember?'

'Of course I remember,' I snap. 'But who *are* you? Why are you visiting my mother? She doesn't know you.'

She looks down at the sleeping form of my mum. 'I do know your mother. I just haven't seen her for a very long time.'

I can't imagine that Mum knew anyone who was homeless, and this woman is a lot younger than Mum.

'I know all of Mum's friends and we've never met.'

'I'm a distant relative,' she says. Her eyes connect with mine and I can see that she's hesitant to give me more information. 'I'm from Adelaide. We haven't seen each other in ten years.'

Neither of my parents have many relatives. They were both only children, so I have no aunts or uncles, no cousins, no family other than the one I've created with Richard. I don't believe this woman for a second, but Nora doesn't know I have no family so I'll wait for her to trip herself up. She'll probably say she's some long-lost niece I've never heard about.

'My dad, Henry, and your mum were cousins. I'm his daughter.'

That answer I wasn't expecting. Mum does have an older cousin named Henry who lives in Adelaide, but when I was growing up they were rarely in touch. Not that I knew of, anyway. I have absolutely no idea if Henry had children or how many.

'When I was little,' she continues, 'we lived in Melbourne for a while and I was very close with your mum. We spent a lot of time with her and your dad. You weren't born yet. Your parents were having trouble conceiving.'

Her eyes pierce mine and I realise it must be true. How else would she know personal information about Mum? I move to sit down in the remaining chair at the small table, and Nora lifts her chair to join me. I'm not sure what to feel right now. Since Dad died and Mum's condition worsened, I've felt so alone, having no other relatives. I guess that's why I hold on so tightly to keep the family I have with Richard together, even though I question at times whether it's worth it. Especially lately. One minute Richard's distant, the next attentive. I'm walking on hot coals half the time, cautious of what mood he's going to be in. But knowing I have a relative puts me at ease somehow.

'I thought it was just me,' I say. 'I mean, I didn't know I had any other family. I'm an only child and so were my parents. But I guess you already know that.'

'I do.'

'So how come your family moved back to Adelaide?' I ask.

'Mum wasn't happy living in Melbourne. She missed her family in Adelaide so Dad ended up transferring back. My parents have both passed since.'

'I'm sorry,' I say. I can't help glancing over at Mum. Even though she's not with it half the time, she's still with me.

'It must be hard for you,' says Nora. 'The nurse explained the situation.'

'Yes, it is.' My fingers fidget on the table. 'She's the only family I have left.'

Nora reaches her hand over, like she's about to take mine, but then she hesitates and places it on the table.

'I mean, she's not my only family, I have my husband and children too. It's just different having your parents around, you know,' I say.

'I completely understand. With my parents gone, I sometimes feel like I'm all on my own.'

'Do you have siblings?' I ask. I feel I missed out on so much, not having a sibling.

'No,' she says. 'Just me.' Her eyes glisten.

'Did you know it was me, that day we met on Glenferrie Road?' It is weird that I've met Nora twice now without knowing who she is.

'I was pretty sure. Your mum used to send us photos of you when you were young, and you look a lot like she did at your age. I guess I was taken aback when I saw you. I didn't mean to ask you for money, but I was worried you'd leave without me having a chance to speak to you, and that's what flew out of my mouth.'

'Why didn't you just tell me who you were?'

'I assumed you didn't know about me.'

I hope I'm not overstepping, but I have to ask her how come she's living in a shelter. Maybe she needs my help. I'm sure even Richard would agree to help family. 'When did you arrive in Melbourne?'

'The day we first met,' she says. 'That's why I was so flustered when I saw you.'

'I don't mean to pry but how come you're living in a shelter?'

She hesitates, as if she's weighing up whether to confide in me. I assume if she's living in a shelter it mustn't have been safe for her to live at home. Maybe she's on the run and she's come to Melbourne hoping to find Mum and me.

'You can trust me,' I say, wanting her to feel comfortable.

'My husband was abusive,' she says. 'I had to leave. I was at a shelter in Adelaide, but then he found me, so I came to Melbourne.'

'That's awful,' I say. 'Do you have children?'

'Two boys. They're teenagers.'

'Are they with you?'

She glances over at Mum. 'No, I had to leave them behind.'

It must have been pretty bad for her to leave her children with an abusive man. I'd be frantic not knowing if my kids were safe.

Her eyes connect with mine. 'He's not like that with the children, if that's what you're thinking. I wouldn't have left them if he'd ever harmed them in any way. It was just me he had a problem with.'

'I'm sorry,' I say, unable to find the right words to comfort her.

'I'll go back for them. I just have to get a few things sorted out before I do.'

'Do you need money, clothing, anything at all?'

'No, I'm fine, but thank you, that's very generous of you to offer. Although I'm not sure I'd fit into your clothing.'

I look down at myself. I miss my curves. 'I need to put on a few kilos, I'm too thin.'

'You look perfect to me.'

I smile at her. I can't believe I have a relative, and she seems so lovely. I'm glad she feels she can trust me with everything going on in her life. She must feel completely alone here in Melbourne.

'Nora, you have to come and meet my family.'

She shakes her head. 'No, I couldn't intrude.'

'It's not an intrusion at all,' I say. 'I'd love you to meet my kids and my husband, Richard.'

Her face pales. 'I'm not sure it's a good idea. I have to be careful that my husband can't trace my steps.'

'Of course, I completely understand. What if I don't tell Richard where you're living?'

'Hmm ... I'm not sure,' says Nora.

'I promise, I won't even discuss your situation with him. It's not my story to tell.'

'Okay,' she says, but I can tell she's uncertain.

'Perfect, come over this Saturday at three. I'll make afternoon tea.' I get up and go to Mum's dresser to find the notepad the nurses use, resting on the top. I write down my address and phone number and give Nora the sheet of paper.

'Thank you,' she says, standing to leave. 'I'll see you then.'

As she walks out of the door, Mum wakes.

'Nora,' I call out. 'She's awake.'

But she doesn't hear me. She's gone.

Chapter 24

Nora

Mum starts to stir while Elle is writing down her address for me. It will be too confusing for her to see double of her daughter, the younger version and the older one, so I get up to leave. Elle hands me a piece of paper with her address and mobile phone number. Obviously I don't need either, but I take it. When I walk out the door, I hear her call after me that Mum is awake, but I don't look back. I keep walking straight to the bus stop and am absolutely relieved when a bus pulls up straight away. I don't even check if it's the right number, I just get on it.

I find a seat next to the window and release the breath I've been holding on to. It was completely surreal to sit opposite myself and hold a conversation with the person I was ten years ago. I had no control over anything Elle said or thought, or any of her actions, as though we were totally different people. And the whole time she sat there having no idea that I'm her. I don't understand it, but it really was like she was a separate entity to me, a beautiful young stranger, so innocent, despite what she's encountered in life so far. I've seen another side now, facing homelessness and having to start over at the shelter. I've endured losing the people I love. All of it has brought with it wisdom that Elle's forty-one years don't have.

At one point in our conversation I almost forgot that she is me. It was like I was taking on a motherly role, and there was this huge responsibility to guide and protect her. I know how hard it's been for her, losing Dad and now watching Mum wither away. What she needs most right now is family, and I want to give her that.

I thought it was best to stick as near to the truth as possible. Mum did have a cousin, Henry, but I have no idea if he's dead or alive, let alone if he had children. Everything that came out of my mouth just seemed to flow, and it worked. It all made complete sense. And I was honest about the husband part. I thought it would be good for Elle to hear my story, because it's her story too. I figured if that part were true, then when I have to actually tell her that I am her, everything Richard has planned for her won't seem so far-fetched. At least I hope so.

I run my fingertip down the window. The cold is setting in, winter will be here soon and in a few weeks Elle will be living on the street, fighting the icy weather, trying to keep warm. Trying to stay alive. Even if I've delayed Richard, he's on a mission, and he won't stop until she's out of his life and their boy's lives.

The last thing I want to do is face the Richard of ten years ago. I hate it when he pays me visits in my world, his face so smug because he knows he's holding all the cards and can call the police at any time, even though none of it is true.

But for some reason, coming back to 2012 and seeing myself again, the woman I used to be, has made me realise how strong I am to have survived everything Richard did. I'm still standing. Richard doesn't intimidate me anymore. I'm not scared of him because I know that, right now, I hold all the cards.

The bus pulls up at a stop I don't recognise and I realise I'm on the wrong route. I get off and while I wait for the bus that will get me back to the shelter, I take the opportunity to call Georgie. She updates me that she apologised to Elle and they're back to their usual easy-going rhythm. I tell her about my conversation with Elle this morning. Even though Elle said I could confide in her, I'm sure she'll tell Georgie I'm a relative, and because Georgie already met me at the workshop, Elle will assume it's okay to mention that I left my husband and children behind. I need Georgie to accept the version of events Elle relays to her, that I'm a distant cousin, as I have no doubt Richard won't like it. He spent so many years ostracising Elle from her friends and went to such lengths to get rid of Georgie, I'm sure he won't appreciate Elle now having a relative in her life. He doesn't want her to have a support system to fall back on when he turns her world upside down.

But the fact is that even though she's going to have one now, she's not going to need it this time round. He is.

'You're a natural at that,' says Heather, watching me apply foundation in the communal bathroom. She's loaned me her make-up bag to use. When I visited Georgie at her place, I gave Heather full access to my face. This time I want to apply my make-up myself. I want it to look the way I used to wear it, the way Elle wears it now.

'Thank you,' I say. 'I used to put make-up on every day.' I run black eyeliner across the outer rim of my lower lids and dip the tip of my finger in soft pink eye shadow, rubbing it across my eyelid, then swipe my lashes with mascara. I line my lips with a brown eyeliner – Heather doesn't have lipliners, only lipsticks – then rub them with some Vaseline to give them a glow.

'It suits you,' she says, handing me a blouse. 'Try this one on.'

I slide into the arms and do up the buttons. It's not exactly my style but it fits nicely, so it's a yes. She's brought some black pants, which I squeeze into, and lets me borrow her jacket, which is nicer than the one I found in the communal clothes cupboard.

I stand on my tiptoes in Heather's black flats to get a better look at myself in the mirror. I'm happy with what I see, a first in a long time. I look mature, almost business-like, which is a good thing. I want to look confident, like a woman in control of her life. I told Heather about Elle – not that I am her, but that we're related and have recently reconnected. She knows I want to make a good impression when I go to Elle's home for afternoon tea. What she doesn't know is that I also want to leave a lasting impression on Richard. I want to cause every nerve in his body to run cold when he sees me.

'They did a great job with your hair,' says Heather, brushing hers back with her fingers. 'Maybe I should give them a try.'

'You definitely should,' I say. 'It's amazing what a good cut and colour does for a girl's confidence.' I can't change the extra weight I'm carrying or erase my wrinkles, but there was one thing I could do to help me look more like Elle and less like Nora. Thanks to Georgie, yesterday I went to the hair salon in North Melbourne that I've passed many times over the last few years. When the hairdresser was finished, I barely recognised myself in the mirror. My hair colour had returned to a honey gold and the trim gave it a flicky look. Georgie insisted on paying for it all, and as much as I don't like taking money from anyone, we both agreed it was necessary for meeting Richard.

I'm so glad I did, because I strode out of the salon feeling like a new woman. I had a newfound confidence, a lightness in my chest. I can't remember the last time I felt so comfortable in my skin, probably before I met Richard and before he made me feel like I wasn't good enough, both in my appearance and who I am.

Heather's reflection in the mirror smiles at me, not just her mouth, but her eyes too. 'You seem different to the woman I met a few weeks ago.'

'I am,' I say, packing up her make-up. 'I'm a woman on a mission.' And I feel it too. Even if I end up back where I was in the future, I'm going to seize the world and get out there. I'm a trained chef, I'll apply for a job at a restaurant or work for a catering business. I'll rent my own place and apply for legal aid so I can take back custody of the boys. And I'll go and find the Georgie of 2022 and reconnect with her. I'll make a new life for myself.

'I have to get back to work,' says Heather, picking up her make-up bag and the other tops she brought with her.

'Thank you for everything,' I say, reaching over to hug her. 'The clothes, the make-up.'

'My pleasure,' she says. 'Enjoy your family reunion.'

'I will.' I most certainly will.

My stomach is filled with a swarm of butterflies as I walk down the street to Elle's house. I am nervous, but not about seeing Richard. In a few moments I'm going to see Charlie and Olly. And not the Charlie and Olly of 2022 – I'll be seeing my boys as I left them. Charlie was eight and Olly only five. It's going to take every ounce of strength in me not to pick them up and devour them. I don't want to show any emotion that might be alarming to their parents. Although Elle knows my story, that I left my boys behind, and may just assume it's because I miss my children, I can't risk becoming too overwhelmed in front of Richard.

I round the corner and look down at my outfit to make sure everything's where it's meant to be. I brace myself and press the doorbell. Footsteps run down the hall to the door, and Elle calls out, 'Olly wait for me.'

The front door opens and there's Olly, his big eyes looking up at me, dressed in a long-sleeved t-shirt and jeans, his caramel hair dishevelled. He's exactly how I left him and my heart fills to the brim. I think it may completely burst with love. I didn't know a person could feel as much joy as I do in this moment.

Elle comes to stand behind Olly and says hello, but I barely hear her. I bend down to his level. 'You must be Olly.'

He nods. 'Mum said you're her cousin.'

'I am. My name is Nora.'

'Dad said she has no cousins.'

'Did he now?' I say, looking up at Elle.

A flicker of embarrassment crosses her face.

'Olly, go tell your brother to come downstairs.' As he runs off, she opens the door wider. 'Please come in. You look lovely, Nora.' She eyes my hair with a smile. 'Can I take your jacket?'

'Yes, thank you.' I hand it to her. My outfit looks better without it. 'You have a beautiful home,' I say, following her through to the living room. I notice the study door is closed.

'Thank you. Make yourself comfortable,' she says, gesturing to the couch.

I sit facing the garden. Elle has set up afternoon tea on the coffee table. She's made an orange cake drizzled with white icing and decorated with candied orange peel, biscuits and a platter of sliced fruit.

'Richard will be a few minutes,' she says, sitting down. 'He had a work call he had to take.'

'That's fine,' I say, relieved to have time with my children without his presence looming over us.

'Where are those boys?' Elle gets up and walks to the bottom of the staircase. 'Charlie! Come down.' She returns to the couch. 'Sorry about that. He's working on a model car, and once he starts, nothing can distract him.'

At the same time as the boys run down the stairs, the study door opens with a creak and I hear the familiar sound of Richard's dress shoes against the floorboards. Even on weekends he always wore his work shoes, but with casual pants and a shirt. I'm too overwhelmed to turn around, not wanting him to see my reaction when I sight Charlie for the first time.

'Charlie, come here,' says Elle.

I turn my head slightly and see Richard in my peripheral vision, but fortunately Charlie gets to me first. He stands in front of me, Elle behind him with her hands on his shoulders.

'Nora, this is Charlie,' says Elle.

He takes my breath away, dressed in beige chino pants and a t-shirt. I'm sure Elle forced him to wear the pants.

'Nice to meet you,' I say, holding out my hand to shake his, barely able to contain my joy. His skin feels soft, warm and so very familiar that it melts my heart. I want to hold his hand forever but force myself to let go. I've daydreamed of this moment every single day I've been absent from their lives. Seeing them like this, the age that I left them, makes it feel like no time has passed at all. But I know that in another lifetime, like me, my children have aged too.

'You look like Mum,' he says.

'I'll take that as a compliment,' I say, smiling at him, so glad he notices the likeness. At the same time I can sense Richard occupying the space behind the couch.

'And this is my husband, Richard,' says Elle, her eyes drawing to him.

I stand as Richard comes over. He extends his hand. I look down at it and swallow. 'I'm Nora,' I say, reaching to shake his hand. 'It's nice to meet you.' His handshake is firm and he grips mine for a moment too long. He looks the same, strong and confident, the line of his jaw hard, his hair slightly greying at the edges, but not as grey as it was the last time I saw him. Just looking at him makes me want to tie him up, throw him in a room and lock away the key for eternity.

'You have a lovely family,' I say, retrieving my hand and remaining poised despite my thoughts.

'Thank you,' he says, then moves to sit on the other couch.

I sit back down and cross my legs.

'Mum, can we have cake?' asks Olly.

'Sure,' says Elle, leaning towards the coffee table to cut it. 'But guests first. Nora, would you like a slice of orange cake?'

'That would be lovely.'

Elle fills a plate with cake and a biscuit and gives it to Olly to hand to me. 'Thank you,' I say. 'It looks delicious.'

Charlie sits on the couch, quiet and waiting politely. It's difficult to draw my eyes away but I can feel Richard watching me.

'What year are you in at school, Charlie?' I ask.

'Year three.'

'Do you like school?'

He nods.

'I'm in prep,' says Olly, coming to stand in front of me. I can't resist touching his arm lightly, his skin as silky soft as a baby's.

'Do you have children?' Richard asks, leaning forward and clasping his hands together in the space between his knees.

'Yes, I have two boys. They're teenagers.'

'How old are they?' he asks.

Elle hands him a plate and he uses his fork to cut a mouthful of cake. I notice Elle doesn't take a slice for herself but nibbles on a biscuit. Actually witnessing it, the control he has over what she eats, I'm appalled with myself that I let it go on for so long. It pains me to see it.

'My eldest is almost eighteen; he's in his final year at school. My youngest is fifteen.'

'What school do they go to?' Richard takes another mouthful of cake. The motion of his mouth chewing is nauseating.

Fortunately I researched schools in Adelaide before I came, so I'm prepared. 'St Michael's.'

'So what brings you to Melbourne?' asks Richard.

'Just here for a visit. I've been wanting to come and see Rosalind for a while now, and to meet Elle, and the timing was right.'

Elle glances over at me. 'Nora, would you like a tea or coffee? Or herbal – I have peppermint and chamomile.'

'A mint tea would be lovely.'

'Richard?'

'Coffee. I'll come help you.'

Richard follows Elle to the kitchen leaving me with my boys, which is exactly where I want to be.

Chapter 25

Elle

'I don't like her,' says Richard, standing next to the coffee machine.

'What's not to like?' I whisper, grabbing two mugs and placing a peppermint tea bag in each.

Richard turns his head towards the couch area. 'I don't like the way she looks at the boys.'

I follow his gaze. Nora is sitting on the edge of the couch and Olly is on the rug in front of her, showing her his Bob the Builder collection, and Charlie has now moved to sit on the couch next to her. I'm sure Nora must miss her boys, given the situation she's in, and that's what Richard's picking up on. Obviously I can't tell him that, so instead I say, 'She's good with kids.'

'It's weird you didn't know you had a cousin. She's popped out of nowhere.'

'Richard, we've been over this,' I say, keeping my voice hushed. 'She's a third cousin, they lived in a different state.' It doesn't seem unusual to me. I'm not sure why he's doubting her. I already told him Mum's cousin Henry lived here when Nora was little but then he lost touch with my parents when he moved back to Adelaide.

'How old is she, anyway?'

'I don't know, maybe mid to late fifties.' I glance over at Nora. She certainly looks a lot younger today than she did when we first met. The blonde hair suits her. In fact, today's the first time I've noticed how alike we look. 'It's uncanny the resemblance, don't you think?'

Richard stares at me, scrunching up his eyebrows like it's the most preposterous thing I've ever said.

'I think it's the eyes, they look like mine.'

'I can't see it,' says Richard.

I sigh and pour boiling water over the tea bags. He can't see it because he thinks there's something untoward going on. From the moment I told him about meeting Nora at Mum's, he's been questioning me about her. Fortunately, I didn't tell him about our earlier meetings. He would be livid if he knew about our first encounter. He already thinks it's strange that all of a sudden I have a cousin I didn't know existed. He even suggested we do a background check on her, but I steered him away from that idea. If he delves into her life, he may end up tracking down Nora's husband, and that would create problems for her. I hope pointing out how alike we look will be enough proof for him.

I carry the mugs to the coffee table and Richard sits on the couch next to me with his coffee.

'So, Nora, what do you do for work?' he asks.

'She's a chef,' I answer for her.

'How interesting. Elle works in catering.'

'Yes, she mentioned.'

'And where are you staying while you're in town?'

'I'm renting an apartment I found on Airbnb.'

I look down at my mug of mint tea, uncomfortable at Richard's questioning, but knowing that if I speak up he'll only say something to embarrass me. So I remain silent.

'How long are you here for?' asks Richard.

'I'm not sure yet. So what do you do, Richard?' asks Nora.

'I work in finance.'

'And your family – do you have any siblings?'

'No, just me.'

'And your parents?'

'They've passed,' says Richard, shifting in his seat.

A small smile plays on my lips. Clearly, Nora can handle herself.

'I'm sorry to hear that. Well, you have a lovely family.' She glances at me and the boys. 'And your home is beautiful.' Nora takes a sip of her tea, then looks directly at Richard. 'You're a very lucky man.'

Richard clears his throat.

'Nora, would you like another biscuit or some fruit?' I ask.

'I will have one more biscuit,' she says, reaching over to grab one from the platter. 'What are they? They're absolutely delicious.' She inspects the biscuit before taking another bite.

'It's a healthy version of a Florentine. They're low in carbs, no cornflakes,' I say, glancing over at Richard.

'Mmm, are they dried cranberries?' she asks.

'Yes, I use them instead of the glacé cherries.'

Nora takes another mouthful. 'How wonderful – they're chewy and crunchy at the same time. Let me guess, you use honey?'

'How did you know? I make them all the time and no one can ever tell.'

'I'm a chef,' she says, then she smiles at Richard.

I think he's warming to her.

The doorbell rings.

'Are you expecting someone?' Richard asks.

'No, I'll go see who it is.' I open the front door to find Georgie. 'Hi! What are you doing here?'

'I left my chopping knife here yesterday.'

Georgie has her favourite knife that she always brings with her.

'I've just got Nora here,' I say quietly.

'Oh, I forgot she was coming. I'll grab it and go.'

She makes her way to the kitchen and I follow her. 'Hi,' she calls out to Richard and Nora. 'Sorry to interrupt.'

She goes into the kitchen and opens the drawer where I keep the sharp knives and utensils.

'Come on, I'll introduce you,' I say to her. I lean over and whisper. 'Remember, you've never met her.'

'Right, yes,' she says, retrieving her knife and holding it up. 'Found it!'

I shake my head, smiling. 'Leave it on the bench.' She places her handbag next to it and follows me to the couch.

'Nora, this is my good friend Georgie. Georgie, this is my cousin Nora.'

'So lovely to meet you,' says Nora.

'Wow,' says Georgie, taking a seat on the other side of Charlie. She looks from Nora to me and then back to Nora. 'You two could be sisters! I can't believe how similar you look.'

'Mum, can we go play upstairs?' asks Charlie.

'Sure. Say goodbye to Nora.'

'Bye, Nora,' says Charlie.

'Bye, Nora,' says Olly, waving his hand in front of her face.

'Bye,' she says as they run off. 'They're adorable.'

'They have their moments,' I say.

The room falls quiet as Georgie watches Nora, Nora looks at me, and Richard stares at Nora. This is awkward.

'So how long are you in town?' Georgie asks her.

'Maybe another week or so,' says Nora.

'We should do something fun, the three of us,' she says, looking at me. 'Elle, we should take Nora out for a girls' day – we can go for lunch and a shop or visit a museum. I love art. Do you like art?' she asks Nora.

'I do,' she says, raising her eyebrows at Georgie.

Georgie is behaving oddly. She seems almost nervous. I assume it's because she knows Nora lives at a women's shelter and they've actually met before, but she has to act as though they haven't. I hope Richard doesn't pick up on it.

I try to catch Georgie's attention but she's too focused on Nora. 'Georgie, did you need anything else, or just the knife?' I ask.

She looks over at me and I motion minutely with my head in the direction of the door.

'Ah, no,' she says, getting up. 'It was lovely to meet you, Nora. I'm sure I'll be seeing you soon.'

'You too,' says Nora.

'Bye, Richard,' says Georgie. She grabs her handbag and the knife from the kitchen bench and I walk her to the door.

'I like her,' she says, peeping over my shoulder.

'Good, now go,' I say, pushing her out the door.

Nora leaves shortly after. Richard offered to drive her home, but she said she was happy to walk for a while and catch public transport. Fortunately he didn't insist because she needs to hide where she's living. We didn't get a chance to make another time to meet, but she has my number if she needs anything.

I'm cleaning the dishes and Richard is hovering. He seems tense.

'Is everything alright?' I ask.

'I don't trust her.'

'Who?' I act like I have no clue what he's talking about, but I assume he's referring to Nora.

He turns to look at me, his eyes intense. 'Nora. There's something off about her.'

'Richard, you're reading into something that's not there.'

'I don't agree,' he says. 'Do you have Henry's number, or any contact information?' He has that look in his eyes, the one he gets when I've done something to upset him.

'No,' I say. 'He died, remember?'

'And his surname was Plankett? He was your mum's cousin on her dad's side, right?'

'Yes, Richard, but please don't go causing trouble.' I would never have invited Nora over if I thought it would jeopardise her safety. If Richard looks into her background, it might lead to Nora's husband finding out where she's living. Maybe I need to tell Richard why she's really in Melbourne. That would solve the problem, but I don't feel I can do that without Nora's consent. 'Just leave it. I'm not going to be seeing her again anyway, she's going home in a week.'

'Fine,' he says. 'But I don't want you befriending her.'

'Richard ...'

'I'm serious, Elle. You're not to contact her again or I will look into her.'

'Okay, I won't.' It's infuriating the way he barks orders at me about what I can and can't do. But I have to keep the peace, especially about this. I can't be the one responsible for Nora's husband finding her.

Richard's phone rings in his hand and he looks down. 'I have to take this,' he says. 'But I mean it, Elle, no contact.' He walks to the study and I shudder at the slam of the door.

Now that I know Richard looks through my phone, I won't even be able to call the shelter to see if Nora's okay. I am worried for her, though – she seemed so happy to have found me and to meet the boys today. She has no family here, she's completely on her own and I can't even be there for her, to help her through this difficult time in her life. I can't imagine what it must have been like for her, having to leave her home and her children.

How can I just abandon her now that I know she's family?

Maybe Georgie can be our go-between. She did take a liking to Nora. I'm sure she'd be happy to check in with her every now and again. Just so I know she's okay.

Chapter 26

Nora

I collapse on the bed. I can't believe I just went to my home, sat on my couch and had afternoon tea with myself from ten years ago, as well as Richard and my children, who hadn't aged a day since I'd left them. It was like having an out-of-body experience but I was still in my body, just an older version of it. I'm trying to process it, but it's absolutely impossible to do so.

The phone vibrates in my hand. 'Hello,' I say, sitting up.

'That was crazy,' says Georgie.

'I know,' I exhale.

'Did you see Richard's face?'

I did. He was as tightly wound as a ball of string. 'I hope we didn't make things more difficult for Elle.'

'It's not her fault she has a cousin.'

'Richard won't see it that way. Everything's Elle's fault.'

'You looked fantastic. He must be able to see that you look like an older version of Elle. No offence,' she adds.

'None taken.'

'So what's the plan?' asks Georgie.

It's a good question. I've been thinking about that since I left the house, and from the vibes I got from Richard, I'm sure he's going to move things along. I may have slowed him down by changing Georgie's reaction to the fiasco with the business, but my gut is telling me he's going to move now, before Elle gets too close to me.

'Now we keep an eye on Elle. We have to work out how Richard drugs her.'

'Can't we just tell her that he's going to drug her? I don't want her to have to go through that,' says Georgie.

'Neither do I, but she survived it the first time, and this time we're going to stop it before it has an effect on her whole system. The day to day of that period was such a blur for me, I have no idea how he did it. I was in bed most of the time. Richard had Patricia looking after the kids after school.'

'I thought you said he hired a nanny?'

'He did. The nanny was Patricia, but I didn't know at the time that she was the woman he was having an affair with.'

'What a bastard. He actually had the other woman pose as the nanny?'

I feel like such an idiot that I had no idea what was happening right under my nose. How did I not see that Patricia was masquerading as a nanny? He wanted the boys to feel comfortable with her, and what better way to ingratiate her into our lives than if Mummy liked the nanny. Of course the boys would think it was okay to like her too.

'He has no conscience. Patricia started making all the meals, so it could have been her drugging me. I have no idea.'

'But when did Richard bring her in as the nanny? Was it before you started feeling unwell? I assume it took time for whatever it was to hit your system.'

'It did,' I say. 'The first five days or so that I felt off I kept going, I just couldn't drive. And I wasn't working anymore, so I reserved my energy for when the boys were home. I can't remember if Richard did the school run or he had her do it, but to answer your question, no, she wasn't in our home yet.'

'That means Richard was the one slipping it into your food. At least at the beginning.'

'I'm not even certain Patricia had anything to do with the drugs. I think he told her I was unstable and she probably believed him. He's convincing like that. Before Daylesford, I just thought I had a virus. But when we came home my health went from bad to worse and he organised the nanny. She eventually took over everything with the boys.'

'He must have increased the dosage after Daylesford,' says Georgie. 'We have to work out how he does it before he takes her there.'

'You're right.' It's good to have another person to work through what happened. Sometimes when you're so close to a situation, it's hard to see it clearly. Having Georgie helps me fill in all the pieces I haven't been able to work out yet.

'Georgie,' I say, every nerve in my body on alert. 'I need you now more than ever. Elle needs you. You have to work out how he's drugging her and with what. When you're at her place doing the orders next week, you're going to have to snoop. Write a list of everything she eats or drinks while you're there too. Don't leave out a thing, even if you think it's something small. Check the medicine cabinet in the upstairs bathroom. Check the drawers. Check Richard's study.' Panic rises in my chest, but I have to stay in control for Elle. 'You have to find out what he's giving her before she gets back from Daylesford.'

'I will. You can trust me, Nora – I don't want this to happen to Elle any more than you do.'

'Thank you,' I say. I appreciate it, but she forgets that it has already happened to Elle, at least in my world. It happened to *me*, and I was all alone when it did. Richard drugged me for more than five weeks and I had no one to turn to for help. The man organised to have me locked up in a mental institution, he took my children from me, he took everything from me. But there's no point getting angry anymore – now it's time to get even. 'Call me when you find something.'

'Will do.'

I end the call. Of course I don't want Elle to go through any of this either, not even for a day. But I have to let Richard drug her initially so she can experience the symptoms. It's the only way I'll be able to convince her.

The day before I left home, Richard had come into my bedroom. 'It stinks in here,' he had said, drawing the curtains back and opening the window. 'When was the last time you showered?'

'I don't know,' I said, barely able to lift my head from the pillow.

'You don't know?'

Was that a laugh? I couldn't be sure.

'Look at you, Elle, you need help.'

'We went to the doctor. You heard him, he doesn't know what's wrong with me. Has he called with my blood test results?' Richard had taken me to our general practitioner again a few days ago. We'd seen a neurologist a couple of weeks before that, and they suggested it was stress-related, probably based on everything Richard had told him was happening in my life: our separation, the business dissolution, my dad dying the previous year, my mum having Alzheimer's, my closest friend not talking to me. When he ran through the list, he almost convinced me too. But there's nothing worse than a doctor explaining away your symptoms as stress when you know something's wrong.

I insisted we go back to see our general practitioner, who had at least acknowledged there was something physically wrong with me, but he couldn't explain it medically. He organised some blood tests, but then Richard suggested it might be depression and recapped our situation to him. I had tried to explain that it had started before I even knew about his affair, but Richard cut me off. He told the doctor that it had started with a virus, but then I'd been fine. The doctor said if the blood tests didn't show anything then it could be depression and he'd refer me to a psychiatrist.

'Yes, he called earlier. He said your results were fine.'

'Why didn't you let me talk to him?' I pulled myself up to sitting.

'You were asleep. Look at you,' he said.

I looked down at myself. I was still in my pyjamas and there were food stains on my top. I ran my hand through my hair to tidy it and the roots were oily, the length tangled.

'You're depressed, Elle. It's time you faced it and saw someone who deals with this kind of thing.'

I ignored him. 'Are the boys home from school?' I asked.

'Yes.'

'I want to see them.'

'You want them to see you like that?'

'Okay, let me shower and get changed first. Can you ask the nanny to come help me?' I didn't think I could manage on my own and I wanted to wash my hair.

'She's not here to look after you, she's here to take care of the boys. Really, Elle, you never cease to amaze me.'

With that he had walked out.

I moved to the side of the bed and stood. I felt completely dizzy and sat back down again. I couldn't remember the last time I'd eaten anything. Maybe this morning when Richard brought me a smoothie.

There was a knock at the door. 'Come in,' I said.

It was the nanny. 'I wasn't sure if you'd eaten so I made you a sandwich,' she said. She placed the plate and a mug of herbal tea on the bedside table. She only came to our house in the afternoons, after she picked up the boys from school. She looked after them until Richard came home, made dinner and then left. Occasionally I'd heard voices downstairs after the boys went to bed, but I assumed it was Richard's girlfriend, Patricia. The man had no scruples, bringing her into my home when I was there. He was probably having sex with her in the study.

'Thank you,' I said to the nanny. 'I really appreciate it.'

'You're welcome,' she said, turning to leave.

'And thank you for taking care of my boys. I don't know what I would have done if you weren't here. I'm not sure what's wrong with me, but I don't feel myself.'

'I'm sure you'll feel better soon,' she had said, then closed the door.

I ate the sandwich and drank the tea. I didn't think I'd even had a glass of water during the day. I kept a glass next to my bed at night, but Richard must have taken it downstairs to wash in the morning because when I'd woken the glass had disappeared. My mouth was parched, so I was probably dehydrated too.

My sugars must have been low from not eating, because when I stood after the sandwich I felt less dizzy, but I'd still needed to hold on to the wall as I made my way to the bathroom. I stripped out of my pyjamas, discarding them on the floor, and turned on the shower. I tipped my head back slightly, letting the hot water cascade over my body. With one hand holding onto the tap to keep steady, I used the other to massage shampoo into my hair, then rinsed, and repeated the process with the conditioner. I dried and dressed in clean clothing and sat on the bed while I brushed my knotted hair. The fresh air from the open window was circulating through my bedroom and I had felt marginally better. In fact, I thought I could make it downstairs to see Charlie and Olly.

I held on to the banister as I made my way down one step at a time, stopping short of the last couple of steps when I noticed the boys and Richard sitting at the table eating dinner. With the nanny. They looked like one happy family. It felt like the tip of a knife repeatedly poking into my chest. I was about to turn around and head back upstairs when Olly had called out, 'Mummy!' and ran to me.

'Hi, darling,' I said, taking his hand.

He dragged me to the table and the nanny stood and took her plate to the sink.

As she rinsed and placed it in the dishwasher, she had asked, 'Can I make you a plate before I leave?'

'No, I'm fine. Thank you.'

I joined the boys at the table and Richard picked up his plate and took it to the sink.

'I'll be off,' said the nanny. 'See you tomorrow, boys.'

Richard walked her to the front door. For the life of me I couldn't remember her name. In fact, I was sure Richard had only referred to her as 'the nanny'.

'What's the nanny's name again?' I had asked Charlie.

'Patricia,' he said.

My entire body had constricted, and in that fleeting moment, the foggy haze in my head cleared completely and I knew without a doubt that Richard was up to something.

Lying back down on the bed at the shelter, my fingers still clenched around the disposable phone, I pray that Elle won't have to experience that.

Chapter 27

Elle

'Ouch!' I say, dropping the knife on the chopping board and grabbing my finger.

'What did you do?' Georgie moves to my side and turns on the tap. 'Run it under the water and I'll have a look.'

It's not the first time I've cut my finger or hand, it comes with the vocation, that and the occasional burn, but for some reason when I looked down at the cucumber I was chopping, my eyes went blurry.

Georgie inspects my finger. 'I don't think you need stitches.' She dries it and wraps it firmly in a clean tea towel to place pressure on it. 'Go sit at the table and I'll grab a bandage.'

We both keep first-aid kits in our homes, as well as an over-supply of waterproof band-aids and bandages. Georgie grabs a band-aid and antiseptic cream from the cupboard above the fridge and comes to sit down next to me.

'I couldn't find the cotton tips.'

I usually keep a box next to the first-aid kit but I must be out. 'There's some in my bathroom. Second drawer.'

'I'll be back in a sec. Keep the pressure on.'

Georgie runs up the stairs.

I remove the tea towel to take a look and the wound opens and begins to bleed again. I wrap it up and apply pressure. I'm feeling a little woozy, probably from the amount of blood on the tea towel, so I move to the couch and lie down, resting my feet up on a pillow so the blood will rush back to my head. At least, that's what I think it's meant to do. I place my hand on my chest, holding my finger up. 'Georgie!' I call out. What's taking her so long?

She comes running back down the stairs.

'You took forever.'

'Sorry, I had to use the loo. Are you alright?' she asks, looking down at me. 'You look a little pale.'

'I'm fine, I was just dizzy. I thought I should lie down. There's quite a bit of blood.' Although the truth is I've been feeling dizzy on and off for several days. I'm probably just overtired; I haven't been sleeping well.

'Stay here,' she says, going to the kitchen table. Georgie comes back and perches on the couch next to my legs. She unwraps the tea towel and applies a thin layer of cream with the cotton tip and then several band-aids.

I hold up my finger. 'It's bigger than my thumb!'

'Sorry,' she says. 'I'll redo it once it stops bleeding. Are you okay? What happened?'

'I cut my finger.' I look at her, bemused. She is being weirdly overattentive.

'Okay,' she says. 'Are you sure you're feeling alright?'

'Georgie, it's a cut. It's not like I haven't cut myself before.'

'I know,' she says. 'You've just been so quiet this morning. Normally you don't stop talking.'

'I'm fine. I've been feeling a little off the last few days.'

'Was it something you ate?' she asks. 'Did you have something you don't normally have or did something taste off or not right?'

I laugh at her. 'Georgie, what's got into you?'

'Nothing,' she says. 'I just want to make sure you're okay.'

'I'm probably coming down with a virus or something.'

'Okay. You stay there and I'll go finish the cooking. Do you want a Panadol?' she asks.

'I think I will.' My head is starting to throb. 'I feel bad you having to finish the cooking by yourself.'

'It's fine, we were almost done. I'll pick up the boys for you this afternoon.'

'No, I'll be right by then,' I say. Georgie's children go to a different school to mine and I don't want her going out of her way. 'I'll just close my eyes for a little.'

When I wake, Georgie's sitting on the other couch staring at me. 'What time is it?' I ask.

'Almost three.'

I sit up. 'What are you still doing here?'

'I didn't want to leave in case you needed me to get the kids.'

'I'm fine,' I say, getting up for a glass of water. My mouth is so dry. I walk to the kitchen and find myself standing in front of the oven before getting my bearings and turning around to the sink. I really am feeling quite off. I hold on to the bench with my free hand and turn the tap on with the other, filling a glass. I drink it in one go.

'You're not fine,' says Georgie, speed-walking to the kitchen. 'You walked into the oven!'

'I did, didn't I?' I thought I'd imagined it.

'Lie down,' she says, steering me back to the couch. 'I'll bring you some lunch then pick up the boys.'

I'm about to protest but then agree; I shouldn't drive like this. 'Thanks, I appreciate it.'

'Do you want a coffee?' Georgie calls from the kitchen.

'Chamomile tea, please.'

She brings me a tea and a bowl of chicken salad. 'I made this for you earlier. I'll get your phone in case you need anything while I'm out.'

'It's in my handbag,' I say, taking a mouthful of salad.

Georgie returns with my phone and sits next to me on the couch. 'Should I call your doctor?'

'No, I'm sure I'll be fine in a few days. It's probably a virus.'

'When did it start?' she asks.

'Um, Monday after you left at lunchtime. But it comes and goes, I'm sure it's nothing. It could be vertigo, Mum used to get that all the time.'

'Okay.' She pulls her phone from her back pocket. 'What are your symptoms?'

I laugh. 'Are you going to check with Doctor Google?'

'Come on, humour me,' she says.

'Fine. Dizziness, dry mouth, my eyes are a little blurry ...'

'Anything else?'

'A bit of a headache. But, honestly, I promise I'm fine.'

'Okay,' she says, checking her watch. 'I'll pick up your boys first then get my kids. I'll be back in an hour, but call me if you need anything. Try not to get up.'

'What if I need the loo?'

'Fine, but for nothing else,' she says, pointing at me.

I finish my lunch and tea and close my eyes.

Later that evening, Richard comes home earlier than usual from work and insists on cleaning the dishes after dinner. He even takes the boys upstairs for their showers and puts them to bed. I can't remember the last time he's helped in the evenings, probably because he never has. I've been sick with colds and the flu before and not once did Richard ever offer to help. Not even a school drop-off or to read to the kids before bed.

'Would you like a warm drink or a snack?' he calls out from the kitchen.

'No, I'm fine,' I say. I'm sitting on the couch watching the news. I didn't feel comfortable lying down when Richard was busy washing dishes, even though my head feels like it weighs as much as a bowling ball.

Richard joins me on the couch with his coffee. 'I have a surprise for you,' he says. He hands me an envelope.

'What is it?' I ask, taken aback. We've been going through a bit of a rough patch lately, but usually when Richard plants a surprise on me it means he's ready to make amends.

'Open it and see.'

I open the envelope, pull out the card and read the note in Richard's handwriting – a weekend for two at the Lake House.

'This is such a nice idea.' We've been to Daylesford once before when Charlie was a baby, but we stayed at a cabin. We loved it, but I've always wanted to stay at the Lake House and try their restaurant. I've read that eating there is an experience in itself.

'It's booked for this weekend.'

'This weekend? But I haven't organised the boys.' I assumed

the note was an IOU for me to book sometime in the foreseeable future.

'It's taken care of. I've booked a nanny for the weekend.'

'A nanny? I'm not going to leave the boys with a stranger!'

'She's not a stranger. She's been working for a colleague of mine's family for years. She's just on loan for the weekend.'

'I don't know. I'd have to meet her first.'

'You can meet her when she comes on Saturday. It's all organised.'

My eyes briefly close. 'Maybe we should wait until the following weekend when I'm feeling better.' If I'm going to the Lake House, I want to be able to enjoy it.

'I'm sure you'll be fine by Saturday,' says Richard, kissing the top of my head. 'It's three days away.'

'You're probably right.' He seems so excited about this, I don't want to disappoint him.

'Great. It's all sorted,' he says, before heading to his study.

Turns out Richard is correct. When Saturday rolls around, I'm feeling almost fine.

Chapter 28

Nora

'He's drugging her,' says a distressed Georgie.

'Hang on,' I say, walking out of the kitchen and past the foyer, with the phone to my ear. I step outside the shelter, the cold air hits instantly, wind slapping my face. As I walk down the street I stay close to the buildings, protecting me from it a little.

'Are you sure?' I ask her.

'Yes, definitely. I spent most of the day at her house yesterday. I couldn't bear leaving her alone like that.'

Part of me feels awful for not stopping this before it starts, but it's crucial Elle experiences the symptoms. I'm afraid if she doesn't, she'll never believe me.

'Did you find anything?' I ask.

'Yes. I found a packet of prescription medication hidden in a drawer under Richard's razor. It was for Endep and it was prescribed to Richard. Do you know if he takes it?'

'Not that I'm aware of.'

'I looked it up and it's used to treat depression.'

'Depression? That's odd. You'd think a medication for depression would have made me feel good. Maybe he was giving me something else.'

'I checked the side effects and a lot of them are what Elle is experiencing and the symptoms you mentioned you had too. And there's something else,' she says.

'What is it?'

'He's taking her to Daylesford this weekend. She told me this morning he's organised a nanny to look after the boys.'

Patricia. I knew the weekend would be coming up but it's still unfathomable to me that he left my sons with his mistress last time around. I remember feeling uncomfortable leaving them with someone I didn't know, but he promised me she had great credentials. I bet she did.

'You said the nanny is the woman he's having an affair with?'

'She is.'

'There's no way I'm letting her spend the weekend with Charlie and Olly. She'll be living in their home, sleeping in Elle's bed.'

'She does after I'm gone.'

'Nora, that's not going to happen again. I'm going to take the boys for the weekend.'

'You'd do that?'

'Of course. I'd do anything for Elle.'

Hearing Georgie say that, and seeing how ferocious she is about protecting Elle, makes me feel awful that I've spent the last ten years being so angry with her. 'Thank you,' I say, knowing that with every action Georgie changes from the past to help Elle, she's hopefully rewriting my future.

I stop walking and realise I'm standing outside the library. Snippets of memories flood in. They say you're the editor of your memories, but I'm not sure if these ones are to be held on to or let go of. I was so far gone when I was last within those walls, but it was also inside the library that I was saved.

'I have to go, but I'll head down there on Sunday,' I say.

'What are you planning to do?'

'I'm going to be there to warn her.'

I hang up and shove the phone into my back pocket while facing the library doors. I haven't been able to set foot in this place since the period when I was sleeping on the streets and the library was where I'd seek refuge. Today I feel different about going inside. Maybe it's because my path is changing, whether it's the path of my past or the path for my future, I'm not sure. But I know my life is going to be different, and I feel I can face anything, even the darkness of my past.

I push through the door, it's nice and warm inside. I spent the first week after I left home curled up in a ball in different nooks I'd find on the street, my body shaking, sweating in the cold as my nervous system tried to readjust as it withdrew from the drugs. I realise now Richard must have been giving me well over the prescribed amount. Five or six days after I fled - I can't remember exactly, but it was when I was finally alert enough to care about my hygiene – I found the library. Initially I just used the facilities to wash my face and under my arms, and to use a clean toilet. Then I found the staff kitchen and helped myself to snacks and water when the librarians were busy. I tried not to be seen, but one night it was storming outside, pelting down with rain, and I snuck back in before closing time and slept there overnight. One of the librarians found me the next morning, curled up across two beanbags in the reading corner.

She saved my life.

I woke to the gentle shake of a hand. 'Are you okay, dear?' the librarian had asked.

I had looked at her confused, not knowing where I was, and lifted my head to check my surroundings.

'Do you know where you are?'

I nodded.

'Is there someone I can call?' she had asked.

My eyes filled to the brim with tears. I shook my head; there was no one. Not one person in the world who she could contact to help me.

'Stay here. I'll get you some water.'

She returned with a glass of water and a few dry crackers.

'You don't look like you belong here, dear.'

I was still dressed in my jeans, cashmere jumper and canvas runners, and I'd used my puffer jacket as a blanket. Even though they weren't clean, I guess she could tell they were expensive. My hair, which hadn't been washed in at least ten days, had the type of honey-blonde highlights you can't get from a supermarket bottle.

The tears I'd been holding on to flowed. 'I don't.'

'There's a shelter for women not far from here. Let me take you there.'

She helped me to my feet.

'What about the library?' I asked.

'Another staff member will be here soon,' she said. Her brown eyes were warm and comforting and gave me some small hope.

I had no energy and was unsteady on my feet. She held on to my arm as we walked, bearing some of my weight. I'm sure that even if I was more stable on my feet, she still would have held onto me.

'We donate books to the shelter,' she'd said, chatting until we arrived at the entrance to a building. 'Here we are.' She pressed the intercom. There was a click and she pushed the door open with her free hand. She sat me down on a chair and went to speak to the lady at the front desk.

Before I knew it, I was surrounded by Sheena, Mary and the librarian. I wasn't alone.

The librarian who took care of me that day is at the front desk now, tending to visitors. Her tortoiseshell glasses sit atop her grey shoulder-length hair.

'Hello,' I say, as I walk past.

'Hello,' she replies. Of course she doesn't recognise me. She hasn't met me yet.

I wander down the aisles of books. The reading corner is still scattered with beanbags, and there's also several mini-sized tables and chairs for children. A young mum is sitting at a table reading to her child while he colours in. The kitchen and bathroom are at the back of the library, but I don't venture that far. Those memories are imprinted in my brain and living them once was enough.

I head back outside into the brisk air and make my way to the shelter. Even though Georgie researched the medication Richard might be giving Elle, it doesn't explain how it works and why a medication for depression would have such terrible side effects. But I know someone who might have the answers.

'Is Mary with anyone?' I ask Sheena when I walk into the reception area.

Sheena checks the computer. 'She is. She'll be free in about twenty minutes if you'd like to wait for her?'

'Thanks, that would be great.' I head into the lounge and make a cup of tea, then sit in the chair outside Mary's office.

When her office door opens, a woman walks out who I haven't seen before. As she walks past I see a faded bruise across her jaw. I stand up and knock on Mary's open door as she sits at her desk typing into her laptop.

'Mary, do you have a minute?' I ask.

'Sure. How are you, Nora?'

'I'm good, thanks,' I say, taking a seat on the couch.

'How can I help you?'

'I was wondering if you know anything about a medication called Endep.'

Mary gets up from her chair and comes to sit next to me on the couch. 'It's used for depression.'

'How does it work?'

'It corrects the imbalance of certain chemicals in the brain.'

'Sorry, I'm not sure what that means.'

'Your brain sends messages to every part of your body, and the medication works by changing those messages. So for instance, if you're feeling pain somewhere but there's no physical reason for the pain, say it's a phantom pain, Endep will rewire the way your body receives messages so you don't feel that pain. It can be helpful for depression because it can change your mood.' Mary leans back into the couch and crosses her legs. 'It does take a while for the benefits to kick in and often a patient will experience side effects at first, so it needs to be monitored by a doctor or psychiatrist in case the dose has to be altered. Usually patients start with a small dose.'

'What are the side effects?' I ask.

'The most common are drowsiness, dizziness, headaches, blurred vision, dry mouth. Some patients may experience weight gain and constipation. There can be more severe side effects too, but they're very rare.'

I endured many of those side effects and, from what Georgie said, Elle is experiencing them now.

'Have you been prescribed it before by a doctor?' asks Mary.

'No,' I say. 'What would happen if it was taken by someone who wasn't depressed?'

'Most likely they'll experience the side effects.'

'And what if they're given too much?'

'Nora,' says Mary, leaning over to touch my arm, 'was someone medicating you before you came here?'

'I think so,' I say.

'That would explain your confusion when you arrived.'

Mary doesn't know the half of it. She's referring to when she met me weeks ago and I was acting crazy because no one here recognised me. When Mary met me the first time I arrived here after the librarian brought me in, I was experiencing severe symptoms of withdrawal from the drug Richard had been poisoning my body with. It was clear right away to her then that I'd been on drugs. She just assumed I'd been taking them willingly.

'What happens if you stop taking the medication suddenly?' I ask.

'It depends on the dosage you were on, but most likely you would experience withdrawal symptoms like nausea, muscle aches, fever, chills, anxiety, issues with memory, hypersensitivity to your environment ... There are a whole host of symptoms. That's why a doctor would wean a patient off it slowly. The amount would be tapered down over several months.'

Several months? I swallow the lump in my throat. I recall experiencing most of those symptoms when I was living on the streets, some lasting for months after I arrived at the shelter.

'Nora, if someone was giving you medication without your knowledge, you need to tell the police.'

'But I have no proof.' There's also the fact that it happened ten years ago, but I can't tell her that. I wish I'd been stronger back then. If only my head had been clearer and I'd been thinking straight, I would have been able to put together everything that was happening to me. I would have relied more on the staff here to help me stand up to Richard. But I was too afraid, and I know that I have to forgive myself for that because, the fact is, I did my best at the time. Back then, my goal was simple: survive each day.

Mary's lips form into a tight line. 'It's too late to do a blood test now. If you were drugged, it would only show up in your system for maybe a week after you stopped taking it. You've been here for over a month.'

My eyes widen. A blood test.

'Thanks for explaining everything to me,' I say, getting up. 'I appreciate your help.'

'I feel like I haven't been much help at all,' says Mary, walking me out.

'Trust me, you have.' The Eleanor standing in front of her has no drugs in her system, but now I know for sure that the Eleanor of 2012 most certainly does.

Chapter 29

Elle

Check-in isn't until three o'clock, so when we arrive in Daylesford we visit a gallery. The surrounding gardens are gorgeous, covered in red and yellow hues, with a spectacular view of the Central Highlands. The gallery itself is an old convent and boarding school, that was converted in the early 1990s and exhibits both contemporary and traditional art. We walk up the narrow wooden staircase and along the Baltic pine floors, exploring each room. Richard stays a few paces behind me, distracted by his phone. There are paintings on each wall, some sculptures too, but it's the character of the building, the arches and stained-glass windows, that catches my eye. The history seeps through every surface. If only walls could speak, I'm sure there would be stories to tell.

After exploring the gallery we go to the café at the entrance for lunch. 'This room is divine,' I say, as we sit down. I stare up at the tall glass-fronted atrium and the aqua green walls that look like the backdrop of a canvas. The wrought-iron chairs are painted electric blue. 'Richard?'

'Did you say something?' he asks, placing his phone on the table.

Finally I have his attention. 'Never mind,' I say, picking up the menu. 'I'm so glad we left the kids with Georgie. I wouldn't have felt comfortable leaving them with someone we don't know.'

'It's just one night,' says Richard. 'They would have been fine.' He glances at his watch.

'But Georgie's like family.'

Richard humphs.

'What are you getting?' I ask, glancing over the menu.

'The soup of the day.'

'Will that be enough?'

'I'm saving myself for dinner,' says Richard. We have a four-course dinner booked at the Lake House this evening.

'I think I'll get the calamari salad.' It sounds wonderful, served with gremolata on a bed of Greek salad.

A waitress comes to take our order. I'm so glad to be feeling better today, almost myself. It's a relief that the virus has passed so I can enjoy our time away. We don't often do this, and I feel like I've hardly seen Richard lately. He's been so busy at work the last couple of months, going into the office at least one day on the weekend, and work dinners have been more frequent too.

While we're eating our meals, the waitress walks past our table with a plate of fresh scones and cream. My nose follows her; they smell fresh from the oven.

Richard stops her on her way back. 'Excuse me, can I order a serve of scones for my wife?'

My eyes practically bulge. Richard frowns upon me eating

dessert. When we're out with friends, I restrict myself to a mouthful as a taster. This must be the first time he's ever actually ordered a dessert for me.

He seems to register my confused expression.

'What? Can't I do something nice?' he asks.

'Sure,' I say, although most of the time there's a catch, and I'm always the last to find out what it is. I ignore the uneasy feeling that washes over me, and when the scones arrive I allow myself one with a spread of raspberry jam and a scraping of cream.

After lunch, we drive to the Lake House and check in. The receptionist leads us along a cobbled path to a row of two-storey weatherboard cottages. She unlocks the room and hands us two keys.

'Enjoy your stay.'

'Thank you,' I say.

The room is gorgeous, with white shutters leading to a balcony with timber railings overlooking the lake. The bed is made up with a navy throw and green velvet scatter cushions lined flush against the pillows.

'What do you want to do?' asks Richard, unpacking his black wheelie case and placing his book next to the side of the bed he's chosen.

'Should we walk around the lake?' I ask.

'Sure.'

We change into sneakers and head out. As we walk through the outdoor patio area set up with tables and enclosed within white timber railings, I glance through the long windows of the restaurant that overlooks the lake. The staff are setting the tables for dinner and I smile at a waiter, who acknowledges me with a nod of his head. We make our way down the steps leading to the path around the lake and head off in one direction.

The sky is a clear blue, and the trees that surround the entire lake reflect on the glistening water. A family of ducks paddle past, and a stand-up paddleboard occupied by a man clad head to toe in a wetsuit glides by. It's serene.

'You're awfully quiet,' I say to Richard as we walk in stride.

'I have a lot on my mind,' he says.

'Anything you want to talk about?'

'No.' His voice is heavy, so I refrain from chatting and just enjoy the surroundings.

After our walk, I spend the rest of the afternoon curled up with a book in the cosy library bar opposite reception. There's a fire blazing, and the room is fitted out with mismatched armchairs and vintage couches, coffee tables, artwork and bookshelves. The central light fitting is wrapped with organza in the design of a flower, the golden light at its centre the pistil. I spend most of the time sipping my tea and admiring the gorgeous room as opposed to reading. It's all very comforting.

Dusk sets in and I go back to the room to dress for dinner. Richard is lying on his back, hands crossed at his waist, asleep. I shower and put on a fitted navy dress and heels, and when I emerge from the bathroom, Richard is sitting on the couch by the window. He's changed into pants and a shirt and is wearing a blazer.

'You ready?' he asks.

'Yes.' He doesn't comment on my appearance like he usually does when we go out, but I shrug it off because he seems so distracted. It is nice not having my outfit assessed.

The lighting in the restaurant is dim. A long banquette seat runs below the windows that line one side of the restaurant, and each place is allotted a mauve velvet cushion. The tables are pristine, set with a white tablecloth, silverware and sparkling glasses. Richard orders a bottle of red wine and the waiter pours it into a glass decanter before filling our wineglasses.

'All our produce is freshly harvested and mostly locally grown,' says the waiter as he runs through tonight's menu. 'Our fermented sourdough is baked daily at our farm.'

Richard and I select a dish for each course, and when each one is presented at the table, it looks like a work of art. I turn the plate, inspecting every ingredient before trying to decipher all the flavours. By the time we get to dessert, I think Richard is a little frustrated with me assessing and commenting on each dish.

'I've never seen anything quite like it,' I say, studying their famous dessert. It looks as smooth as a Granny Smith apple, the stem made from chocolate, sitting on an edible nest.

'Are you going to eat it?' asks Richard.

'Yes, I'm going to eat it.' Really, his impatience is becoming more prominent the older he gets. But I choose to ignore it, assuming he has work on his mind. Even though the dessert looks too pretty to eat, I slice through the crisp shell to the creamy centre and take a mouthful. It not only looks but tastes like heaven. 'How's yours?' I ask.

'Very good.'

Richard ordered the sorbets, two perfect quenelles of raspberry and pistachio on a bed of crumbled chocolate served with fresh berries sprinkled with gold leaf. I'd love to taste it, but know his plate is off limits. He doesn't like sharing his food.

'I was thinking we should take the boys away for a few days during the school holidays. Maybe up to Queensland,' I say between mouthfuls.

'I'm not sure I'll be able to get time off, but you can take them.'

'Oh, okay, if you don't mind us going without you.'

He wipes the corners of his mouth with the napkin. 'Why would I care?'

'I just ... never mind.' I thought a family holiday was for the family, but I guess Richard feels differently. 'I'll book something when we get back.'

'Just check the cancellation policy and make sure it's refundable.'

'Okay.'

It's a little after ten when we get back to the room. I change into my nightie and get under the covers. I feel awkward. I don't want to feel uncomfortable with my husband, but I do. We're on a romantic weekend away and usually we'd have sex, but Richard and I haven't been intimate for at least four weeks. And it's been much longer than that since I've felt close to him when we're having sex. He's there performing the act, but he's not present and there's no emotion, it's cold. In fact, I can't remember the last time there was any passion in our relationship.

I don't have too long to think about it because Richard turns off the lamp on his side of the bed and reaches for me.

So I'm utterly shocked the next morning when, sitting at breakfast, a mouthful of poached egg on its way to my mouth, Richard says, 'I'm leaving you, Elle.'

I almost choke on the egg, but gather myself and take a second to respond. Perhaps I've misinterpreted him. 'What do you mean?'

He leans over. 'I mean, I want a divorce. I've already spoken to my lawyer.'

My jaw drops. 'You've spoken to a lawyer? I don't understand.'

'How much clearer do I have to be?' He looks frustrated with me. 'I want to divorce you and I've notified my lawyer. He says we have to be separated for twelve months before it can be finalised.'

I glance around at the surrounding tables, barely able to breathe. There's a couple in their sixties at the table next to us. They sit in parallel, their heads naturally leaning towards each other as they chat, their comfort with each other evident. A young couple elsewhere sit opposite one another, each with a hand stretched across the top of the table, their fingers touching. You can feel the love surrounding both couples – it's almost contagious – although clearly it has no effect on Richard.

I look back at him, filled with fury. 'You made love to me last night!'

'It was goodbye sex, Elle. Nothing more.'

'Goodbye sex?' I change my tone, putting on a deep voice, and say, 'Let's have one for the road, shall we? Keep you going for a while.' My voice returns to normal, but it's elevated. 'What the fuck is goodbye sex?'

Heads turn at the other tables. I take a moment to collect myself again, and then it becomes perfectly clear: Richard has someone else. He must. He's the kind of man who needs to be looked after. He also needs his ego stroked, and he wouldn't go through with this if he didn't have a fallback.

'Who is she?'

'Would you lower your voice? People are staring.'

'That's why you're telling me here, isn't it? In a restaurant, so that I remain calm.'

'You're not exactly calm, Elle. You're hysterical.'

I'm certainly not hysterical, but I am mad. He actually had sex with me last night and is leaving me today. 'You could have given me an STD.'

'I didn't give you an STD. Stop overreacting.'

'I'm the one who's overreacting? You're cheating on me and leaving me for another woman! Who is she?'

'No one you know.'

So there is someone. The bastard. 'I can't be here right now,' I say, pushing my chair away from the table.

'Where are you going?'

'For a walk. And don't even think about following me.'

I storm through the restaurant, past reception and out the door, sprinting down the stairs that lead to the lake path. I stand with my hands on my hips gasping for air, practically gulping it, which probably isn't the best way to steady my breathing. I cannot believe Richard is cheating on me and wants a divorce, after everything I've put up with. I didn't expect this. Not at all. I'm the one who's always giving in to him; I practically mollycoddle the man so that life runs smoothly. If anyone should be leaving anybody here it should be me, not that poor excuse for a human being.

I head off on the path around the lake, my arms swinging fiercely by my sides. 'I hate him, I hate him, I hate him,' I repeat under my breath. I pass a closed café, painted red, on the opposite side of the Lake House, near a small playground for kids. I pass a woman walking in the opposite direction to me. She says good morning, but I don't respond. Then I feel guilty for not saying good morning. The path becomes hidden with shrubs and trees and a group of chatty women walk past, their lives going on while mine is falling apart.

I can see the Lake House on the other side and keep walking towards it.

I'm fuming inside. How could I not have seen it? It's all beginning to make sense: the extra work dinners, Richard going into the office on weekends, the change in his behaviour, like the day after Georgie's dinner party. Richard had been so angry with me for not telling him about the business expansion. I'd spent the night in Olly's room and the next day Richard was at work all day, even though it was Sunday. Then he came home so chirpy, like all was forgiven, which wasn't like Richard at all. He was probably so happy because he'd spent the day fucking some woman. And yesterday, was he stuffing me with scones and food because he doesn't care how I look anymore, because I'm not going to be his wife? How did I not know all this was happening right in front of me?

I decide to go right back in there and unleash every thought I've ever suppressed to keep the peace. I look for the steps to the Lake House but can't see them. I keep walking for what feels like ages and find myself back in the carpark near the café again. I look across the other side of the lake and there's the Lake House. 'What the ...'

The woman I ignored earlier passes me again.

'Excuse me,' I ask her, 'I'm trying to get back to the Lake House but I seem to be going around in circles.'

'It's a loop,' she says. 'If you take the road on the other side of the café, it will take you there.'

'Thank you.' I walk towards the road on the other side of the café and that's when I see her standing in the carpark, watching me.

'Nora, what are you doing here?' I ask, walking over to her.

'Hi, Elle,' she says.

She's definitely not surprised to see me, which is odd. In fact, she looks as though she's been waiting for me.

'How did you get here? How did you know I'd be here?'

She smiles at me. 'I took the bus this morning. I knew you were going to need me.'

The truth is, it's a relief to see a familiar face. I've never felt more alone than I do right at this moment. But how could she possibly know not just that I was in Daylesford, but that she'd find me walking around the lake this morning? *I* barely know where I am.

She must sense my confusion because she places her hand on my elbow. 'Let's go find somewhere to sit.'

She steers me towards the enclosed playground, and I sit next to her on a bench seat. 'Is everything alright?' I ask her. 'Did Georgie tell you I was here?'

'No, I knew you would be here.'

'I'm not following.' I glance towards the other side of the lake, reflexively checking Richard isn't lurking about, watching me. He forbade me from seeing Nora again. But then I realise it doesn't matter what Richard thinks anymore.

'I came so I could be here for you when Richard tells you he wants a divorce.'

My pulse quickens, my eyebrows furrow. 'How ... how could you possibly know that? He just told me half an hour ago.'

'He also told you that he's been having an affair.'

'What's going on? How do you know that?' I stand, panic rising in my chest. 'Did Richard tell you he was planning this?' I ask, although I already know the answer will be no. Richard was wary of Nora. He wanted to investigate her. The last thing he would do is confide in her.

'Elle,' she says, her blue eyes penetrating mine, 'there's something I need to explain to you and I think you should sit down.'

'I'm too mad to sit. Just tell me.'

She takes a deep breath. 'Elle ... I am you.'

'What do you mean? That we're in the same situation?' I know her husband was abusive and she left him.

She shakes her head. 'No. My name is Eleanor Plankett. I'm fifty-one years old. My mother's name was Rosalind and my father's Stuart. I have two sons; Charlie is almost eighteen and Olly is fifteen. My husband is Richard Harrison and I was here with him exactly ten years ago today. He told me he wanted a divorce.'

I think Richard may have been right about Nora. She's clearly not stable.

Chapter 30

Nora

Elle is staring at me like I'm a crazy person. She looks infuriated too.

'I can't deal with this today, Nora. I have enough going on in my life right now. I've got to go.'

She starts to walk away from me but I can't let her go yet. This will be my only chance to get through to her and I have to do it now. I follow and reach for her arm.

'What are you doing? Let go of me,' she says.

'I can't, Elle.'

She huffs and stops to stand in front of me. 'So one minute you're a homeless lady asking me for money, the next you're my cousin Nora from Adelaide, daughter of my mum's cousin Henry, and now you're trying to tell me you're *me*. I don't get what you're playing at here. Is it money you want?'

This is going to be harder than I thought. 'No, I don't want your money. Look, I lied about being Henry's daughter, I'm Rosalind's. I've never even met Mum's cousin Henry, I have no idea if he's alive, let alone if he has children. But I had to give an excuse when you found me with Mum that wouldn't scare you away. And I am homeless. I don't have a real home. I've been living at the shelter in North Melbourne for the last ten years. I work in the kitchen there and in return they give me free accommodation and meals. I lost everything, Elle, my children, my friend, my business. I don't want that to happen to you.'

'I'm sorry you're in that situation, but my life has nothing to do with yours.'

I emit a resigned sigh and drop my head. This is not going how I'd planned, but I can't give up. I look into her furious eyes. 'You buried a treasure with the boys last summer. It was a time capsule. Charlie put a model car in it, Olly a Bob the Builder figurine and you put in the beaded bracelet the boys made you.' I hold up my wrist with the beaded bracelet wrapped around it to show her.

She stares at it, her eyes wide. 'How ... ? It's not possible.'

'You each wrote a note and you buried it in the garden below the cubbyhouse window.'

Elle's jaw drops. 'How could you possibly know any of that?'

'The boys wanted to be able to keep watch over it from the cubbyhouse when they played. I can tell you what they wrote in their notes.'

She looks at me bewildered. 'I didn't read their notes.'

'I have.'

She holds out her palm in front of me like a stop sign and shakes her head. 'No, stop ... Please, Nora, this is ridiculous.'

'A month ago there was an open for inspection at the house and I retrieved the time capsule from the backyard. That's why I have this bracelet.'

'Richard's selling the house?'

'He sold it years ago. The owner who bought it from him is selling it in my time, in 2022. Look, I don't know how this works, all I know is that after I dug up the capsule, I bumped into you at the shopping strip. I was as shocked as you are right now. At first I thought I was hallucinating, but when I got back to the shelter, nobody recognised me. I had no room, no belongings and I discovered that I was back in 2012. And Mum was alive.'

Elle pales. 'She's dead?'

There's no way to soften the blow. 'She dies in 2017.'

Her eyes well, but I can see she's trying to remain composed.

'Look, Nora, I get that this all makes sense to you, but it's too unbelievable for me to even consider that you're me from 2022.'

'I get it, I really do, but you have to understand, that when this all happened to me I eventually realised that I was being given a second chance. As unexplainable as it was, the universe was giving me an opportunity to save you, Elle, to save myself. Richard tried to sabotage your friendship with Georgie. He set you up for fraud. When he changed over the business software, he botched the accounts so it looked like you were only breaking even, and then he transferred the money from your business bank account to your personal account.'

'Did Georgie tell you about that?' She looks at me accusingly. 'Our software was hacked, but the money went back.'

'It did,' I say. 'Because I warned Georgie what was going to happen so she didn't react the way she did last time around. Last time, she thought you stole from the business. I went to her after you came in to do the cooking workshop at the shelter and told her everything. She didn't believe me at first either, but she does now, because everything I told her would happen did.' My heart is galloping, but I have to convince her.

'Georgie would never think that I stole money from her.'

'She did, and it destroyed your friendship and the catering business. That was Richard's plan, Elle. He didn't want you to have any support when you go through the separation. He wanted you to feel alone, helpless.'

Her eyebrows scrunch together. 'Are you some kind of fortune teller?'

'No! I'm you!' This isn't working. I'm going to have to try a different tactic. 'Okay, fine, don't believe me, but at least listen to what your husband is up to. You didn't have a virus during the week, Richard was drugging you, and whatever dose he gave you then, he's going to double it when you get home.'

'That's crazy. Richard wouldn't drug me. I know he's done some pretty awful things, but that's going a step too far, even for Richard.'

'When you go back to the dining room, he's going to tell you that he thinks you should both live in the same house for now, for the sake of the boys. He's going to drug you until you're so incapacitated that you can't even look after your children, and then he's going to hire a nanny, who is actually Patricia, so she can get to know Charlie and Olly.'

'Patricia?'

'Yes, the other woman. Go,' I say, my head gesturing in the direction of the road. 'Find out for yourself. But, please, just do one thing for me: don't let on to Richard that you know what he's going to say. And don't mention the drugs, because if he thinks you know then he'll just find another way to get rid of you, and I won't be able to help because I won't know what his plan is. Your future will end up being the same as mine, and me coming back to the past will have been for nothing.'

She stares at me for a moment, considering. 'Fine, but you're wrong,' she says.

'I'll be waiting here for you,' I say. I sit on the bench, watching her storm off.

Chapter 31

Elle

'She's a crazy woman,' I mutter to myself as I walk up the road. 'Freakin' crazy.'

My brain is telling me this, but some part of me is wondering how Nora could possibly know everything she did. I can explain how she knew about the business easily enough – Georgie must have told her. I'm not surprised that she was able to convince Georgie of her story, because she's more naïve than me like that. But I never told Georgie about the time capsule I made with the boys. Only Charlie, Olly and I know about our secret treasure. And the bracelet did look similar to the one the boys made me, but at the end of the day, it's just a beaded bracelet. She could have made it herself.

I do believe in premonitions, and maybe that's what this is, though, it's preposterous to think Richard would drug me. I had a virus.

I take two stairs at a time until I'm on the patio next to the restaurant. I can see Richard through the window still seated at the table, reading a newspaper and sipping a coffee. There's a half-eaten Danish pastry on his plate. He looks as he would on any other day, completely relaxed, unperturbed, not like a remorseful man who has just told his wife he's having an affair and wants a divorce.

I open the door to reception and make my way down the stairs. The bartender behind the bar smiles at me as I pass, but I don't return his smile. I sit down at the table and Richard, acknowledging me, folds up the newspaper.

'What's her name?' I ask.

'It's not important,' says Richard.

'Tell me her name now!'

He glances around the restaurant at the other guests. 'Don't make a scene.'

'If you don't want a scene then you'll tell me.'

'Patricia. Her name's Patricia.'

My blood runs cold. Nora knew her name.

'I want you out tonight,' I say.

'I'm not moving out, Elle.'

'Excuse me? You expect me to leave?'

'No, I think we should both stay where we are, for the sake of the boys.'

My heart gallops. Strike two for Nora, she's on a winning streak. But I'm more focused on what Richard is proposing. 'For the sake of the boys? If you cared at all about our family, you wouldn't have done this.'

He rolls his eyes like I'm overreacting. 'All that matters now is Charlie and Olly. They're young, so I think we should ease them in to us not being together.'

I cross my arms over my chest. 'And how do you propose we live under the same roof?'

'You can have the main bedroom —'

'How generous of you.'

'I'll set myself up in the study. We'll explain to them that we're not husband and wife anymore but we're still a family and can all live together. It's what's best for the children.'

'How would you know what's best for them? You're hardly around.'

'Why do you have to make everything difficult?'

I point my finger at my chest. 'I'm the difficult one here?' Really, he's got to be kidding. The nerve of him.

'My lawyer said it's quite common for parents of young kids to stay in the home together until the divorce comes through.'

'And how long does your lawyer say that takes?'

'You have to be separated for twelve months before it's finalised.'

'There's no way I'm living with you for a year! But I guess I'll work that out with my lawyer,' I say, standing up. 'I'll meet you at the car in an hour.'

He nods and I walk off. I don't have a lawyer, but I'll find one.

I practically sprint down to the playground near the lake. I can see the back of Nora's head. She's sitting on the bench seat where I left her. She turns around before I'm even close enough for her to hear my footsteps and she gives me a small smile. When I reach her, I sit down.

'How did you know?' I ask.

My hand is resting on the wooden seat between us and she places her hand on top of mine. My skin tingles. Her hand feels warm, and when she laces her fingers through mine, I close my eyes. It feels as if our hands are melding together, as though we're one. A wave of calmness envelops me, and when I open my eyes she's looking at me, her blue eyes a reflection of mine. The outline of her face, her cheekbones, the shape of her nose and mouth, it's all mine. How could I not have seen it before? She holds up her hand for me to place my palm against hers. They're the exact same size. Slowly I move my head, so I can see around both of our hands: the skin colour is the same, the shape of our fingers, though mine are slightly thinner, the same burn scar below our thumbs.

'I can feel a vibration around our hands,' I say.

'We must share the same energy field,' says Nora. 'I felt it when you shook my hand at the cooking workshop.' She drops her hand to her side. 'Maybe we shouldn't touch. I don't know how this works.'

'Is this real or am I dreaming?' I ask.

'I asked myself the same thing after we met. It's real, Elle.'

'Why did you change your name?'

'I was trying to prevent Richard from finding me. It was Nan's name.'

'I know,' I say. 'I remember.'

'Are you ready to listen?' she asks.

I take a deep breath and nod.

Nora tells me everything that happened to her, from the moment she came back from Daylesford with Richard until the day she ran into me in Glenferrie Road. She fills me in on the changes to my past that she's already made with the help of Georgie. That she's saved our friendship.

Nora gives me a few moments to digest all this information, and then she tells me her plan for Richard. I sit there in a daze, trying to absorb everything.

By the time I walk back to our room, I'm shaking inside and out. I'm completely overwhelmed, from finding out who Nora is, this morning's events with Richard, and hearing from Nora everything Richard has in store for me. Even though part of me still doubts what she's told me, the reality is that time will tell. I'll find out for sure soon enough.

I unlock the door to the room and it's empty. My bag and belongings are gone. How dare he touch my things – he has no right to anymore. It crosses my mind that maybe he's left without me, but after I return the key to reception I see the car in the carpark, Richard at the steering wheel. As much as the idea of being in close proximity to him for an hour and a half sickens me, I open the passenger door and strap myself in.

It's a very long drive home.

The first thing I do when I get home is call the carpenter to come tomorrow to install a lock on my bedroom door. After everything Nora has told me, I wouldn't put it past Richard to kill me in my sleep.

Chapter 32

Elle

Georgie arrives the next morning just as I'm letting the carpenter out. I fall into her arms before she's even had a chance to put her handbag down. 'Richard's divorcing me – he's having an affair!' My heart is breaking from the sheer force of the events of the last twenty-four hours.

'I know. I'm so sorry, Elle,' she says.

I lift my head to look at her. 'You know? How could you know? It only happened yesterday.' I swipe under my eyes.

'Nora told me.'

'When?'

'A week ago?'

I let go of her. 'You've known for a week and you didn't tell me? Why didn't you warn me? I could have been prepared for this.'

Georgie places her handbag on the bench. 'Would you have believed me?'

I release a frustrated breath. The truth is, of course, I wouldn't have believed her. I'm still struggling to wrap my head around everything Nora told me. I was awake half the night trying to process it. 'No, I wouldn't have. The whole thing is absolutely insane.'

'You see? You would have just got mad at me.'

'Do you think she's telling the truth, that she's really me from the future?'

'I do,' says Georgie. She takes my hand and we go to the couch. 'Obviously I thought she was crazy at first. But then she told me everything that was going to happen with our business down to the smallest of details, and it all did happen, every single little thing. Plus there were the events and things about my life that only you know.'

'I feel like I'm delusional to even be considering that what she's saying is true,' I say, 'but I think it is. When our hands joined yesterday, there was this overwhelming connection between us. I actually thought my hand was going to dissolve into hers it was so powerful. And she has the exact same scar.' I show Georgie the scar on my hand. 'It was weird but in that moment, when we were linked, it was like I knew all her thoughts too.' I didn't tell Nora this, but I seemed to glimpse into the life she's led. All the pain she's endured, the sense of loss. In that very instant, I felt it all as my own, which I assume one day it might be. My body tenses at the thought. 'She thinks that Richard's drugging me and that was why I was unwell last week.'

'I know, she told me too.'

I run my hand through my hair. 'I ... I just can't believe that he would do that. That he'd drug me to keep me from my children.'

Georgie rubs my shoulder. 'I'm so sorry. I don't know what to say to make it better.'

'The only thing that will make it better is if it's not true.'

Georgie picks at her fingernail, casting her eyes down.

'What? What are you not telling me?' I ask, afraid of what else there could possibly be.

'Well, we're not completely certain, but I found a prescription drug called Endep in Richard's bathroom drawer. It's used to treat depression.'

'Depression? Does Nora think Richard's depressed? Is that why he does this to me?'

'No, she thinks that's what he drugs you with. We've checked the side effects and they're similar to all the symptoms you had last week.'

'It could be a coincidence, though. I mean, they were also common symptoms for a virus.'

'Maybe,' says Georgie. 'I guess we'll know soon enough.'

That's the scary part. Nora told me that her symptoms worsened after Daylesford. She thinks Richard upped the dosage he was giving her to speed things up.

'Nora said we should write down everything you eat or drink that Richard may have tampered with. We know he's not going to put it in anything the boys might eat, but you should keep an eye out when you get up from the table during dinner in case he adds it then.'

'Lately I've been having dinner with the boys. Richard's been coming home so late from work, or he's had work dinners.' Although now I know that it's probably all lies and he's most likely been with Patricia.

'Can you think of anything else he could be putting it in?' asks Georgie.

'I keep a glass of water on my bedside table overnight. But I'd taste it in water, wouldn't I?'

'Maybe.'

'And he makes me a smoothie every morning. But it can't be in that, he makes mine in the same batch as his.'

'He could add it to your glass before you drink it,' suggests Georgie.

'I'm usually in the kitchen when he makes it,' I say, my thoughts processing. 'But I don't drink it straight away. I have it midmorning.' I can't stomach the thick liquid so early in the day. It smells as putrid as it looks.

'Well, that would give him a chance to put it in when you're not there.'

She's right. Richard would have plenty of opportunities to add it to my smoothie. I'm running around all morning before we even go to school, going upstairs to wake Charlie and help dress Olly, in and out of the laundry putting on washing. Even on the days when he leaves for work before we go to school, it would be easy for him to slip it in the smoothie without me noticing.

I get up and go straight to the fridge, Georgie one step behind me. I open the fridge door and there it is, sitting on the top shelf in a glass. My hand trembles as I reach to grab it and place it on the bench. Both Georgie and I stare at it like it's a treacherous villain, our enemy, because if that glass is filled with what we think it might be then it will poison my body, leading to my downfall. A huge part of me still prays that it's not, that there's some other explanation for Richard's prescription for Endep that doesn't involve him feeding it to me. That this whole thing is just some crazy hoax, and at any moment Richard will jump out of a closet and say, 'Fooled you,' and life will go back to normal.

Georgie places her hand on my back.

'I can't do it,' I say, and not because I'm worried about feeling ill again, although I am. I can't do it because I don't want to know the truth.

'You don't really have a choice. It's the only way you'll know for sure.' Georgie's face is etched with sympathy, her eyes glistening.

I pick up the glass and sniff it, although I doubt I'd smell anything over the strong aroma of the smoothie. 'You know what, I think we should cook the orders for today first, otherwise Sarah will get here and they won't be ready.'

I put the glass back in the fridge and go to the pantry in the laundry and take out today's ingredients. As I tie up my hair and put on my Notch apron, Georgie puts on some music and we get started.

By the time we've finished cooking, the kitchen is filled with the smells of garlic and ginger and spices. Georgie has made fresh pitas and we're standing at the bench pulling apart the meat on the lamb shoulders for the shawarmas. We fill containers with condiments and the meat, and wrap the pitas with foil. Georgie assembles a spare pita with leftovers and tears it in half, handing me one.

'I don't think I could eat anything,' I say, as my stomach rumbles at the mouth-watering smell.

'Eat,' says Georgie. 'If there is medication in the smoothie, it's better not to have it on an empty stomach.'

I take a bite, the tahini and juices oozing out of the side of the pita. I wipe my mouth with the back of my hand and let out my breath, feeling marginally calmer.

'You see?' says Georgie. 'Pure comfort.'

I finish the shawarma and pack the mini raspberry friands and jaffa muffins that have been cooling into containers. Georgie wipes down the benches until they're shining. The kitchen is so clean there's no evidence of this morning's cooking marathon.

By the time Sarah comes to pick up the order, everything is packed and ready to go. There's only one thing left for me to do.

An hour later, the dizziness sets in, and by the time school pick-up comes around, my head feels like it's being banged against a wall.

The truth stares me in the face. There's no getting away from the fact that my husband is drugging me and I'm probably going to end up homeless and then living in a shelter without my children, just like Nora did.

'It's come on quicker than last week,' I say to Georgie as she walks over to the couch with two paracetamol for me. She hasn't left my side and will get the boys from school after she picks up her kids.

'I assume Nora's right and he's upped the dose,' she says.

I wipe my brow where beads of sweat have formed, probably because of the anxiety engulfing me as opposed to the medication.

'I feel awful,' I say.

'It's unbearable to watch you like this.' Georgie holds the glass for me until I've popped the tablets onto my tongue.

'Thanks,' I say, taking the glass. 'Can you help me upstairs? I don't want the boys to see me like this when they get home.'

'Of course.' She places her arm around my waist as we make our way to my room and then I climb into bed.

The daylight coming through the window feels like an ophthalmologist is shining a light into my eyes. 'Do you mind closing the curtains for me? I'll try to sleep it off.'

She places my phone on the bedside table and moves to close the curtains. 'Text me when you're awake. I don't want you coming down the stairs on your own.'

She's about to close the door when my phone rings. She comes back over and picks it up.

'It's Richard,' she says. 'What should I do?'

I can't remember the last time he's called me during the day. I hold out my hand for the phone and answer. 'Hello?'

'Hi, it's me. How are you?'

'Actually, I'm not feeling too well.' I know he's checking in because he won't want me driving the boys if the medication has affected me.

'What's wrong?' he asks.

'I'm not sure. It feels like the virus I had last week, only worse.'

Georgie rolls her eyes.

'I'll pick up the boys,' he says. 'You have a rest.'

'That's okay. Georgie offered to get them.'

'Okay, I'll leave work early.'

'Georgie's going to give the kids dinner here. We're all sorted,' I say.

There's a pause on the other end of the line. 'Alright, I'll see you later.'

I drop my head on the pillow, exhausted.

Georgie takes the phone, turns it to silent and closes the door.

Chapter 33

Nora

Elle's lying on the couch, a throw blanket over her. She looks dreadful.

Actually witnessing it, seeing her feeling so ill because of Richard, makes me want to strangle him.

'You were right,' she says, looking up at me. 'Everything you told me, it's all happening.' Her eyes overflow with tears. 'I didn't want you to be right.'

I sit down on the couch opposite her. 'I'm sorry you have to go through this, I really am, but it's the only way to get proof,' I say. Richard has been drugging her for three days now, clearly with high doses of medication.

'She's booked in for a blood test tomorrow,' says Georgie. 'I'm taking her to the clinic I go to so Richard can't trace it.'

'Good idea,' I say. 'He was in contact with our family doctor last time.'

'I can't lose my boys,' says Elle, her voice croaky.

'You're not going to,' says Georgie, sitting on the end of the couch near Elle's curled-up legs. She places a hand on Elle's thigh and looks over at me for confirmation.

'Georgie's right. We're not going to let that happen again,' I say, hoping to sound convincing.

'I feel like my whole world is crumbling and I'm holding on by a thread,' says Elle.

'You're almost there,' I reassure her. 'Tomorrow you can stop drinking the smoothie.' Georgie called me on Monday as soon as they discovered how Richard was getting the Endep into Elle. I'd spent countless hours after Richard told me that he'd drugged me, trying to work out how he managed to do it. I guess I was so traumatised by everything that had happened that I couldn't see that the answer was so simple, and ironic - the healthy smoothie.

'And then what? If he realises I'm not drinking it, he'll slip it into something else,' says Elle.

'You're going to have to fake it so he doesn't work it out,' I tell her.

'Pretend to be sick?' asks Elle.

'Yes. When he's around, you have to make him believe you're unwell. Hold on to the furniture, the walls, lie down, whatever you need to do so that he thinks he's still drugging you.'

'For how long?' asks Elle.

'Until I've found a lawyer to get everything in place for you.' I've been calling family lawyers over the last few days. I want to find one who Elle will feel comfortable with for the long term.

'That will just anger him more if I organise my own lawyer.'

I get up from the couch and kneel in front of her. She's clearly petrified of Richard. I know that feeling – I was too for so very long.

'Elle, I need you to trust me on this. If Richard is divorcing you, it's only natural that at some point you would organise a lawyer.

And he isn't going to know about it until everything is in place, and he's going to be so out of it himself by then that he won't realise what's happening until it's done.'

'What do you mean, "out of it"?' asks Georgie.

'We're going to give Richard a taste of his own medicine,' I say.

'As in literally?' asks Georgie, her eyebrows raised.

'Yes.'

Elle lifts her head off the cushion. 'You want me to drug him?'

'You're just switching the smoothies,' I tell her. 'Technically, Richard's drugging himself.' Although at some point she is going to need to add it to his food as well.

Elle glances over at Georgie.

'Nora's right,' says Georgie. 'You're not putting it in there, you didn't buy the medication. He's doing it to himself.'

'But won't he realise when he starts to experience the same symptoms as me?'

'Not at first, he'll probably just feel a bit off. And there's no way he'll think you're drugging him because he's got no idea that you know that he's drugging you.' I go back to the other couch. 'It's only for a little while, until all the arrangements have been made.' Although the reality is, I don't know how long it will take until we sit down with a lawyer.

Elle drops her head back on the cushion. Her face is pale as her eyes flutter close.

'Georgie, could I have a glass of water, please?' I ask.

'Of course,' she says. 'I'll make us tea too.'

Georgie goes to the kitchen and clatters away, making more noise than is probably necessary to give me some time with Elle. She's clearly distressed, which is understandable. She's just found out that her husband is cheating on her, he wants a divorce and he's drugging her. It took me years and years to process what happened, and I'm only starting to let go of it now, because I can do something about it.

'Elle, I know this is hard for you, but there's something else you need to know.'

She looks over at me, her face full of worry.

'Richard never divorced me,' I say.

'What?' She bolts upright at the same time as something bangs in the kitchen.

'Sorry,' calls out Georgie. Clearly, she's equally stunned by this reveal.

'But ... he asked me for a divorce.' Elle's mouth is practically hanging open.

'He did, but he never served me with papers. The whole time he knew where I was living, where he could find me, and he didn't go through with it.'

'Why? What possible reason could he have for not doing it?' asks Georgie, handing me a mug of tea.

'Thank you,' I say. She hands another to Elle before sitting back down, cradling her mug. 'I assume because divorcing me would involve court proceedings and mediators. The shelter would have organised a legal aid lawyer for me. He'd already admitted to drugging me, so that might have come out. And staying married to me meant he was in control. He was my next of kin, so if he said I was a danger to myself he could organise to have me committed at any time.' I take a sip of tea.

'But what about Patricia?' asks Georgie. 'Is he still with her in 2022?'

'He is. Not divorcing me probably also gave him a legitimate reason not to commit to another marriage. He already had his children so there was no point, and that way it would be easier for him to walk away when he was ready for a newer model.'

'They've stayed together for all that time?' asks Elle.

'Yes,' I say.

'Does she live with them?' Elle looks horrified.

'Yes, I think so,' I say, feeling a pang in my chest. I know how awful it is to know that another woman is being a mother to your children.

'Elle, just focus on the boys. You're doing this for Charlie and Olly,' says Georgie.

'Okay, there's not really any choice then,' says Elle. 'And Nora's right, he's drugging himself.'

'He is,' says Georgie.

The oven timer beeps. Georgie checks her watch. 'Sorry, I have to finish up in the kitchen. Sarah will be here in half an hour.'

'I feel so bad I can't help you,' says Elle from the couch.

'I can give you a hand if you need?' I offer.

Georgie glances over at Elle, who nods her head.

'Sure,' says Georgie.

I follow her to the kitchen and she hands me an apron. As soon as I wrap it around my body, it really does feel like I'm back in 2012.

'What can I do?' I ask her.

'It's mostly done, I just need to garnish and dress the salad and pack everything in containers,' she says as she removes a tray of freshly baked rolls from the oven. They're perfectly golden on top and look light and fluffy. The smell fills the room.

I sprinkle the salad with the chopped chives and toasted pine nuts before coating it in dressing, then dust the mini flourless chocolate cakes that are cooling on the rack with icing sugar.

Georgie and I move around each other in sync, like no time has passed.

I miss this, and for a moment I feel like the old version of me. But it is exactly that, just a moment. In my world, Georgie isn't in my life anymore and I don't live here. Richard did everything he could to make sure of that.

Chapter 34

Elle

'Drink it,' says Georgie.

'What's in it?' I ask.

'Ginger, celery and lemon. It'll help detoxify your system.' She fills a glass with water. 'And drink this when you finish.' Georgie drove me to the medical centre for my blood test this morning.

'Yes, ma'am,' I say, although secretly it's nice to have someone take care of me for a change.

'Actually,' she says, going to the cupboard and retrieving a jug and filling it with water, 'just to make sure you've had enough, I'll leave this on the bench. We have to flush everything out of your system.'

'Thank you,' I say. 'And not just for this, but for everything. Helping me with the kids, cooking dinner for us, taking me to the doctor. I don't know what I would have done without you.'

'You don't have to thank me,' she says. 'There's one more thing we need to do, though.' She goes to the fridge and takes out the smoothie. 'I'll let you have the honour.'

We both watch as I pour it down the sink. Georgie turns on the tap and clears the thick liquid that sits around the drain, washing any traces of the smoothie away.

'Now go upstairs and have a sleep while I cook,' she says.

Sarah is coming to help her prepare the orders this morning, so I don't feel bad leaving her to it.

Throughout the day, Georgie makes me several more juices, and by the time Richard comes home from work that evening, my body feels drained but not as awful as it has the last few days. But for Richard's sake I lie on the couch, appearing worse than I am, watching television with Charlie and Olly snuggling around me.

'Boys, upstairs to bed,' says Richard, clicking his fingers like he's calling a dog.

'Mummy, I want you to put me to bed,' whines Olly.

'Mummy's not well,' says Richard.

Olly's mouth quivers.

'Mummy's fine, sweetheart, it's just a virus. Come give me a kiss.'

Olly bends his head to kiss my cheek and I pull him in for a hug. 'I'll be better soon,' I whisper in his ear.

'Goodnight, Mum,' says Charlie, kissing me too.

'Love you,' I call out as they follow Richard to the staircase.

Richard comes back five minutes later, clearly not having bothered to read to them. He plonks himself down on the couch opposite me.

'I think we should hire a nanny,' he says.

'A nanny? Why?'

'Elle, you're not well. It's not a virus.'

'I'll make an appointment with the doctor.'

'I think that's a good idea. I can take you,' he says.

'Georgie will take me.'

He runs his hands over his head. 'Georgie has her own family to take care of. She's been here every afternoon this week.'

'She's been helping me,' I say.

'I don't want her here.'

'It's not up to you, Richard. You're the one who left our marriage and Georgie's the only family I have.'

'She's not your family, Elle.'

I sit up. 'Maybe I should call Nora then.'

His eyes grow dark. 'Nora? She's probably long gone by now. Do you think she's going to leave her family in Adelaide to come and help a woman she barely knows?'

'Actually, we spoke the other day. She's still in town.'

Richard gets up and comes to stand over me. 'You are not to call Nora, do you hear me? I don't want that woman in my home. I don't trust her.'

And I don't trust you! But I don't say that out loud. Nora has warned me to be careful. If I rebel, I may change my future, but not to my benefit. Richard might speed things along or, worse, try another tactic to get rid of me. 'Fine, I won't call her, but Georgie's already committed to picking the boys up tomorrow. If I'm still not well by the end of the weekend, I promise I'll let you hire a nanny.'

'Good,' says Richard. His shoulders relax. 'I'm going to the study.'

'Goodnight,' I say. I wait until I hear the door close before I go upstairs. I look in on Olly and he's curled in a ball, teddy clutched to his chest. I lean over and kiss his forehead. 'Mummy will never leave you, my sweet boy,' I whisper.

I go to Charlie's room where he's fast asleep on his stomach, the doona half off the bed. I pull it up over his body and kiss the top of his head. He stirs in his sleep. 'Love you,' I say.

I change into my nightie, lock the bedroom door and tuck myself under the doona. Georgie said that Nora has found a lawyer she's sure I'll gel with and we're meeting her on Monday. It does feel strange, having someone else take on this task for me, especially one that's so monumental and life-changing. But Nora knows exactly how life-changing it will be for me if each step isn't meticulously planned out. The stakes are high for her too. I have to trust her, because in effect I'm trusting myself. She told me that ten years ago she left this house with fifty dollars in her pocket. Last time around she didn't have the finances to seek professional advice, but fortunately I do. That's why I called the bank to set up a personal account for me.

I haven't told Nora or Georgie this, but after what Richard did with the business account, I wouldn't put it past him to empty our joint account and leave me with nothing so that I'm dependant on him. I haven't transferred any money into it yet; I have to wait until Richard's not in his right mind and forgets to check it. But next week I plan to start making transactions out of our joint account and into mine. Some of that money is what I've earned over the years from my business, not to mention what I've earned for being Richard's devoted wife. I'm sure Richard has accounts and assets out there that I don't know about. But he can keep it, I don't want it. I just want what's mine.

The next morning, I'm feeling a lot better. I'm assisting Georgie and Sarah with the cooking when the doctor calls.

'Hello,' I say, making my way out the back door and into the garden, towards the cubbyhouse.

'Hi, Elle. I'm calling with your blood test results,' she says.

'Yes?'

'It shows traces of amitriptyline in your blood,' says the doctor.

Amitriptyline is the main ingredient listed on the front of the Endep packet.

I swallow. 'Will I have any symptoms now that I've stopped taking it?' I know that Nora experienced severe withdrawal symptoms, but Richard had been giving her the drug for close to six weeks.

'You should be fine; it was only a short period that you were given it. You might just feel a little off for a few days. I'll have the report emailed to you today. Please call if you need anything.'

'Thank you,' I say, dropping the phone to my side. I'm relieved and devastated at the same time. I know I've had all the side effects from the drug, but there must have been some infinitesimal part of me that was hoping Richard wasn't really drugging me. I turn around and Georgie is standing there. I nod and her hands fly to cover her mouth. She must have been feeling the same.

'He did it. He really did it,' I say to Georgie, my eyes filling to the brim.

'I'm so sorry,' she says, hugging me, then taking hold of both of my shoulders and bending her head to look me in the eyes. 'But this is a good result. Now we have evidence.'

My head nods repeatedly as I sniff. 'Can you call Nora's number for me, please?' I ask, handing her my phone.

She takes it, dials and then hands the phone back to me.

'Hello ... Nora ... you were right. The blood test results came back and they were positive. He really is drugging me.' I can hear the desperation in my voice.

'Thank goodness it showed up,' says Nora. 'I was worried there wouldn't be enough of it in your system yet. How are you feeling?'

'Better today. I did a juice cleanse yesterday. But, Nora ... Richard's given me until the weekend to get better and then he's planning on bringing in Patricia. I think I should swap the smoothies tomorrow and get things moving.' I can't go on like this for one moment longer, living in the same house as a person who is drugging me and wants to cause me harm.

'Elle, I know this is hard, but you have to wait until Monday. Richard's a smart man. If you swap the drinks now, he might catch on before we're ready. It's a risk.'

'Okay, okay.' I'm completely jittery and anxious, but it's also probably from coming off the medication.

'Elle, I know you can do this. Trust me, you're braver than you think. Look at me – I survived it, and I won't let Richard win this time around. I've already had a preliminary chat with the lawyer. She understands the urgency of the situation and she's made a plan for everything that needs to be done.'

'Okay,' I say, looking over at Georgie.

'It will all be over before you know it,' says Nora. 'I'll see you Monday.'

'See you then,' I say.

I hope that Nora is right.

Chapter 35

Nora

It worked. I can't believe it, but I actually have proof that Richard was drugging me. 'Everything okay?' asks Heather, coming into the kitchen.

'Huh?'

'You look like you're lost in another world.'

'I am.' I'm literally lost in another world, trapped in another time, and I have no idea what's going to happen to me when this is all over. Am I going to go back to 2022 when Elle's life is resolved? Will I still be me, Nora, or will I be Elle? Will the last ten years be erased, like the person I am today never existed? I came back to the past after digging up the time capsule. Do I need to return it to go back to my world? Do I want to go back? And even if I change her life now, will Elle still end up in the same position in 2022 but via different circumstances?

Who knows if I can really change the past? Maybe I'm just delaying the inevitable, her destiny. Or should I say mine. There are so many questions that I can't possibly know the answers to. Maybe I never will.

'Anything I can help with?' asks Heather.

'No, just a few things on my mind,' I say, grabbing the plastic wrap to cover the afternoon tea leftovers. 'How are you?'

'I'm looking forward to the weekend. It's been a busy week.'

'It has,' I say. There was a new intake of women with young children this week and it can take a while for them to settle in.

'What are you up to this weekend?' she asks.

'I think I'll spend some time with my mum. And I might do a little cooking.' Cooking relaxes me, that is when I'm not rushing to get it done like when Georgie and I would for the catering business. When I have time to potter and experiment with dishes, make something new, it can be quite mesmerising.

'How is your mum doing?'

'Pretty much the same. Some days she's good, some days not so great.'

'It can't be easy.'

'It's not, but even when she doesn't recognise me, she doesn't mind the company.'

'Well, I'll see you Monday.'

'See you,' I say, not knowing what Monday will bring. I sense that my time with my mother is limited. When I go back to my world, she's dead, and I'll go back to missing her. But today, she's alive, so I'll spend as much time as I can by her side.

I've been trying not to focus too much on this morning, but the vision board in my head is difficult to get away from. Over the weekend I could see it so clearly, with lines leading from one point to another, circles for the more important items, everything laid out in chronological order of when it needs to happen. If it was a physical vision board it would be colour-coded and highlighted, but in my mind it's black and white. I would have put pen to paper, but I couldn't leave anything like that around in case it's found when the universe sends me back to 2022 or obliterates me from life altogether. It's a comfort that Georgie has written down notes for everything that needs to be done. She says it's safely hidden away in her underwear drawer. I'd feel better if it were in a home safe, but it will have to do.

I check my watch every thirty seconds while I wait for Elle. She finally walks into the foyer at five minutes to ten.

'Sorry,' she says. 'I forgot how long it takes to park in the city.'

'How are you feeling?' I ask her.

'Much better, thanks. My head is clearer and I feel like I can do this.'

'How did you go this morning?' I ask.

'Good. I pretended there was a knock at the front door, and when Richard went to get it, I swapped the smoothies. I'll have to come up with something better for tomorrow. He wasn't impressed that I made him get up from reading the newspaper to answer the door to nobody.'

I'm not surprised. 'And you're acting like you have all the side effects?'

'Yes, I'm holding on to the walls and furniture for balance.'

I press the button for the lift and we step inside.

'What's her name?' asks Elle.

'Mina Holesman. I think you'll like her.'

'Well, if you like her, I guess I do too.' She gives a little laugh, but I can tell she's nervous.

We're both quiet as we sit in the waiting room outside Mina's office, on edge with anticipation. When her door finally opens, I glance at Elle, and she looks petrified. I would have felt the same even a month ago, but today I don't. I know this is how it was meant to be, how it should have played out back then, and now I get a redo, not just for me, but for my children. I miss them terribly, and they're the ones who have suffered the most from being without me for so long. When I saw Charlie and Olly exactly how they were when I left them, I knew I would go to any lengths now to protect them from what the Charlie and Olly in my time have had to endure.

'Hi, I'm Mina.' Dressed in a black pants suit, she extends her hand to shake Elle's and then mine. 'Please come in.' Mina closes her office door behind us and we sit in the leather armchairs that face her large mahogany desk. There are certificates lining the walls and a lush artificial plant stands boldly next to a filing cabinet in the corner. She has a file laid out on her desk next to her computer.

'Would you like a glass of water?' Mina asks, gesturing to the jug of water and glasses resting on a tray.

'Yes, please,' says Elle.

'I'm fine,' I say.

She pours a glass and hands it to Elle. 'Nora has filled me in on your situation and I've put together a plan of action that I'd like to run through with you.'

Elle nods.

'Please stop me at any time when you have questions. Do you have a copy of the blood test results?'

Elle rummages through her bag and pulls out a folded piece of paper. She opens it and it's full of creases. She hands it to Mina.

'Thank you.' Mina puts on her glasses, reads the page and adds it to the file. She places her elbows on the desk and leans slightly forward, picking up some papers. 'I've filled in the application for the parenting agreement, giving you sole responsibility for both of your children and stating that they will live with you. It stipulates that the father, Richard Harrison, will spend three supervised hours per week with the boys until they're eighteen.' She hands a copy to me and one to Elle to look over.

'Both you and your husband have to sign the agreement and then I'll submit the document to the Federal Circuit and Family Court.' She glances from Elle to me. 'I won't ask how you plan on getting him to sign it.'

I don't fill her in and instead ask, 'How long does it take to be in effect?'

'It can take two weeks to be sealed and the order is then set in place. But I've had cases when it's gone through in a matter of days.' She turns her attention to Elle. 'I'm going to organise a family violence intervention order for you too.'

Elle looks over at me, her eyebrows creased, concern etched all over her face. She turns to Mina. 'But he wasn't violent, he didn't physically harm me.'

'Violence is a basic violation of human rights. It includes physical violence, emotional and psychological violence, it can even include economic abuse. Any controlling behaviour that makes the person feel unsafe, and it definitely includes drugging another person without their consent.'

'Okay,' says Elle.

'You will be named as the affected family member,' explains Mina. 'And both of your children will be named on the order as well. If they've seen or heard any violence or if they've been affected in any way by Richard's actions, they have a right to be included. That will mean that your husband won't be able to see them either while the FVIO is in effect.'

Elle glances my way, but our eyes don't connect. I know what she's thinking: she's sheltered the boys from Richard's behaviour. But my boys haven't been protected, they've both been victims of their father's actions, and she knows hers will be too if she doesn't do this, so she remains quiet.

Mina leans back in her chair. 'Richard won't be able to communicate with you or approach you or the children. It's a civil order, but if he breaks it then he's in breach and it becomes a criminal offence, and he can be charged by the police.'

'How long does it stay in effect for?' I ask.

'A minimum of twelve months, on average two years, but I've had cases where a magistrate has agreed to a five-year order with no recourse or appeal. The duration is at the discretion of the magistrate, and in your case it would be reasonable circumstances, in my opinion, for the judge to agree to a lengthier FVIO.'

'So does that mean Richard won't have any access to the kids, even though the parental agreement allows for a few hours a week?' I ask.

'Yes, that's correct. When the FVIO ceases then he will be allowed access.'

It's a lot to take in, and Elle, sitting beside me, is shifting in her chair, crossing and uncrossing her arms and legs.

'Once we issue it with the magistrate's court, you'll need to give a statement to the police via a video interview, so they can make their charges against him.'

Mina has already told me this, but I can almost feel the rolling wave in Elle's stomach, and the nausea that goes with it, as she digests what she has to do.

'The police will serve a copy of the application to the respondent, which is your husband. You both have to then appear in court and, given everything Nora has told me about your husband, there's every chance he might contest the order.'

Elle's face drops and so does mine.

'But we have proof,' says Mina, tapping on the piece of paper with the blood test results. 'And Nora said you have a witness too.' She flicks through her notes. 'Georgie?'

'Yes,' says Elle. 'She found the Endep prescribed to Richard.'

'Georgie also knows in detail what Richard did with regard to their business fraud,' I add. 'She has records of everything.'

'She does? I thought Richard corrected the system,' Elle says to me.

'I asked her to make copies of everything before she came to you.'

Elle's face is full of surprise.

'Your case is pretty watertight. It's very unlikely that a magistrate would deny the order,' says Mina.

It's a relief to hear Mina say that. I need everything to be cemented in place so that Elle doesn't have to ever worry about losing her boys again. 'Mina, if we have proof that Richard is drugging Elle, and proof of the fraud, won't he do jail time?'

'Yes, that's where the criminal offences come into play. Most likely he will be charged on several counts – unlawful assault, and reckless conduct endangering serious injury. Then there's the charge for fraud – obtaining financial advantage by deception. Even if he returned the money, the crime was still committed.'

Elle reaches for her glass of water and takes a sip. Hearing the list of charges is like music to my ears, but I'm sure for Elle it's breaking her heart. A week ago, Richard was the man she was spending the rest of her life with. Even though their marriage was filled with more lows than highs, she was committed to it. To him. And now she's coming to terms with the fact that her husband is capable of a whole list of crimes.

'Remember, the FVIO is a civil action,' says Mina. 'The police will deal with the criminal behaviour.'

I know Elle won't want to hear this, but I need to know. 'How long will he go to jail for?'

Mina crosses her hands in her lap. 'It's likely some of the charges will be whittled down by the defence. It may end up that he's charged on only a couple of counts. In most circumstances, the case will be heard by a judge and jury, and the sentence would be an aggregate of the charges, so somewhere in the vicinity of five to ten years.'

Mina looks to Elle and Elle looks at me, her eyes pooling.

'But if Richard admits guilt, and consents to the case being heard in a magistrate's court,' Mina continues, 'they're limited in sentencing and it would be a maximum of two years.'

'Can he do that?' I ask.

'His lawyer may advise him to, especially if he's committed the crimes.'

Elle's shoulder's slump in what I assume is relief. I know what she must be thinking – that Richard is still the father of her children, and she doesn't want Charlie and Olly to be visiting him in jail. But the alternative, doing nothing, means the boys may lose their mother.

There's still one more item that hasn't been discussed yet. 'What about the divorce?' I ask.

'The best thing right now is to put everything in place to protect Elle and the boys, make sure they're under her care and limit Richard's access to them. The divorce is just a document. With the FVIO, he won't be able to set foot in her home or have contact with Elle or the children.'

Words have never sounded so good to my ears. 'Thank you, Mina. Thank you for everything,' I say.

Elle gets up from the armchair with effort, as though she's carrying a barbell. 'Thank you,' she says to Mina.

Mina stands and comes around to the other side of her desk. 'Call if you need anything. I'll be in touch soon.'

Chapter 36

Elle

Nora walks next to me, moving as if years have been taken off her life, but I feel like I'm carrying the weight of the world. Part of me is filled with relief in knowing I have someone like Mina on my side and that everything will be set in place to safeguard my future. But, even so, the pain is unbearable that this is even happening at all. And it's not just the inexplicable sadness of it, it's compounded by the immeasurable betrayal of my husband, the person closest to me, and the anger surging through my heart at what he's done.

'Isn't she fantastic?' Nora is practically beaming.

'She is. Very professional and efficient.' We're almost at the bus stop. I offered to drive Nora back to the shelter, but she insisted she prefers to take the bus and to walk.

'I knew you'd like her. I wanted to make sure I found someone you'd feel comfortable with, long term.'

'Thank you,' I say, trying to keep my emotions in check. I don't want Nora to think I'm ungrateful for everything she's done. 'I really appreciate you organising this.'

'I'd do anything to make sure you don't lose Charlie and Olly.'

I nod, and when we arrive at the bus stop, from the way she's looking at me, I get the feeling this may be goodbye.

'You're going to be okay,' she says. 'Just remember what a strong, capable woman you are and don't ever let a man walk over you again.'

'I won't.'

'You know my story now and how fragile life can be. It can change in an instant. Make the most of it, Elle.'

'What will happen to you? Where will you go?' I have no idea how this works. Will Nora go back to 2022 or has her life, my future, now completely changed?

'I'm not sure, but I think I'll find out soon enough.'

The bus pulls up and she moves to get on.

'Nora,' I call. 'Thank you for everything. You saved me.'

She smiles at me. 'I saved *us*, Elle.'

She steps onto the bus, but I can't walk away until she's out of sight. She turns around one last time. 'Make him pay,' she calls out.

By the time I get home, I'm exhausted. It's after twelve and Georgie's cleaning up the kitchen from the morning order. Thank goodness there's no sign of Richard.

'Hi! How did it go?' Georgie pulls off her gloves and wraps her arms around me.

'Good. My brain is still processing all the information, but the lawyer was lovely. She said to contact her anytime.'

'I'll make us tea and you can fill me in.'

She goes to put on the kettle and I place my handbag on the bench. 'Richard's not here? I was worried he might be feeling unwell and come home.'

'No, all clear.'

We sit down at the table and I run through everything Mina explained to Nora and me. I'm sure I've forgotten a few things, but Georgie gets the gist. I show her the parental agreement that Mina gave me. 'Now I just have to get him to sign it and this will all be over.'

'Keep it somewhere safe until you do,' says Georgie, taking a sip of tea. 'Put it in your underwear drawer.'

I laugh. 'That's not exactly a great hiding place, George.'

'You have a lock on your bedroom door, so that will help.'

'It's on the inside of the door, so that's no help if I'm not in the room. It's only for a few days, though. I plan on doing this quickly.'

'I'll be relieved when it's all over. I hate keeping secrets from Tye.'

'He wouldn't believe you if you told him. Well, maybe the part about my husband drugging me, but definitely not about Nora,' I say.

'No. That he would not understand,' she says.

'She really is amazing,' I say.

Georgie takes my hand and squeezes it. 'She's amazing because she's you.'

I squeeze her hand back. 'Thank you for being in this with me.'

'Always,' she says. 'But now I do have to go, I have errands to run.'

'Go,' I say, getting up from the table. 'I'll see you tomorrow.'

She kisses my cheek. 'Call if you need anything.'

'I will.'

Georgie lets herself out and I take the papers for the parental agreement upstairs to hide them under Olly's mattress, tucked inside the elastic edge of the mattress protector.

This morning before work, Richard said he was going to go ahead and organise a nanny, but I told him Georgie would help out this afternoon. I don't need her to, of course, but I'll let Richard think she's picked up the boys from school and stayed to babysit us and prepare dinner. I'll have to find Patricia's number on his phone so that when he does organise for her to come, I can cancel. I don't want that woman anywhere near my children.

Richard walks in the front door at seven o'clock, goes straight to the study and emerges several minutes later in fresh pants and a shirt. I notice the colours don't match.

'You just missed Georgie,' I call out from the couch when I hear him in the kitchen. 'The boys are playing upstairs.'

'Where's the Panadol?' he barks. 'I've had a splitting headache all day.'

'Cupboard above the fridge.' I don't get up; I'm meant to be feeling unwell. 'Georgie left you a plate of dinner in the oven.' As if she would, she wouldn't want to feed the man.

'Thanks.'

I pop my head over the couch and he's opening the oven door.

'Ow! Shit!'

He's grabbed the hot plate without an oven mitt.

'What did you do?'

'I burned myself!'

He's wincing like a baby. 'Run it under some water. There's Savlon in the box with the Panadol.' I don't offer to help. He's not my responsibility anymore. 'I think I'll go up, I'm exhausted.' I hold on to the side of the couch as I walk past and do a little wobble as I make my way to the staircase, aware that he's watching me.

'Still dizzy?'

'A little. It comes and goes.' I climb the staircase.

'Tell the boys to go to bed,' he calls out.

'Okay.'

It's not even seven-thirty and I have no intention of telling Charlie and Olly to put themselves to bed. They're playing on the carpet in Olly's room with the train set. I sit down and join them. 'Do you want to stay up late tonight?' I ask them.

Olly's eyes widen as he looks up at me. 'Can we?'

'Yes, but we have to be very, very quiet,' I say. 'Daddy has a headache.' Since Richard relocated to the study, he's only been coming upstairs to put the boys to bed because I haven't been 'well'. Other than that, he uses the downstairs bathroom, which fortunately has a shower. 'Go brush your teeth so you're all ready and then we can play.'

Charlie and Olly go to the bathroom. The tap runs. 'You're messing the toothpaste,' says Charlie. Olly always squeezes too much.

When they come back we play for a little while and then climb into Olly's bed so I can read to them. I lie in the middle and Charlie nestles his head in the crook of one of my arms and Olly in the other. Despite all that is going on in my world right now, this moment is perfect.

I come to the end of the chapter and kiss the boys goodnight. Charlie goes to his bedroom and I tuck Olly into his doona then switch off his bedroom light. 'Sleep well. I love you.'

'Love you too, Mum,' he says.

Charlie is already tucked in when I go into his room. I place my hand on his head and bend to kiss him again. 'Love you.'

'Love you, Mum.'

I think of Nora and everything she went through, being separated from her children for ten years, not being able to do all the little things like kiss them goodnight. Knowing that could be my fate causes an ache in my body. I still don't understand how it happened, but if we pull this off, I'll be thankful for the rest of my life. And I intend to make the most of every minute, for Nora, and for myself.

Chapter 37

Nora

After leaving Elle, I took the bus to Balwyn to see Mum. I didn't mention anything to Elle, but when I said goodbye to her at the bus stop, my entire body was tingling. I'm so relieved when I walk into Mum's room and she's sitting at the table working on a needlepoint.

'Hi, Mum.'

'Elle, darling, it's so good to see you.'

I kiss her cheek and sit down with her, reaching over to touch her hand. It's felt kind of strange being called Elle again. No one has called me that for so many years. In fact, if someone called out that name, I don't think I would even turn around anymore. 'That looks pretty,' I say.

'I used the wrong colour thread here.' She points to a spot.

'I think it makes it look even better,' I say. 'Do you feel up to a little walk?'

'That would be lovely.'

'To the garden or the lounge?'

She smiles at me, her eyebrows raised.

'The garden it is,' I say, going to get her walker from next to the dresser. I slip her shoes on her feet and help her get up. We walk down the hall and the staff who pass by greet her. Mum gives them a smile and says to each one, 'Have you met my daughter, Elle?' Her words are full of so much pride and my heart fills and aches at the same time. I've already had my last moments with Mum five years ago, but then she was lying in bed, frail and withering away, and she didn't know who I was. As much as it hurts, I'm so thankful that this time the last moments I may spend with her are like this, with her knowing who I am and us chatting and walking together in the garden.

'Aren't they beautiful,' she says, stopping at a tree with pink camellias.

She lets go of the walker and I hold her arm so she can get closer to the tree. She reaches for a flower and inhales, either having forgotten that they have no fragrance or what flower it is. Most likely both.

'Do you want me to pick one for you?' I ask.

'No, darling, let it bloom. If we cut it, the flower will die within a week.'

She's right: if we leave the flower on the tree it will live and flourish, at least for a lot longer than it would in a vase. I think back to my younger self, when I was married to Richard. He tried so hard to break me, to stomp down the person I was. He didn't want me to thrive. But now things are changing. I can feel in my body that it's happening already. Soon, Elle will be free to bloom too.

We walk back to Mum's room and she settles at the table. I hug her goodbye and tell her how much I love her. Before I leave, I watch her for a moment from the doorway. She's busy with her needlework. 'Until I see you again, Mum,' I say under my breath.

Back on the bus, I'm feeling weird sensations throughout my body. I don't even know how to describe it, it's like pins and needles, but not like pins and needles, because it doesn't feel uncomfortable. There's a kind of numbness, but not in a heavy way so that I can't move, I just feel very light and floaty.

As soon as I get back to the shelter I go and lie down, but I'm too afraid to close my eyes.

Heather walks past the bedroom and knocks on the open door. 'Are you okay?' she asks.

'Yes, just feeling a little light-headed.'

'Can I get you anything?'

'Actually, would you mind calling a friend of mine? Her number is on my phone. It's in my handbag.' My handbag is on the end of the bed, and I don't want to alarm Heather but I feel like my limbs wouldn't work if I tried to get up, let alone dial a number. My body is as light as a feather. 'Her name is Georgie. It's the only contact on there. Can you please ask her to come and see me as soon as she can?'

Heather puts the phone to her ear, waiting for Georgie to answer. I see Heather's worried face and I know she's concerned but trying to remain calm. 'Hi, Georgie? This is Heather, a friend of Nora's from the shelter ... Yes, she's asking for you ... Okay ... Bye.' Heather puts my phone on my bed. 'She's on her way. She said to tell you to wait for her.' Heather looks down at me, frowning. 'Is everything okay?'

'Yes, I'm okay.' I smile at Heather; I don't want to worry her. I know this Heather has only known me for a little while, but even in that short amount of time, we've become friends.

'Is there something I can do?' she asks.

'Just stay with me until she comes?'

'Of course I will,' she says, sitting next to me on the bed.

'You've been such a good friend to me,' I say. And she has – Heather's been a wonderful friend since I arrived at the shelter the first time around, and this time too. I think of her doing my make-up for me when I went to visit Georgie, then dressing me in her clothes so I'd look nice for Elle. I can't imagine that Elle's path will cross with Heather's in the years to come. I'm certain our friendship has come to an end, but that doesn't mean it wasn't worth it for the ten years it existed.

'I've enjoyed your company,' says Heather. 'It's rare to find someone who you get on with like you've been friends forever.'

'It is.' If I could move my hand to squeeze hers I would. She sits with me until a very puffed Georgie arrives at the bedroom door.

'Nora ...' Georgie's face is flushed, as though she's run a marathon to get here.

Heather gets up. 'I better get back to work.' Her hand lightly touches mine. 'I'll see you later.'

'See you,' I say.

Heather closes the door behind her and Georgie falls to her knees beside my bed, her hands gripping my arm.

'Are you okay?' she asks. 'What's happening?'

'Elle's changing her future.'

Tears flood Georgie's eyes: she understands what this means for me. 'I'm going to miss you,' she says.

'I'll miss you too. Can you write a note for me?' I know she keeps a notebook and pen in her handbag.

'Sure. Who's it to?' She opens her handbag and digs around.

'The staff here.'

Perching herself on the edge of the bed, she crosses one leg over the other and leans there to write. 'What do you want to say?'

'Dear Heather, Mary and Sheena, I can't thank you all enough for taking me in, giving me a place to call home. You've helped me get back on my feet, and now it's time for me to move on. Love, Nora.'

'Done,' says Georgie. She rips the sheet from the notebook. 'Where shall I leave it?'

'On the end of the bed. Will you take the phone with you? I'm not going to need it anymore.'

'Of course.' She places the mobile phone in her handbag.

'And there's a box in the cupboard, top shelf.'

Georgie opens the cupboard and holds up the domino box. 'This?'

'Yes.' I've already returned all the contents to the box. They belong to Elle. 'Can you give it to Elle for me?'

Georgie looks at it oddly. 'What is it?'

'She'll know. Georgie ...?'

'Tell me, what can I do?'

'You've done so much already. Just believing in me and believing in Elle is changing her future.' I look into her beautiful eyes and smile. 'You've changed my past and now Elle won't have to know what it's like to be without a home. She won't lose everything in her life, she won't lose you.'

'I don't want you to leave.' Georgie wipes a tear from her cheek and takes my hand in hers. I can barely feel it.

'I'm not leaving you, George. You'll see me tomorrow.'

'I know,' she says, sniffing. 'I know you're Elle, but you're different in so many ways that I forget you're the same person.'

'We are the same person – our heart is the same, and the friendship you have with me is based on the foundation you have with Elle. Never let her go.'

'I won't. I promise you I'll look after her.'

'I know you will.'

'And you don't have to worry about Richard. I know everything I have to do.'

She does. Her love for Elle is fierce and I can leave this world with the comfort that Georgie will protect her.

'I love you, Georgie.'

'I love you too,' she says, bending to kiss my forehead.

'I'll see you tomorrow,' I say, smiling at her.

'See you tomorrow.'

I watch her leave and then I close my eyes and let go.

Chapter 38

Elle

I'm in the kitchen finishing the boys' lunches when Richard comes to the bench to make our smoothies.

'You look better today,' he says, surprised.

'I'm a little dizzy, but I think I'm getting used to managing with it.'

'The nanny's picking up the boys from school today.'

I clear my throat. 'Okay. I'll text you later though if I feel up to it.'

Richard's hand hovers over the blender button. 'Would you stop putting off the inevitable? You need help, Elle. There's something wrong with you and you're not managing looking after the boys. It's not just the dizziness, you've been confused.'

'Have I?' I'm almost looking forward to hearing what possible lie he's going to spin.

'The school phoned me yesterday – they said there was a nut bar in Charlie's lunchbox. You know there's a kid in his class who's anaphylactic. We're lucky the teacher found it before he opened it.'

I do buy nut bars for the kids to eat at home, but there's no way I put one in Charlie's lunchbox. And, anyway, Charlie is rigid when it comes to his lunchbox; he likes the same food in it each day. There's also the fact that if there's an issue at school, I'm the one they contact, never Richard. But I play along. 'That's awful. I'll email his teacher to apologise later.'

'No need. I've taken care of it. But you do need to be more careful, Elle. You're not yourself.'

Of course he'd say the issue is resolved. He wouldn't want me emailing the school only to discover that he made it all up.

'I'm going to the doctor later, hopefully he'll work out what's wrong,' I say.

'Good,' he says, switching on the blender.

I go upstairs to Olly's room so Richard can spike my smoothie without me watching.

Last night I scaled Olly's drawers like Spiderman and put his school jumper on a high shelf that I can't reach from the ground. 'Where's your school jumper?' I ask him now, searching his room. I open his cupboard. 'There it is. Can you call Dad? I can't reach it.'

Olly runs to the top of the stairs. 'Dad, I can't reach my jumper,' he yells.

I pass Richard on the staircase and hold on to the banister. 'Sorry, it was up high and I didn't think it was safe to climb with the dizziness.' I have to say that since I came home from visiting the lawyer yesterday with Nora, I feel a newfound confidence. I have my team and I'm not alone in this. But the next part of the plan depends on me.

Richard's smoothie is sitting on the kitchen table next to the open newspaper. I can see he's had at least a sip because some of the thick, dark green mixture runs along the top of the inside of the glass. I grab my smoothie from the bench and tip a little in the sink so it runs down one side of the glass too, then swap it with his. I wipe the rim of Richard's glass with a tissue and place it in the fridge. Richard comes back downstairs and sits at the table. He picks up his glass and my hands clutch the kitchen bench, my body tense as I watch him drink it. My heart is pounding, I can't wait for this to all be over. But I have to admit, it's kind of thrilling to watch him unknowingly drug himself.

Richard empties the glass and licks his lips. 'I'll take the boys to school,' he says, pushing back his chair. He walks down the hallway and closes the bathroom door. I wait until I hear the shower running and then pick up his glass and place it in a resealable storage bag. When the idea to test the smoothie glass came to me, I contacted Mina straight away to find out if it was possible. She spoke to the police and they've organised for it to be tested with a forensic laboratory. Mina said that the more evidence we have, the stronger our case will be. I can't wait to tell Nora. I think she'll be impressed.

The boys are brushing their teeth when I go upstairs. 'Quickly, let's get ready. Georgie will be here in a minute to take you to school,' I say. I don't want Richard driving them to school with a double dose of Endep in his system.

'How come Georgie's taking us?' asks Charlie.

'Dad and I have a meeting,' I say.

'Is it for the divorce?' he asks.

'Yes, just to plan a few things. Everything's okay, though.' We sat the boys down on Sunday and explained the new living arrangements as simply and gently as possible. Olly didn't seem too fussed, but Charlie has been questioning things the last few days. I'm trying my best to put his mind at ease, but it's a difficult age to have your parents divorcing. Richard wanted to discuss with the boys that we're getting a nanny, but I've asked him to hold off for the moment. I hope I can stall that happening for a couple more days. I may have to get inventive.

'Come on, let's go,' I say, taking Olly's hand as we run down the stairs and to the front door. The boys pick up their schoolbags next to the entrance table just as I hear the downstairs shower turn off. I'm relieved to see Georgie's car waiting in the driveway. She climbs out and bundles the boys into the back seat.

'I'll see you later,' she mouths, knowing Richard is lurking somewhere in our house.

I close the front door and, on my way down the hall, knock on the bathroom door. 'Richard, Georgie called to offer to take the boys to school on her way.'

The door opens and Richard stands with a maroon towel wrapped around his waist, his hair wet. 'What? I said I'd take them.'

'I thought it would be easier for you, so you won't be late for work.'

His eyes are cold as he stares at me. He shakes his head then slams the bathroom door.

I'm relieved, I was expecting worse.

I make my way upstairs, and after showering, I dress in jeans, a shirt and a cardigan. As much as I love wearing make-up, I don't put any on. I can't be looking too well when Richard comes home.

Yesterday I went to our local pharmacy to see if they had a repeat script for Richard's medication on file. Nora's idea, of course. She said Richard drugged her for almost six weeks so there must have been repeats on his prescription. She was right, and I purchased another packet so he wouldn't notice any tablets missing from his box. I've hidden the medication in the pill box in my bathroom drawer. I'm going to add a dose to his dinner tonight on top of whatever he took this morning that was intended for me. His prescription says to take one tablet twice a day, so I figure that's what he gave me the week before Daylesford. From what Nora told me, her symptoms worsened when they returned, so I assume he increased that dose for me last week. It had the desired effect on my body size, but Richard's a lot bigger than me so he can probably handle more. Nora suggested adding an extra dose in his evening meal. Killing him won't help me, so I double-checked with Doctor Google just to make sure.

I remove two tablets and head back downstairs. In the kitchen I place them in a small resealable bag, release the air and crush them with a meat mallet into a fine powder. Then I place the bag in the inside zipped pocket of my handbag.

I wash my hands and take out the pantry ingredients for today's menu, setting up the chopping boards and mixing bowls. Georgie was doing the fresh produce shop for me. We're making caramelised leek and mushroom tarts, pumpkin and goat's cheese mini frittatas, individual salad wraps and a beetroot, walnut, feta and rocket salad. For dessert it's fruit skewers, and chocolate and pecan brownies.

The front door opens. 'I'm here!' calls out Georgie.

'Hi,' I say, going to help her carry the shopping.

'How did you go this morning?' she asks.

'Good, he drank it all up.' I go to the fridge and take out the other smoothie. 'But I will throw this out just in case. I'm going to drop his glass to the police station after we finish. They're having it tested. The more evidence we have, the better.'

'Clever,' she says. 'Before we start, can we sit for a minute?' Her face looks serious.

'Is everything okay?' I ask.

She places her handbag on the kitchen table and pulls out a chair. I sit down next to her.

'It's about Nora,' she says.

'Is she okay?' I ask, already knowing the answer. We've already changed so much of Nora's past, which I hope means I'm changing my future. But it suddenly hits me what that means for Nora.

'She's gone, Elle.'

Emotion builds inside me. I can feel my eyes brimming with tears. 'I'm being ridiculous, aren't I?'

'It's fine to be sad,' says Georgie. 'I was sad too.'

'This feels so weird – I'm crying like I've lost her, but she was me.'

'It's okay. I get it. I feel the same,' says Georgie. She pulls a box from her handbag. 'She asked me to give you this.'

My mouth drops open. 'The time capsule.'

'I assumed so, but I wasn't sure.'

My fingers glide over the lid of the domino box.

'I'll start prepping,' says Georgie, going to the kitchen to give me some time.

I slide off the lid and empty the contents onto the table. We only made this in the last summer holidays, so I know what's in there. My idea was to open this with the boys in ten years' time. They wrote the letters to their future selves, so I don't want to read them and invade their privacy. I already know what I wrote in my letter to myself. I decide to just put everything back in the box, but when I pick up the folded papers, I notice there are four instead of three. My heart races in my chest. The boys have drawn pictures on their folded notes, so I put them back in the domino box. There are two left, both in my handwriting. One I recognise from January, although the paper is now creased. The other is new, from Nora.

My hands trace the familiar writing on top of the note. It says, 'For Elle, to be read in 2022.' I immediately feel there's no way I can wait ten years to read this note – it's the only thing I have left from her. But Nora has requested that I do, and I assume there's a reason for it. I place both my letter and Nora's in the box and put the lid on. 'I'll be back in a sec,' I say to Georgie, who's busy cooking in the kitchen.

In my bedroom I empty a shoebox of its wedge heels and wrap the domino box with the tissue paper the shoes were in. I push the armchair from the corner of the room to the cupboard to stand on, pull some jumpers from a high shelf and push the shoebox to the back, then fold the jumpers and stick them back in front of the box. I have no idea how I'll be able to go to sleep at night knowing it's there, a letter from my future self. When I think about it, it's really the reverse of my letter, although both are to be read at the same time. I close the cupboard, a sense of contentment washing over me.

That moment of peace changes when I get downstairs and see Richard sitting at the kitchen table.

'What are you doing home?' I ask, heading to the kitchen. I put my Notch apron on and start slicing the mushrooms.

'I was feeling nauseous.'

'Oh, that's not good. Do you think it's a stomach bug?'

I look anywhere but at Richard, and Georgie keeps her head down, whisking eggs. I can feel him watching us.

'It's not a stomach bug,' he growls.

I lift my head and look directly at him. 'Okay, it's just that we're cooking for other people. Just in case, do you mind staying in the study?'

If looks could kill, I'd be dead, but he gets up and heads to the study.

'I'll bring you a chamomile tea later,' I call out after him.

The door slams. Georgie and I stop chopping and look at each other. We both let out a snort of laughter. 'Shh, he might hear us,' I say, so we giggle quietly. I don't know why we're laughing, there's really nothing funny about the situation. I'm drugging my husband, and Georgie is my accomplice. I guess it's all the nervous energy releasing. So much has happened these last few weeks. My life has been like a roller-coaster and I can't wait for the ride to come to a stop.

I wait until the cooking is done and we're washing dishes to make Richard a chamomile tea.

'Let me take it to him,' says Georgie. 'I'll say you weren't feeling well and have gone to lie down.'

'Should I put the Endep in now? I was going to make a mine-strone soup and put it in that later.'

'Maybe wait in case it has a taste. The tea's practically water.'

'But he's organised Patricia to pick up the kids from school.'

'Leave it to me.'

I watch her walk down the hall, holding the mug. She turns back to look at me then knocks on the door. 'Richard, it's Georgie. Can I come in?'

'Yes,' he barks.

'I made you a tea. Elle's gone to lie down, she said her head was spinning. I'll pick the boys up from school for you.'

'No need. I've organised a nanny to do it.'

'I insist. It's on my way to get my kids. I'll bring them back and help Elle with dinner. You just rest and feel better.' She steps out of the room before he can speak and says, 'Holler if you need anything.'

Later that evening, I take Richard a steaming bowl of minestrone soup for dinner. I suggest he stay in the study so the boys don't catch whatever bug he has. When I go in to collect his dishes half an hour later, he's out cold on the study couch, snoring. His phone is on his desk, his laptop open. Now's my chance. I slide his phone into my back pocket, pick up the dishes and go back to the kitchen. The boys are watching television on the couch.

I'm not sure where I've seen this – maybe on a television crime show or something – but I hold Richard's mobile phone so that it's facing towards the light and lying flat in my palm. I turn it on and, when it directs me to enter a password, I see fingertip marks over the numbers two, three, six and nine. I try a few combinations of these and, on the third, it opens. I'm officially a sleuth.

I know he's out cold, but regardless, adrenaline courses through my body. I find Patricia's number in Richard's contacts and write it in the notes on my phone, along with his password. When I open the study door, he's still snoring. I return his phone to the desk and join my boys on the couch. At least I don't have to put on an act for the rest of the evening.

Chapter 39

Elle

Richard's asleep when I take the boys to school the next morning. I made his smoothie for him and left it on the bench and when I return home, the empty glass is in the sink. The downstairs shower is running, so I make myself a coffee and one for Richard. I make his stronger than usual, just in case he detects a taste, but I doubt he will. His morning coffee is the only time he allows himself sugar, and he drinks it with milk. Today, I'm not going to bother spreading the dosages out over the day, he can have the other dose now. I crush the tablets and add the powder, letting it dissolve in the boiling water before adding the milk. I leave it on his desk for him and wait.

I'm not sure what to do with myself. I check and recheck the time, listening out for sounds of movement. My mind has been consumed with everything I have to do, and I can't think or concentrate on anything else, even work. I know how important today is for my future. Everything comes down to this.

I've been having the same nightmare every night. I'm asleep on the concrete footpath outside our home, curled up in a foetal position, trying to keep warm, and I wake to a large faceless figure looming over me. My hand reaches up to touch the figure, hoping for help, but when I do, the figure turns to dust, particles descending to the ground in a heap, until all that remains is a pile of grey dust on the footpath. Then I wake in a cold sweat, my heart pounding.

My heart's pounding now, too, knowing I've given Richard such a large quantity of Endep in one go. Hopefully he won't keel over and die. As much as I don't want him in my life, he's Charlie and Olly's dad. And if I end up in jail for murder, not only will my boys have no parents to care for them, but I'll be letting Nora down as well. And myself.

I panic when I hear footsteps coming down the hallway. I open the drawer and take out a frying pan and saucepan and place them over the stove, pretending not to notice his presence, although my whole body stiffens.

Richard places the empty coffee glass in the kitchen sink. 'Can you book me an eye doctor appointment?' he asks.

It's only then that I look at him. His eyes are glassy. I assume his vision is either blurred, like mine was the other week, or he's seeing double, which is one of the possible side effects that I read in the packet information sheet.

'I'm not your wife anymore, remember?' I say, placing a chopping board on the bench, and grabbing knives and utensils from the drawer.

'Fine, just text me the number,' he scoffs, filling a glass of water and drinking the lot.

I can probably add dry mouth to the list of symptoms Richard's experiencing, because he rarely drinks water. I check my watch: the medication should kick in sometime in the next hour.

Richard stands there staring at me. 'You're looking well,' he says.

I swallow. 'I'm feeling a bit better, thanks.' He must know that with the amount he's giving me, I should be practically catatonic.

He turns to leave and then comes back and looks at me again for what feels like an eternity. My whole body freezes.

'It's strange that you're so much better and now I haven't been feeling well.'

'Maybe you have the same virus. I must be at the end of it.'

His eyes bore into mine. 'Are you doing this?'

'Doing what?'

He hesitates. He can't come right out and ask if I'm drugging him because it would be admitting that he's been drugging me. I pick up the olive oil and drizzle it in the pan.

Suddenly he grabs my arm forcefully.

I look down at his hand. 'Let. Go.'

Richard releases my arm and walks off to the study.

I let out my breath. He knows. I'm sure of it.

The front door opens and Georgie calls out, 'Sorry I'm late, the traffic was crazy.'

I rush down the hall to warn her that Richard is home at the same time that his study door flies open. I make it to the front door just in time to see a wobbly Richard point his finger at Georgie.

'How did you get in here?' he screams. Aggression was also listed in the extensive list of possible side effects, though I'm not sure it counts if it's a pre-existing condition. 'You didn't ring the bell.'

'Ah ...' Georgie looks over at me.

Normally she's handy with a quick response, but we're both out of our league with what's happening in my life right now.

This is my responsibility, so I step in to take the attention away from her. 'I gave her a key last week so she could let herself in with the boys if I couldn't get up.'

Richard looks from me to Georgie like we're conspiring, which of course we are, but my explanation sounds totally reasonable to my ears.

He holds out his hand. 'You won't be needing it anymore. Pa ... The nanny will pick them up from now on.'

Georgie hands him the key and he closes the study door with a bang.

I link my arm through Georgie's. She's visibly shaken.

'I think he might be on to us,' I murmur.

'That's impossible,' says Georgie. 'If it weren't for Nora, you'd have no idea about the drugs.'

'I know, but he realises I'm not as sick as I should be. Maybe he thinks I just came up with the same idea as him.'

'To drug him and have him committed? Elle, there's no way.'

'I've just got this awful feeling.'

'The awful feeling is Richard.'

She's probably right. I'm beyond anxious now and completely on alert. I'm probably just being paranoid.

'I can't believe you've had to live with that for all these years,' says Georgie.

My lips draw into a thin line. I never really thought there was another possibility until I met Nora. I made a commitment and I had two children to think about; leaving never seemed an option. I make us tea and put on some music to calm my racing heart while we work.

'You know, at first I didn't believe her,' I say.

'Who, Nora?'

I nod. 'I know Richard's far from the perfect husband, but I couldn't wrap my head around the fact that the person I shared my life with could do all the things she said he would.'

Nora said Richard had even shown her a self-inflicted knife wound that he'd blamed on her, but for all we know he could have bought a fake scar from a costume shop and stuck it on his stomach. And the physical abuse that he said happened the day she left, I'm doubtful of whether he really harmed himself then too. Nora didn't actually see the police evidence of bruises on Richard's body, she just believed what he said because she was so fragile and living in fear at the time. Learning everything that Richard was capable of, it wouldn't surprise me if he made up that part to keep her away from the boys. He probably falsified the doctor's referral to the hospital too. It breaks my heart to think she spent all those years without Charlie and Olly, especially when Richard's threats were most likely just lies.

Georgie grimaces. 'And now?'

'Now I can imagine him doing every bit of it.'

She puts down her knife and hugs me. 'I'm so sorry, Elle.'

'Me too.' I wipe a tear from my cheek. 'I guess I'm one of the lucky ones.'

'How so?' she asks.

'The women we met at the cooking workshop at the shelters, they don't get a redo.' Those women were so brave, leaving volatile situations to save themselves and their children. Nora did that too, and I understand, because she is me, that things must have been dire for her to get to the point where she left her children behind.

Richard must have pushed her beyond limits. She had no choice but to leave to save herself.

'You're right, but maybe we can help in some way to make their future a little brighter.'

I hope we can too, and from now on I won't need permission from Richard or anyone else to do it.

We wait an hour for the Endep to fully kick in before Georgie goes out the back door and down the side gate to ring the front doorbell.

'Coming,' I call out. I open the front door. 'Oh, hello,' I say to the empty air. I glance behind me and Georgie is already returning inside through the back door. 'He's resting, but I'll make sure he signs it when he's awake. I'll call you when it's ready to be picked up. Thanks, Kyla.' I close the front door and knock on the study door. Richard is asleep on the couch, drool seeping from the corner of his mouth.

'Richard.' I shake his shoulder.

He groans, his eyes half open as he tries to focus on my face.

'Kyla dropped off these papers to be signed.' I look for a pen on his desk then grab a book from the shelf to rest the papers on. I want Richard's signature to be as clear as possible.

He lifts his head, but I can see he's having trouble focusing. He has to sign both pages of the order as well as another section. I hold the pen out for him and he takes it as I point to the first spot. His hand is shaky but he signs it. The signature is half decent. I want to pound the air in victory, but I'm not done yet; there's two more signatures to go. He signs the next page and then drops his head back onto the cushion.

'Last signature,' I say. I notice that my hand is slightly shaky too, and my insides are racing. He holds out his hand and I guide the pen to the paper for him. 'All done. I'll call Kyla to pick them up.'

'Mm,' he mutters and closes his eyes.

I grab his phone on the way out.

I wave the papers in front of Georgie as though I'm holding a prize, and I am. 'It's done. It's all over.' Well, almost. He's still here.

'Well done,' she says. 'Who knew we were so devious.'

'Richard's a good teacher. I'm going to put these in a safe place.' I'm lost for new places to hide things so I take a leaf from Georgie's book and bury them in my underwear drawer. It's only until this afternoon. I'm delivering the papers to Mina's office after Sarah picks up the delivery.

Mina has issued the family violence intervention order and the police will serve Richard with a copy of the application tomorrow. She's also sent them my blood test results and they're waiting on the results from the smoothie sample, but I know it will show traces of Endep.

After I hide the papers, I remember I have one more thing to do. I pull Richard's phone from my back pocket and put the passcode in. A stream of unanswered texts pop up from Patricia, asking if everything's okay and to call her. There are also several missed phone calls from her. I type out a reply that all is well and that he'll pick up the boys from school today. I even add a heart emoji. Who knew Richard could be so sweet.

I turn off his phone, sit on my bed and take a moment, gathering my thoughts. I have full custody of Charlie and Olly, I have a roof over my head, I have Georgie in my life and I have my business. I'm not going to live the life Nora did. I feel like one very lucky woman right now, and I have Nora to thank for it. She did it. I did it too. And so did Georgie.

Chapter 40

Elle

I refrain from drugging Richard the next morning. As much as he deserves it, if I do then he won't be able to converse with the police when they arrive. I also want to see the look on his face as it all sinks in.

For the first time in years, Georgie rings the doorbell when she arrives. After I let her in, I hear movement in the study.

'How are you feeling?' whispers Georgie when we're in the kitchen.

I hold out my trembling hand. 'My whole body feels like this.'

Her face is full of empathy. We both go quiet at the sound of footsteps coming down the hall. The bathroom door closes and the shower runs. I put on some music and turn up the volume.

'George, do you think I'm doing the right thing? Maybe I've gone too far with the intervention order and getting the police involved.'

She takes both my trembling hands in hers. 'Elle, it's just nerves.'

'But maybe it was enough just getting the parental agreement in place.'

'You know he would have hired expensive lawyers to contest it. Listen to me: Richard was drugging you, he committed fraud and stole from our business. They're criminal offences, he deserves to be punished.'

'I'm just worried about the boys. They won't have a father.' I turn away, tears pooling in my eyes.

'Elle, look at me.'

I look into her consoling eyes.

'You know what Richard has planned for you. He intends to lock you away in a mental institution for the rest of your life.'

'I know, but ... It's just not me, all this,' I say.

'Of course it's not, because you're a good person. But trust me, Richard is getting off lightly compared to what he did to Nora. He deserves every bit of what's coming. If you don't follow through, he's going to find another way to take the boys from you. You'll never see Charlie and Olly again. He will never stop, and those precious boys won't have a mother.'

I take a breath and collect myself. I know she's one hundred percent right. Richard is the kind of person who will do whatever it takes to get what he wants. The truth is, I already knew this before I met Nora, I just didn't know the lengths he would go to.

'Look, I get that you're having cold feet, but you're not alone in this. I'm with you every step of the way,' says Georgie. 'And I know that Nora isn't physically here, but she's still here.' Her hand touches my heart. 'She lives in you, Elle. Her journey may have taken a different turn to yours, but you're still the same person with the same heart and soul. So when the police come, just think of Nora, that you're saving her from the fork in the road that changed her life forever. You're saving yourself from heading down that same path.'

'Thank you,' I say, hugging her. 'I needed to hear that.' I have no choice but to follow through with Nora's plan. She came into my life to save me from my future and I have to believe that my destiny can be changed. At the very least, I have to try. Nora was concerned that our lives are predetermined, and that whatever we do now may not change where I end up, that I might just arrive there in a different way. But I'm sure that every decision and action I take can lead to a different outcome. I may make the wrong decisions at times and diverge from my path, but if I'm aware I've taken a wrong turn, I believe I can find my way back. I can keep trying to make the most of this one life I have.

Georgie squeezes me tight.

The bathroom door opens and we keep holding on to each other until we hear the study door close.

'I guess I should make him his last smoothie.' I fill the blender with ingredients and switch it on. I remove the lid and look at the thick, dark green liquid. 'It really is hideous.' I pour it into a glass and walk down the hallway.

I knock on the study door. 'Can I come in?' I open the door enough to see that Richard is sitting behind his desk. His face is pale, and as I move towards him I can see that his eyes are dilated. 'Are you feeling better?' I ask, placing the smoothie on his desk.

'I know what you're up to,' he says.

I scrunch my eyebrows, feigning ignorance. 'I don't know what you're talking about.'

'You think you're smart, but you have no idea who you're up against.' He makes a fist and lifts his hand to hit the desk but misses. He looks down at his hand then moves it to rub his temples.

'Do you still have a headache?'

'Stop acting innocent. I know you've been drugging my smoothie.'

'Richard, you're being paranoid. Where would I get such a crazy idea? Not to mention I don't mix with drug dealers.'

He scoffs. 'Drink it then.'

I pick up the glass. 'I've always hated your smoothies, Richard. If there's one good thing to come out of our separation it's not having to drink this awful thing.' I smell it and turn up my nose. 'But to prove you wrong ...' I take several sips then put the glass back on the table. 'See, it's just a smoothie. Maybe you should have a rest. You really haven't been yourself lately.'

Richard stands. 'You're nothing, Elle. Nothing without me!' He picks up the smoothie and throws it against the wall.

'Richard!' I scream. Glass shatters everywhere, and the thick smoothie covers the wall and carpet like green mud.

Georgie runs into the study. She takes in the mess. 'What's going on?'

'Richard has gone insane,' I say.

'The only crazy person here is you! You can lie until your blue in the face, but I'll find those drugs.' He storms out of the room.

We follow him down the hallway and up to my bedroom. I stand at the door, and Georgie's arm secures itself around my waist. Richard is in the bathroom, opening drawers and banging them closed. My heart vibrates in my chest. He comes out and opens the bedroom closet, pulling my jumpers from the shelves, tossing them on the carpet.

'Where is it, you bitch?' he screams, his face flushed. He opens my drawers, rummaging through my underwear. Thank goodness I dropped the parental agreement to Mina's office yesterday. He comes up empty-handed, and huffs back to the bathroom.

The sound of the doorbell fills me with relief. Georgie and I glance at each other. I nod and she runs downstairs to answer it.

I go to the top of the stairs to listen. 'Is there a Mr Richard Harrison here?'

'Yes, please come in. I'm Georgie, Mrs Harrison's friend.'

Richard storms out of the bedroom holding up the packet of Endep in his hand. 'This! This is what you've been drugging me with.'

He holds it in front of my face and I take it from his hand. I placed the packet of Endep that I purchased in Richard's drawer last night. I assume he has the packet he was drugging me with because it wasn't there anymore.

I lean forward to take a closer inspection of the packet, like I have no idea what it is. 'This medication is prescribed to you. I didn't know you were taking anything.'

He stares at me, then at the packet, confused.

'Why would I drug you with a medication you're already taking? It doesn't make sense.'

'Elle, Richard,' Georgie calls out. 'Can you come down? There are people here to see you.'

Richard pushes me out of the way and holds the banister as he runs down the stairs, tripping on the way. 'Fuck,' he mutters.

I wish I'd gone ahead of him so I could see his face, but the look on Georgie's when I get to the bottom of the stairs is enough. Her eyes connect with mine and her lips purse. Two police officers are standing next to her.

'Are you Mr Richard Harrison?' the older female police officer asks Richard. The younger male officer moves to stand next to me.

'Yes,' says Richard. 'What's this about?' He stuffs the Endep packet in the pocket of his pants.

The officer hands Richard some papers. 'You've been issued with a family violence intervention order,' she says. Despite the fact that she's about a foot shorter than Richard, her stature is grand. She has that 'don't mess with me' look about her.

Richard turns to me, his face crimson. He looks aghast. In fact, I think his eyes might pop from their sockets.

Instinctively I move closer to the police officer standing next to me, and the police officer closes the gap too.

'The court date has been set for next week, but until then you're not to be in contact with your wife or children,' she says.

Richard gathers himself. 'Look, Officer, there must be some kind of mistake. My wife hasn't been well recently, she's not herself. You see, we separated and she's not coping.' He hands the forms back to the police officer. 'This won't be necessary.'

'It's already been issued, Mr Harrison,' says the officer.

'Well, unissue it!' he yells.

Georgie, standing next to the kitchen bench behind the officer, flinches.

'We'd like to take you down to the station for questioning,' continues the officer.

'I'm calling my lawyer. He'll straighten this out,' says Richard, turning to go to the study.

The police officer shifts to place her hand in front of Richard, barely centimetres from his chest, while her other hand rests on her gun in the side of her belt. The younger officer moves to stand behind Richard.

'I'd hoped to do this the calm way.' She nods to the younger officer, who moves to pull Richard's arms behind his back. 'Mr Harrison, you are being charged with inflicting bodily harm and with fraud. You have the right to remain silent, to speak to a relative or a lawyer, and to have an interpreter if required. Anything you say or do can be used in a court of law.'

I walk over to Georgie, my heart thumping. She pulls me in next to her as we watch this play out.

'This is outrageous. I've never laid a finger on her.'

'Mr Harrison, we have evidence that you've been drugging your wife.'

Richard glares at me. 'You bitch! You did this!'

I let go of Georgie and gather every ounce of strength in me as I take a few steps towards Richard so I'm right in front of his face. 'No, Richard, you did this. It was all you.'

The police escort him out the door and I watch as they drive him away and out of my life. I close the front door and lean back against it, my legs weak. As I slide to the ground, long breaths of relief escape me.

Georgie sits down on the floor next to me, her arm wrapped around my shoulder and legs stretched out in front. 'He can't hurt you now,' she says, planting a kiss on the side of my head. 'It's over.'

'It's over,' I repeat.

The last couple of weeks have been a whirlwind: meeting Nora, everything I discovered, everything I then had to do, building momentum like a crescendo until I reached this pivotal moment. The relief that it's finally done is utterly overwhelming. I feel like the shackles have been removed and I'm free. Free to live my life.

Epilogue

Elle 2022

'**W**elcome, everybody, and thank you so much for coming today. My name is Elle Plankett and this is Georgie Roberts.'

I'm standing behind a podium in front of eighty guests, Georgie by my side. The ten rectangular tables that fill the hall have each been set with cooking utensils and bowls, fresh produce and pantry items. Eight guests stand around each table with aprons on.

For the last ten years, Georgie and I have been running intimate cooking workshops at women's shelters in Melbourne. We've also had other chefs and home cooks volunteer their time to run them so that we could expand our reach. But today the women standing before us aren't in crisis; they're safe and have a home. Today we're holding the fundraiser we run every year on the Sunday before Mother's Day to build awareness, as well as funds, for our program at the shelters. What better way to share what we do with people than for them to experience firsthand how the program works?

'Before we start cooking,' I say, 'I'd like to tell you a story about a woman who one moment was living her life to the fullest and the next found herself homeless. Her name was Nora, and she was one of the bravest people I've ever met.'

Since we began these fundraising events to expand our program, I've been retelling Nora's story, the story of a woman who lost her whole world and then through utter determination and will reclaimed it. Because the fact is, even if Nora hadn't been able to change her past, she was set on changing her future, and I'll forever be inspired by her.

'If it weren't for a few kind helping hands and the safety of a shelter for women,' I continue, 'Nora's life may have turned out differently.'

I look over at the table in the back corner where Charlie and Olly stand with Tye, Holly and Max. They're joined by Heather, Mary and Sheena from the shelter in North Melbourne that became a home to Nora. Olly gives me a thumbs up and I can't help but smile. My boys only know Nora as my cousin from Adelaide.

After the divorce came through, I changed my surname back to my maiden name. As Mina predicted, Richard consented to being tried in a magistrate's court and he received the maximum sentence of two years. They were two very blissful years.

But it is wonderful to know that even with Richard not behind bars, I can still live my life and we can co-exist. When he was released from jail, he contested the parental agreement in a civil proceeding, but it was declined. As stipulated, he's allowed to spend three supervised hours per week with the boys. In the beginning it was in the company of a social worker, but these days Tye takes on that role so spending time with their father can feel more normal for Charlie and Olly.

Georgie takes the microphone and instructs the guests, step by step, how to make the first dish. I move around the tables assisting and chatting with everyone about our volunteer program. Many of our volunteers have come from these fundraisers. At the end of the session, the women share the meal they've made, and the room is filled with noise and love.

Back home, the boys help me unload the car, carrying in boxes of dirty bowls and utensils as well as leftover staples that we can use for the workshops at the shelters.

'I'm going to get changed before I start cleaning.' I walk to my bedroom at the front of the house opposite the lounge room.

A year after the divorce, I sold the house I shared with Richard. Everything about it was filled with memories of him. We downsized to a one-storey Edwardian with a nice-sized garden for two growing boys. I slip out of my shoes, remove my black pants and shirt, and put on jeans and a sweater. I rummage through my shoeboxes until I find the one I'm looking for. I unwrap the tissue paper and take out the domino box, the time capsule we made ten years ago. Technically we should have opened it in January, but it felt more fitting to wait until now because it's ten years since Nora added her note to our treasure.

I put on my slippers and take the box to the kitchen table. The boys are sitting on the couch playing a video game.

'Boys, come here for a minute. I want to show you something.'

Charlie and Olly join me at the table. 'Do you remember the summer we made this? You were eight,' I say to Charlie, 'and you were five, Olly.' They were so little then, and now my boys tower over me.

'I remember this,' says Charlie, turning the domino box over in his hands and looking at the drawings. 'How did you get it? We buried it in the backyard at our old place.'

'I dug it up before we left.' Technically it's true. 'We said we'd open it in ten years' time and it's ten years now.'

Charlie slides off the lid and tips out the contents.

'My Bob the Builder,' says Olly, reaching for the figurine.

'You both made me the bracelet for Mother's Day.'

I slide it onto my wrist then pick up the letters and give Charlie and Olly theirs to read. I take the other two letters and first read the one I wrote to myself that summer. Then I pick up the letter that Nora wrote to me in a time where we both existed and hold it for a moment. I take a breath and unfold the page.

My dearest Elle,

I hope when you read this letter that you're living where you're meant to be, with your children, and I hope that you are fulfilling your dreams and have expanded the business with Georgie. I don't know what kind of strange magic or higher power allowed me to alter our fate, but I know in my heart that you will be making the most of this second chance we've been given.

Love Nora

I fold up her letter and place it in my pocket, my heart swells. Together we changed our destiny.

The boys go back to their video game, and I get up from the table and head to the pile of dishes they've stacked beside the sink. 'Tacos for dinner?' I call out.

Recipes

Georgie's duck spring rolls

Nora's chocolate brownies

Elle's healthy Florentines

Georgie's duck spring rolls

Ingredients:
  1 teaspoon five-spice powder
  1 tablespoon mirin
  2 tablespoons soy sauce
  2 duck breasts, skin intact
  1 tablespoon olive oil
  4 spring onions, finely sliced
  8 shitake mushrooms, diced
  handful of bean shoots, roughly chopped
  2 teaspoons soy sauce
  ¼ teaspoon cinnamon
  3 teaspoons hoisin sauce
  20 wonton wrappers
  oil for frying

Preheat oven to 160°C (315°F) fan-forced.

To prepare the marinade, mix the five-spice powder, mirin and soy sauce in a dish. Add the duck breasts and rub the marinade over them well, then leave to marinate in the refrigerator for an hour.

Heat a frying pan with a drizzle of oil on high heat and brown each side of the duck, then place on a tray and cook in the oven for 40 to 45 minutes. Remove from the oven and leave to rest for 20 minutes, then remove and discard the skin and dice the meat.

Heat the tablespoon of oil in a wok or frying pan on medium heat and sauté the spring onions and mushrooms for 3 to 4 minutes until tender (you may need to add a drop of water). Turn the heat to low and add the bean shoots, soy sauce, cinnamon (dissolve in the liquid in the pan) and the hoisin sauce. Add the diced duck and use a wooden spoon to combine well. Place the mixture in a bowl and leave to cool for a few minutes.

To assemble the spring rolls, lay a wonton wrapper point upwards and place a large teaspoon of mixture in the centre. Fold the wrapper up from the point closest to you to cover the duck mixture, then fold in the sides before continuing to roll. Dip your finger in some water to rub at the end of the wrapper so it holds. Continue the process for the rest of the mixture and wrappers.

To cook, cover the base of a frying pan with ½ to 1 centimetre of oil over a high heat. When the oil is hot, carefully add the spring rolls. When golden (approximately 3 minutes), turn to brown the other side. When cooked, remove the spring rolls to paper towel to drain excess oil. (If you prefer to deep-fry the spring rolls, heat a large saucepan with approximately 8 centimetres of oil and cook until golden.)

Makes 20 delicious duck spring rolls with a little hint of ... cinnamon. Serve with hoisin sauce, plum sauce or soy sauce.

Nora's chocolate brownies

Ingredients:

125 g (4½ oz) butter

1 cup (200 g/7 oz) sugar

160 g (5½ oz) 70% cocoa cooking chocolate

2 eggs

½ teaspoon finely grated orange rind

¼ cup (30 g/1 oz) cocoa powder

½ cup (63 g/2 ¼ oz) self-raising flour

Preheat oven to 170°C (335°F) fan-forced.

Melt the butter, then add the sugar and whisk together. Melt the cooking chocolate and combine with the sugar mixture. Add the eggs and orange rind and mix well, then add the cocoa powder and flour and gently mix.

Line the base of a 20-centimetre (8-inch) square brownie tin with baking paper, oil the sides and pour in the mixture. Bake for 35 minutes.

Allow to cool in the tin before slicing into squares. Makes 16.

Em's healthier version of Nora's chocolate brownies

Ingredients:

3 eggs

⅔ cup (165 ml/5 ½ fl oz) light-flavoured olive oil

120 g (4½ oz) 70% dark cooking chocolate
⅔ cup (190 g/6½ oz) honey
½ teaspoon finely grated orange rind
¾ cup (120 g/4½ oz) wholemeal (wholewheat) self-raising flour
¼ cup (25 g/1 oz) almond meal
¼ cup (60 ml/2 fl oz) milk

Preheat oven to 160°C (315°F) fan-forced.

Beat the eggs and oil together. Melt the chocolate and then mix the honey into the chocolate until dissolved. Add the chocolate mixture to the egg mixture and beat well. Mix in the orange rind. Add the flour, almond meal and milk, and stir until combined.

Line the base of a 20-centimetre (8-inch) square brownie tin with baking paper, oil the sides and pour in the mixture, spreading it evenly. Bake for 30 minutes.

Leave to cool in the tin for 20 minutes, then remove and leave to cool further on a cake rack before slicing. Makes 16.

Perfect with a cup of tea!

Elle's healthy Florentines

Ingredients:
¾ cup (90 g/3 oz) slivered almonds
½ cup (70 g /2 ½ oz) dried cranberries
¼ cup (40 g/ 1 ½ oz) wholemeal (wholewheat) plain flour
¼ cup (60 ml/2 fl oz) light-flavoured olive oil
¼ cup (75 g/2 ¾ oz) honey
80 g (2 ¾ oz) 70% cocoa cooking chocolate

Preheat oven to 170°C (335°F) fan-forced.

Mix together the slivered almonds, cranberries and flour. In a separate bowl, mix the oil and honey until the honey dissolves, then mix thoroughly into the dry ingredients.

Line an oven tray with baking paper. Using a teaspoon, place heaped dollops of the mixture onto the tray (allow room as they spread). Bake for 13 to 15 minutes.

Allow to cool on the tray before using a spatula to lift off each biscuit to a cake rack. Melt the chocolate and dip the base of each crisp biscuit into the chocolate. Place upside down on the cake rack to allow the chocolate to set.

Makes 12.

Store in the refrigerator for a chewy and crunchy texture. Then the challenge is to stop at one ... or two!

Acknowledgements

This story was inspired by a woman I met at the shopping strip where I buy groceries. Just like when Elle first meets Nora, she accompanied me into the bakery, and while we waited to be served, I was conscious of the right thing to say to make her feel comfortable. Having worked with Our Village Kitchen, a charitable organisation that makes meals for families in need, I was aware of the many circumstances that could lead to someone being in this position. But when I came home, I kept thinking about what might have happened in this woman's world. I also kept thinking about the fragility of life, how in a moment your whole world can change.

In my story, Nora gets a redo, a second chance to change her fate. For most people, that isn't the case. If you or someone you know are experiencing domestic violence, please contact the helpline 1800 RESPECT in Australia, or if you are in immediate danger, contact the police on 000.

This was the first time that I have written a manuscript while workshopping it along the way with other writers. Thank you to Amelia Ullmer and Bronwyn Venter for all your suggestions and edits, and for being on team Nora and Elle from the get-go.

A huge thank you to my son, Jack, for graciously playing the piano music that took me to my character's world. Every time you played, 'Creep' by Radiohead, for me, the scenes just flowed. Love you mate.

Thank you to Romy Bursztyn, who took on the task of reviewing this manuscript in the same way she does everything – wholeheartedly. I'm so grateful for your advice and encouragement along the way. Thank you to Amanda Smorgon for your wonderful feedback, for reading all of my manuscripts and always offering to read them again after I rework. It is greatly appreciated.

Thank you to editor Simone Ford for your amazing feedback and guidance, which pushed me to take my manuscript to the next level. I do love a challenge! Thank you to Lauren Finger for your thorough proofread.

My initial research is usually online, but I always like to speak to 'real' people to check my facts. A huge thank you to the lovely family lawyer Jacquelyn Parnell, who worked through Nora's case with me like she was a real client. I thoroughly appreciate the time you spent with me. Thank you to Rachel Vainer for checking the banking details and making sure Richard's fraud would work. I should declare that any mistakes are entirely my own!

My parents, Viv and Leon, and my parents in-law, Marion and Mick, have been so supportive of my writing journey, and I can't thank them enough for listening to me talk endlessly about all aspects of writing and publishing. I love you all. Thank you, Mum and Marion, for reading and devouring this one at full speed.

And lastly, though you always come first, to my husband, Barry, and our kids, Jess, Ally, Jack and Gracie. Thank you for your constant support of all my endeavours, for the twenty-four-hour tech support and for listening to what's happening in my make-believe worlds over dinner (and on walks, car rides and, really, any time of the day). A special thanks to Baz for the smoothie inspo – I never drink his!

Love, Emily